A MEMORY OF MURDER

Nichelle Seely

To Aaron, the love of my life.

1

My gun is in my right hand, the butt gripped securely and the safety off as I turn the key in the lock to my inheritance. It's been a forty-eight hour, thousand-mile journey on featureless highways, the Glock and the meds sharing the passenger seat, and I've finally reached my destination: Astoria, Oregon — the place where I can begin a new life.

The house on Rhododendron Street smells stale. All the furniture has been taken away, the pictures removed from the walls, and the carpet pulled off the floor. My boot heels clack against the bare painted wood. Windows along the south wall admit a spill of late afternoon light. The single-hung sashes have been left open a smidge, and I intend to shut them, but instead I push the sash as high as it will go, admitting a gust of fresh cold air and a faint fishy odor I associate with the exposed mudflats along the shore. The ebb tide has sucked the water from the shallows of the Columbia River to the depths of the Pacific Ocean. The view is stunning. So much water.

The damp breeze caresses my cheeks and hair with invisible clammy hands. I shiver. It's been a long time since I've been in Oregon. The last time, my aunt's house was filled to bursting with books and pictures and rugs and seashells. It's mine now, an unexpected legacy — the house, but not the contents. Clean and clear of memories and the relics of someone else's life.

A great blue heron soars over the roof with coiled grace, scooping wingfuls of wind from the thickening air. I've seen the same birds in Colorado, hunting for prey in lakes and park ponds and roadside swales, when I could take a few precious hours away from the murder and mayhem that characterized my career as a detective with the Denver Police Department.

A wave of anxiety descends. My heart rate spikes and muscles clench. I shouldn't have opened that door to memory. I look over my shoulder, check that I've locked the door, and do a sweep of each floor, clearing the rooms with weapon drawn. The upper story with its slanted ceiling and two tiny bedrooms is secure; ditto the concrete cave of the basement with its naked wall studs and single finished room in the corner. There's no one here; it's safe.

Breathe in, breathe out. Calm.

I make sure my gun is secure in the shoulder holster before returning to my car to unload a suitcase, a fold-up camp cot and chair, card table, and two grocery bags of food. The table and chair I leave in the empty room next to the kitchen. The cot and suitcase I manhandle upstairs. Food goes to the kitchen and into the refrigerator and open shelves; soap and toothpaste into the bathroom, along with my medication.

I look into the mirror of the medicine cabinet for a long time, charting the new lines across my forehead and the padding beneath my chin and cheekbones; the shadows under my eyes that echo the shadows in my mind. My body aches with a fatigue that scrapes against my skeleton. I never seem to get enough sleep. It's the pills, of course. Their fault also that I've gained upwards of twenty pounds in the last six months. I'm so done with all this — the worrying, the lying, the general feeling of malaise and fuzziness.

With savage abruptness, I open the medicine cabinet and glare at the single orange plastic bottle with its white child-proof lid and cleanly lettered label.

Rx: 25428040
    Patient Name: LAKE, AUDREY
    ZYPREXA/Olanzapine
    1 tablet per day or as needed to suppress hallucinations

I'm supposed to take these until my psychiatrist tells me to stop. Or until the symptoms cease of their own accord. But I don't know when that will be. How can I, with the pills pulling a blanket between me and the rest of the world? Meanwhile, I'm always sleepy and soft, and getting softer, and I've left my doctor back in Denver.

Rubbing my eyes, I try to dislodge the shadows. I'm used to walking the razor's edge of danger, riding the rocket of focused adrenalin. I hate feeling muddled and cottoned away from the world.

It's been months — surely the visions are gone. I only had a couple, under extremely stressful circumstances. I'm better now, I'm sure of it. The bad place is just a memory. It's over. And I'm far away from anyone who will be keeping tabs on my medical condition, or laying down rules as to how I should live my life. Better to make a clean break to match the new beginning.

I take down the bottle. The contents rattle. With grave deliberation, knowing that it's probably wrong, I twist off the top and spill the small white pills into the toilet. They float in the bowl, seemingly inert, and I press the flusher hard. Again. Again. Until nothing remains, not one errant dose.

The empty bottle goes back into the cabinet and I shut the door firmly. I avoid looking into the mirror again, but I feel lighter and more buoyant already. Like I've taken one step closer to The Way Things Were Before. Before the hospital, before the incident in Denver, before Zoe. Back when I knew who and what I was.

March arrives. Springtime. I've forgotten the date. I spend the days walking, reading, and cooking complicated meals that require a lot of chopping. Without the meds my precision has improved. More carrot and less finger. Bonus. Today, when I look through the window, morning sun is gleaming on the wide blueness of the Columbia River. The fog has burned off, and a big red and white freighter with a long extended bow skirts the line of buoys that mark the main channel. Closer in, a few cars move down on Marine Drive, and further up the hill a ginger cat suns itself on the macadam of Alameda Street.

I haven't been to Astoria in years. The last time, my mother and my twenty-something self stayed with Aunt Sandy for a week in this very house. Mother dragged me around a walking tour of the neighborhoods while she identified all the historic architectural styles and took what must have been thousands of pictures of houses with closeups of fascia trim and railing details. I remember thinking: ye gods, do we have to, as Mother insisted on 'just one more block,' and me wondering why couldn't she have been a cop like my father, instead of an architect?

I turn from the view and survey my immediate surroundings. Spring sunlight brightens the great room, illuminating the fine layer of dust which fuzzes the windowsills. The canvas camp chair and card table are set up near the windows that overlook the river; a book lies open on the tabletop. Watching the motes that swirl in the sunbeam, it's easy to slip into a daydream of warmth and serenity.

The heavy tramp of boots sounds on the basement stairs. I glance down at my hand and see my gun. I don't remember grabbing it, and fear needles through my earlier complacency. The door creaks open on painted-over hinges as the furnace roars to life, gusting warm air through the wrought iron wall vents. I stuff the weapon down the back of my pants under my shirttail before he sees it.

The building inspector — because of course, that's who it is, since I let him in earlier — strides into the main room. Here by appointment; it's the normal thing to have someone check the condition of the house. He begins to write notes on his clipboard, talking.

"Okay Ms. Lake, here's what I've discovered. You've probably noticed that the building has a low corner."

I nod, still trying to get my head around my unpremeditated gun-grab. Try to take in what he's saying. A low point. Yes. Greatest in the kitchen, where I often lose my balance bending over the thirty-inch counters, built at a time when people were shorter.

He continues. "That's because the foundation is cracked, and so is the basement slab. You've probably had some ground recession — I see an old stump right next to the house. Being on a hill doesn't help." He licks his pencil. "But you'd be hard put to find a house in Astoria that isn't on a hillside, or that doesn't have foundation problems."

"How bad is it?" I ask.

"I've seen worse. I'm guessing six inches of sag. Bad enough that you should get it fixed, or at least stabilized. Not necessarily today, but soon."

"What else?"

"Some of the siding is rotten. Stands to reason, the house is over 100 years old, and even old cedar heartwood can only stand so much rain. You'll need to replace it, and check to make sure the underlying structure isn't also rotten."

My inheritance is apparently not without problems. Sigh.

"The asphalt roof shingles are starting to curl. I don't see any signs of water intrusion, but you'll want to re-roof."

I tune out the additional issues with the roof and porch. What I thought was going to be a safe haven is suddenly a money pit. I just want a safe place to live without issues to deal with. Is that too much to ask?

"Make sure the contractor uses some waterproofing. It rains occasionally here." The inspector chortles, and assures me he'll send a complete report with items of concern listed.

Waterproofing. When this house was built, back in 1917, such things probably hadn't been invented.

I heard something funny the other day, while shopping at the grocery store. Two people were talking in the checkout line, and one was complaining about the weather. The other said, "Stop exaggerating. You know it only rains a couple of times a year. The first time for four months, and the second time for six months."

On my drive home from the store, I noticed the moss growing on the shoulder of the asphalt; the mildew on the shady side of a weatherbeaten Colonial Revival. So, I'm a little worried about rot. I have visions of the place collapsing like a house of cards while I sleep. But. I just can't deal with it now. There's too many other broken things to get my head around.

It's easier to cope with the inspector than I feared. He doen't seem to expect friendliness or warmth, just an email address for his report and a credit card to swipe on his phone. The bare minimum of exchange. I wonder what he concludes about the emptiness, the few pieces of temporary furniture, the scattering of dishes on the open shelves of the kitchen. But perhaps he doesn't think of it. His job is to glean and process information about things, not about people, and he walks away without a backward glance.

When I was working undercover, constant evaluation of the volatile individuals around me was the order of the day. Balancing situational awareness without acting like a cop. Pimps and dealers, prostitutes and users, addicts and runaways; every one ready to lash out or pull an unexpected weapon.

My heart speeds up, sending a pulse of pain through the scarce-healed knife wound on my upper right chest. Sweat breaks out, and I rub my hands on my pants legs. Enough. That's over. Time to move on. That's why I chose not to sell this house, but to live in it. A safe space to heal, physically and mentally. Change my life. Focus on the future.

Maybe that's the problem. Time, as in: too much of it. I'm not used to unemployment. I need more structure to my days, not to mention an income stream so I can afford to repair my house. Cash from the inheritance won't last forever. I need a job, some meaningful work. As soon as I can face the unpredictability of other people. As soon as I can trust that I'll be fully aware the next time I draw my gun.

I walk everywhere. Miles every day. On the beach. On the forest- and fern-lined trails of Fort Stevens State Park. On the winding streets of Astoria with their blind corners and secret stairways and sagging historic architecture. I'm trying to lose the weight, and get tired enough to ward off the insomnia that plagues me every night. Over two weeks have passed since I ditched the drugs and withdrawal symptoms are hitting hard. I cry for no reason. Or for too many reasons to count. I'm anxious and often bathed in sweat. It's difficult to separate the synthetic chemical symptoms from the PTSD. So I don't even try.

Walking helps — a change in my surroundings, something else to focus on besides tumultuous memories and a constant headache that feels like being lobotomized without anesthesia. But it also makes my chest hurt beneath the knobby pink scar.

If I hadn't flushed the pills, I'd be so tempted to swallow just one. Just to take the edge off. Except I've seen too much of the ugliness of addiction. A homicide detective sees the end of that downward spiral all too often. So I tell myself I can get through this. Just take one step after another, and one day I'll be back to normal.

The Riverwalk is less crowded in the evenings. Dog-walkers and bicyclists have gone home to make dinner, or swell the sparse off-season clientele of bars and restaurants. I like the industrial feel of the west end of the trail, the weed-choked railroad siding, the metal-sided warehouses rusting in the rain. Today I keep going, past the fish processing plant and the brewery and under the complicated framework of the Megler Bridge soaring two hundred feet above the Columbia. The damp wind sprinkles tiny drops of condensing mist against my cheeks. The deep bawl of a foghorn comes from downriver, beyond the giant concrete bridge abutments. Heavy fog lies over the water. To my left is a tiny beach scuffed with footprints and driftwood. Wavelets slosh against the shore, created by the rising tide or maybe a passing freighter, unseen beyond the gray curtain of mist.

I'm still getting used to how much moisture permeates the air and how green growing things spring from every cranny. Sprawling rosemary hedges line the shore and fill the air with an aroma that makes me think of my mother's roast chicken. The steel girders of the bridge arch over my head, barely visible. I can hear the muffled rumble of traffic on the concrete deck, far away, just like the life I left in Colorado.

I walk down to the beach. Moisture oozes around the rubber soles of my boots as I add my prints to the palimpsest of sand. A seagull cries. I close my eyes. The isolation, the dank damp cold, the scent of rosemary and car exhaust and water — it cleanses my soul as I concentrate on simply breathing and being and belonging. Not thinking, and above all, not remembering.

Footsteps, running. Indistinct voices. I have to squinch my eyes tight to stop myself from investigating and cataloguing the sounds, letting the noise wash over me instead of becoming a point of distraction.

You're not a detective now, Audrey. No need to get involved.

The footsteps come closer. Voices, arguing. Right on top of me. A blow strikes my temple. I stagger, head ringing with pain. I catch my balance and run, looking over my shoulder at a looming figure. Why is it so dark? I trip on a piece of driftwood. Hands seize the shoulders of my coat, arresting my fall.

"It was just a game! You see that, don't you?" The voice is jagged, harsh, thick with rage. So dark — I can't see my attacker. Terror claws at me. I try to pull away. A distant part of me screams to resist, to fight. But I don't know how.

Hands tighten around my neck. Shaking, twisting. Pushing. There's a chemical smell, sharp and familiar but I can't place it. I fall on something hard and cold. Lights explode in my vision and pain beats against my temple.

The voice, hissing anger. "You won't wreck my life with your lies."

Stunned, I can't fight back as someone picks me up and thrusts me into the river. The water is an icy shock. Can't move my arms and legs. Can't turn over. Water gushes into my mouth, flooding my chest, turning my body into a dead weight as I sink down, deeper and deeper. I seem to hover outside my body, watching myself descend. Long dark hair twists in the current. I don't recognize my face. It recedes into blackness like a dream.

Then I'm on my knees, coughing, gasping for air. The river laps at the fabric of my jeans and covers my hands with insistent cold. The darkness of my vision gives way to the filtered, foggy light of late afternoon. It's just me; there's no one else here. And I'm alive. Not falling. Not drowning. Not dying.

Hallucinating.

Oh, no. It's happening again.

2

The morning following my hallucination, my face looks as though I've been on a three-day bender. I'd spent the previous evening listening to the radio, refusing to think about the experience. And as a result, I'd spent the night dreaming about it. After doing a quick perimeter check of the house to make sure all the openings are closed and locked, I go to the kitchen. This one room, at least, has begun to feel like home. And I'm feeling more like myself, and less like a disembodied spirit. Maybe the meds are finally out of my system.

Coffee is the only solution to quell the morning monster, and as I fill the press I wish I could inject it directly into a vein. Except that makes me think of drug abuse and Zoe and the Baxter Building, and all the rest of it. So when a knock sounds against the door I startle like a new perp in prison. Someone is trying to break into my solitude before I am ready to breach it myself. This person is using the knocker rather than the doorbell, making a distinct metallic clank.

In seconds my gun is nestled in my hand. I keep it out of sight when I crack open the door. An older white man, heavily built, with silver hair and shrewd blue eyes stands on the porch. His barrel shape, bristling eyebrows and alert expression remind me of a great horned owl. He has a bunch of yellow flowers and a plate covered with a gingham cloth.

"Hello," he says. "I'm your next-door neighbor." He gestures to the right with an elbow. "Welcome to the neighborhood."

Is he for real? I'm suspicious of strangers and must look doubtful, because he smiles, deepening the creases in his cheeks.

"I hope I didn't wake you up. You don't have to invite me in. I just thought you'd like some fresh flowers — these daffodils come from my garden — and my wife sent over some cookies."

So then of course I feel like an idiot and I open the door a little wider. "No, it's fine. I'm just a little disorganized now." Wait, did he say he thought he'd woken me up? I realize I am still in my pajamas. And I have a gun in my hand. I close the door back down to a crack before he can step inside.

He says, "We really liked Sandy, the previous owner. Did you know her at all?"

"I'm her niece. She left this house to me." Even to my own ears I sound defensive. But I still don't invite him inside. Because, you know, pajamas. And firearm.

"We saw the van taking away all the furniture."

"Her own daughter got all the contents. I got the building." And that's all *you're* going to get, Mr. Nosy.

"Interesting." He squats to place the plate on the porch, and lays the flowers next to it. "Come on over when you've got a little time on your hands. We'd love to make your acquaintance." He stands. "I'm Judge Lincoln Rutherford — retired, so you can call me Link. My wife is Dr. Phoebe Rutherford. She still does the occasional therapy session at home, so she might not be available for a casual drop-in, but I'm usually pottering around. We'll be seeing you." He smiles again and walks off up the concrete stairs to the street.

I shut the door and rest my head against it, until the anxiety fluttering in my belly subsides.

Nice going, Lake. Barely here any time at all and you've already advertised your weirdness to the neighbors. And a judge to boot. You don't do things by halves.

The voice in my head is sardonic and strident; it sounds like it belongs to somebody else. But it's right — I shudder to think I'd almost threatened him with a weapon. And I realize I didn't tell him my name.

No one is in sight, so I step out onto the porch and retrieve the cookies and flowers. I put both on the card table. I'm obviously not ready to meet people yet, not socially. Certainly not a shrink. I've had enough of that for a lifetime, and none of them had been able to help me.

Plus, there's too much to think about. The house and all it needs. The vision of yesterday evening. My static bank account. The money won't last forever. And I don't think it's enough to replace a foundation, or completely rebuild a roof. My aunt's legacy, which seemed like such a godsend, is now revealed to be less of a sanctuary and more of a trap. With big leg-snapping teeth.

Like it or not, I need to look for a job, and there's only one thing I know how to do. But. That means going back into the underbelly, seeing the worst the world has to offer, and depending on people to have your back. And then maybe discovering that they don't.

Yeah, I'm probably not ready to be a full-time detective again. But maybe I can be a consultant. Breeze in, offer expertise, breeze out. That seems less stressful. Perhaps an informal visit to the Astoria Police Department is in order. Meet the local cops, develop some relationships to help me when a position opens up for real, or when they need some extra help. You know, network. Like an actual professional person.

The APD shares a bunker-like concrete building with the fire department, and the two departments share a lobby with a single plastic chair and fake tropical plant. When I walk in at 1:13 and ask to talk to a detective, the woman at the front desk looks at me as though I have an eyestalk growing out of my head. But she eventually calls someone on the phone, and I find myself in a drab conference room with the senior detective, who introduces himself as Steven Olafson.

I intend this to be an informational interview only, so I can find out about the local law enforcement and get the lay of the land. Present my bona fides. Tell some war stories. Let them know I'm available to help. Except, I've never actually done this before — gone fishing for a job. I'd gone from the Denver Police Academy straight to the Denver Police Department and stayed there. Hopefully, I can learn something about the local process; find out who makes the big picture decisions.

I decide the best approach is straight-up cop-to-cop honesty, and so I tell Detective Olafson about my twenty years of work in the Denver Police Department, and my rise as a successful homicide detective within that jurisdiction. It sounds good — I'm feeling hopeful, and closer to normal than I have in days, here in a place I know the ropes. Plus, wouldn't it be nice to have colleagues again, people to shoot the breeze with who know what it's like to be in law enforcement.

Olafson leans back in his chair, hands behind his head. He's a bulky man, but I doubt much of it is fat. His hair is dark blond, nicked off in a brush cut that ends at the top of his ears. He's clean-shaven, but his tie is at half-mast. The overhead fluorescents don't do his complexion any favors.

"Sounds like you've seen some action in Denver," he drawls. "We don't get much in the way of murders here. There's just a couple of us detectives, and we handle everything that comes our way. Robbery, drug busts, the occasional missing person. We don't specialize. Can't."

I nod. "That's pretty standard for small towns. I wouldn't mind having less violence in my life, that's for sure. One reason I wanted to get away from Denver."

"Can't back away from what comes," he says. "Gotta be willing to take the cases on, regardless."

"Of course," I say. "I wasn't implying —"

"The fact is," he rolls on, looking at the ceiling tiles, "I find that it's the relationships I have with the community that are responsible for most of our success in solving crimes. I've been here all my life, and I know the people. They trust me."

"Sometimes an outside perspective, an outside experience, can be valuable. That's where I could lend a hand."

"Sometimes. Maybe. Haven't seemed to need it much, myself." He places his palms flat on the table. "I appreciate that you've had a successful career, maybe a good solve rate, and you've probably seen more dead bodies than all of us here at the APD put together. But we know our territory. And that's not something you can fake. It's something you need to build, and develop."

I struggle to control my annoyance at his patronizing tone. "I'm aware of that, thanks."

"No need to be touchy." Olafson smiles. His canine teeth seem overlong. "But you're not from here," he continues. "You've got no local connections whatsoever. And that matters. Believe me, it matters."

Before I can say anything more, another detective walks in to the interview room. She's younger than me, but with a hardness around the eyes and lines that run from her nose to her chin. She walks with a bold aggression that makes the air seem to wrinkle in front of her.

Detective Olafson says, "Ms. Lake, meet my partner, Detective Jane Candide. Jane also started out in the big city — in her case, Portland. So, we have all the urban experience we need."

We shake hands. Jane's fingers are cold and hard. I'm trying to be congenial and mask my anger, which I'm aware is out of proportion.

"Jane, Ms. Lake is looking for a job as a consulting detective."

"Really. I wasn't aware we needed any help." She looks at me like a ferret eyeing a Roosevelt elk. Wondering if it has what it takes to bring the bigger prey down.

"We don't." Olafson's voice is decisive. "Ms. Lake, I appreciate your coming in to acquaint me with your qualifications. If we ever need someone with your capabilities, we'll be in touch. Jane, please show Ms. Lake how to find her way out."

The plate glass door clicks shut behind us. I'm shaking, surprised at my own reaction but unable to moderate the feelings of humiliation, anger, disappointment — a thousand tiny barbs that make me want to lash out, or get away to some dark hole like a wounded animal.

What the hell is wrong with me? The overcast sky is uniformly bright and I squint against the glare.

Detective Candide has followed me outside. Now she tugs her blazer closed against the chill and says, "Sorry about that, but he's the big dog. You know how it is."

So does that make her the bitch?

My inner voice has a warped sense of humor. I struggle not to guffaw and end up making what is probably a strange grimace. "I take it I won't be getting a call any time soon."

"'Fraid not. And it's true, we don't really need any help. Why did you come here?"

"To learn about the department. See if I can help you guys out." My voice shakes, and I have to swallow. I'm hyped on adrenaline, and now that the interview is over I'm jittering down. Candide probably thinks I have a whole host of weird tics.

"I mean, why did you come to our town? To Astoria?" Jane waves a hand, taking in the wide river with its anchored freighters and the hillside covered with pre-World War II houses. "Why would you want to leave Denver?"

I certainly can't tell her the truth. At least, not all of it. "I got tired of the big city. All the stress."

"I'm surprised. Tecs like us thrive under pressure and steam. To hear you tell it, you crushed that job."

Shrug. "You left Portland." I've never been to the Rose City myself, but I've heard it's on a lot of top ten lists.

"I had my reasons. And I'm still wondering what yours are." Candide's hands come down to rest on her belt. Although still youngish — I guess early thirties, ten or so years younger than me — permanent cynicism stamps her features. I've seen it before, in older cops who've spent too much time on the mean streets. "You didn't have to come here."

"What division were you in? In Portland?"

Her eyes flicker, and her lids droop momentarily. But she answers: "Narcotics. You want to tell me why you left Denver PD?"

Her reaction to my question is interesting, but I can't really pursue it now. "My reasons are my own."

I could tell her about the inheritance — it won't make any difference to me and might defuse her suspicions — but the younger woman irritates me with her aggression, part of the breed of female cops who think they have to act tougher than their male brethren to be thought half as good. Can't blame her though. I get it.

"Look, Detective, I'm not here to cause any trouble. I'm just trying to scope out the possibilities. Learn things."

"Like what?"

I cast my line. "Like, what's your caseload like?"

"As stated, not so busy that we can't handle it."

"Homicides?"

"You heard Steve in there. A little bit of everything."

"What's on your plate just now?"

"Nothing I'm prepared to share with you."

We stand there, staring at one another. It's not friendly. "So you've no murders on the books, then? No suspicious deaths?" The memory of dying, water invading my lungs, is still fresh. The hallucination seemed so real and detailed. So many sense impressions. I find myself asking, "Drownings?"

She shakes her head. "Nope. Now, why don't you go on back to your hotel? Ask the concierge for some sightseeing tips before you go back home." Her voice softens by about one degree. "I'm sorry you've had a wasted trip."

For some reason, that tiny peace offering makes the rejection worse. "You don't understand," I say through gritted teeth. "I live here now, Detective. I own a house. I'm local. Like it or not, I belong here." I force myself to walk away with the bitter taste of irony in the back of my throat and feel my thin weave of confidence disintegrate. So much for the brotherhood of the thin blue line. Or sisterhood. Contrary to my last words, I've never felt more like an outsider.

3

I'm clenching the steering wheel so hard my knuckles ache; I force myself to loosen my grip as I pull out onto Marine Drive. Candide is still standing outside the station as I pass, watching me leave.

Her attitude is beyond irritating. She's like a little pit bull, defending her territory. What's her problem, exactly? Is she afraid I'm out for her job? Me with my big city badge, which I'd mailed back to the chief before I'd left Denver, with no forwarding address? Hah. One call to my former employer would send my whole house of cards tumbling down. I'd been an idiot to think I could just waltz in and be buddies. I'll just have to pray that curiosity doesn't send either of them to the phone to check too deeply on my bona fides.

Worse, I still don't know what to make of the experience I'd had on the riverside beach. It's not the first time I've had such a vision. No, I had one in Denver, at the Baxter Building, after months of undercover work and dabbling in street drugs. It's what landed me in the psych ward with a prescription for anti-hallucinogens.

So, just refill your prescription. No need to go all ballistic. Meds are your friends.

I hate the insinuating voice in my head, poking holes in my resolve. Drugs are a mask for reality. I smack the steering wheel with my hand, accidentally sounding the horn and startling the man in the car in front of me. He spreads his arms, questioning as he looks in his rear-view mirror. If this were Denver, he would've given me the finger. I wave, mouthing 'sorry.' He shrugs and goes on, and I calm myself enough so I don't have an accident. To top off my day, it begins to rain, and soon the windshield is splotched with moisture..

When I get back to the little yellow house I now call home, I sit cross-legged on the floor with my back to the wall and activate my laptop. The overhead light throws a warm incandescence into the empty room.

Olafson accused me of not knowing the territory. Fine. The website for the Astoria Police Department has an accessible archive, and I spend the next couple of hours scanning through lists of calls. A few break-ins, speeding tickets, emergency responder calls — one instance where a man came home to find his girlfriend's mother putting his possessions out on the front lawn. Surprisingly little violence beyond the odd bar fight or domestic disturbance. The only bodies are accountable as suicides.

Another search under the county reveals two murders in the last dozen years, both victims male. The National Missing Persons database indicates only four missing persons, the most recent eight years ago. I sit back. No wonder the detectives didn't want my help. There isn't anything in the way of major crime. I should have done my homework before offering my services, and not taken their rejection so personally. Come up with a plausible transition story to explain why I'm here. Just waited until I was better, more sure of myself. Now I've ruined my chance to make a good first impression.

I massage my forehead. 'Off my game' doesn't begin to describe it. I slam down the lid of my computer, tired and hungry, but so not up to cooking. Despite the drizzle, I decide to walk down to the Portway Tavern. It's on Marine Drive at the base of the hill. I'll go down there and pretend to be normal; enjoy being around other people without actually having to interact with anyone.

The drizzle has become a screen of thin mist which doesn't do any favors for the neighborhood aesthetic. Not one of the houses along Alameda is newer than the 1940s and most look older. Some have been cared for and sport bright colorful paint and well-tended yards. Some look overcome by the elements, roofs blanketed with shaggy moss and siding smudged with dirt and mildew. It's a mixed neighborhood, trying to be charming and gentrified but stymied by the stubborn residents who don't embrace maintenance or lawn care or even tidiness.

I like it. It feels authentic. Real people living real lives. I wonder what that's like. Maybe someday I'll know them as friends and neighbors, but right now I'm alone on the street.

By the time I reach the Portway Tavern, my pants are drenched and my shoes squeak with moisture. The tiny droplets of mist, which seemed so innocuous when I started out, have the penetration power of a diamond drill bit. The bar is empty except for a lone gambler, a young white man feeding twenties into one of the brightly lit video poker games. A corner of the room is dominated by a huge television screen showing a muted basketball game. I drape my dripping coat over the back of a chair at one of the small tables and sit down opposite.

The bartender is a tall Black woman with close-cropped hair. She nods at me and brings over a menu.

"Burger Tuesday," she says. "Standard burgers cost seven dollars, pint of Bud for three. Craft pint for five. Can I get you a drink?"

"Can you ever," I say. The day has been a long one. "What's on tap?"

She presses a finger to her cheek, thinking. "Alaska Amber. A Buoy Beer American pale, IPA from Fort George Brewing, Widmer Hefeweizen."

Might as well start tasting the community brews, although I do like a good Hef. "I'll take the Buoy pale, and a cheeseburger. Medium well. No pickles."

"No special orders on Burger Tuesday. You gotta take it the way it comes."

"Right. That seems to be the story of my life." Taking what comes. Maybe there's a lesson there, but I'm too tired and hungry to think about it. I mentally calculate the cost of my meal: twelve bucks, not counting tip. I think of my bank account, healthy with inheritance for now, but no fresh infusions on the horizon.

"Don't worry, we've got the best burgers in town. Everybody says so." The bartender/waitress cracks a smile and goes behind the bar to pull my beer. When she brings it to my table, she says, "I'm Claire. Give a call if you want anything else."

Claire goes back to her tasks. The young gambler has emptied his wallet and shrugs on his jacket, looking like a hound dog kicked too many times. He leaves without looking at either of us. Some laminated flyers are tucked between the salt and pepper shakers and the napkin dispenser, and I pull them out.

One is an advertisement for Burger Tuesday, with a photo of a dewy bottle of Budweiser. The second is a drinks menu. The third, not laminated, is an advertisement for a local church. I take a swallow of my pale ale. It has a pleasant citrusy hoppiness without the mouth-puckering bitterness of an IPA. I savor it as I examine the flyer.

"The Church of the Spirit Welcomes You" it reads in a swirly font that looks like it should be on a wedding invitation. "The Spirit speaks to all! Join our worship and be infused with divine creative energy. Pastor Victoria Harkness officiating." Below the words is a black and white head-and-shoulders photo of a white woman, mid-thirties, with long dark hair and penetrating dark eyes. Her Mona Lisa smile doesn't show any teeth. Although her name is completely unfamiliar, I feel a chill frisson of recognition.

This is the woman in my vision.

My throat closes up, and perspiration dampens my upper lip.

Claire sets a plate down in front of me. I look up, blinking. The cheeseburger smells amazing, with an orange slab of cheddar melting down the side and a pile of thick and steaming French fries. I pick one up and take a bite for comfort. Delicious, despite the lack of customization.

She says, "That's my church, if you're interested."

In general, I'm not a religious person. I've seen too much pain and base unkindness and the gross unfairness of the world to have any cozy illusions about the love of God or the possibility of salvation. But now I feel something I don't understand, connection with the woman pictured on the flyer. I'm confused and a tiny bit terrified, but I rope that off into its own corner. Maybe an infusion of spirituality is called for.

"Who is she?"

"Our pastor. She's wonderful. Really gifted. You should come listen to her speak."

"Is she filled with divine creative energy?" I ask facetiously.

Claire nods, not taking offense at my tone. "She is. And so is everyone who comes. It's all about opening yourself to the Spirit, and allowing it to speak to you through your own creativity. People have produced some amazing works."

"Really."

"Yes, really." She leans forward, her hands on the back of the chair with my jacket. "Listen, I know it sounds weird, but she's something else. My husband and I followed the church to Astoria when she moved it from Portland."

Frankly, that sounds like a cult to me. But Claire seems so no-nonsense, not the kind of person you'd associate with a cult. Plus, the woman in my vision.

I say, "You don't seem very busy at the moment. Why don't you sit down and tell me about it?"

People can never resist talking about their churches or their children, and the bartender is no exception. I have no doubt it was she who had planted the flyers. I bite into my juicy burger, mop my chin, and decimate my fries as she speaks. I learn that the Church of the Spirit promotes the message that the Holy Spirit communicates to everybody, especially via creative channels. Every service, Pastor Harkness encourages congregants to bring their artistic efforts to the altar as an offering. They are also invited to share whatever message has been imparted to them.

"Have you ever made an offering?" I ask.

Claire looks down at the small glass of Budweiser she's rotating in her hands. "I'm not an artist. But I really admire those who are."

"Do you have to be a good artist to make an offering? Me, I can barely draw a circle." I sketch one in the pool of ketchup with a fry to demonstrate.

"No, she accepts everything and everyone. One of the reasons I like her."

That sounds too good to be true. Plus, culty. But. I shouldn't be judgmental. We continue to chat periodically as Claire makes occasional forays back to the bar. It's nice, the first real social exchange I've had since I'd arrived in Astoria, and casual enough to be non-threatening. As I finish my meal, Claire says, "You should come to a service. It's Thursday night, because so many people in the service industry have to work on Sunday. Details are in the flyer, and newcomers are welcome."

I lay some cash on the table. "Maybe I will." She'd been right about the burgers. Maybe I could trust her about the church. 'Welcome' is a word I haven't heard in a long time. I want to see this pastor with my own eyes. And it sure beats another night alone.

By the time I get back to the house I'm drenched anew. The street lamps are few and far between, and my little avenue is almost pitch black. I'd remembered to leave the porch light on, and I pause on the sidewalk, watching insects flutter in the glow.

My edginess has softened in the beer's gentle buzz. The little yellow craftsman stirs feelings of fondness, with its tiny detached garage and clapboard siding, looking welcoming in the darkness, rain pattering on the roof and dripping from the eaves. The lawn is patchy with moss, and the tiered flower beds next to the concrete steps which lead down from the sidewalk are a tangle of morning glory.

In the house next door, warm light glows behind the draperies. I think of my neighbors: the judge, and the wife I haven't met yet. Nice people, I'm sure. I'm tempted to go down and knock on the door, return the judge's visit. Except I'm afraid it would be more than an exchange of pleasantries. They would be intelligent, discerning. People whose professions make them adept at ferreting out information. They'd naturally want to know about my past, and I don't want to tell anyone. I want — need — to make a clean break, start fresh. Get away from everything that ruined my life.

Maybe I'll go to the church service tomorrow, talk to Claire again, and meet her husband. And the pastor. I wouldn't have to reveal the truth: that I'm agnostic bordering on atheist.

Yeah, that's how they roll. Cult leaders, pimps, and dealers; hunting for the weak and wounded.

Except I'm neither. Just going through a bit of a rough patch, is all. I'm a homicide cop, and nobody's prey. But sketchy as it is, it still feels good to have a direction, a short path into the future.

I give up my rain-drenched vigil and make my way carefully down the concrete steps, clinging to the cold steel-pipe railing that was made for that earlier, shorter, generation of residents. Once inside, I hang my dripping jacket on one of the many hooks in the hallway. I'm freezing, and jack up the thermostat. Warm air gusts from the old-fashioned grilles. Better, but I still have to brave the basement before I shuck my weapon.

Darkness fills the lower story like a fluid. Rain rattles against the siding and the eeriness doesn't dissipate even after I switch on the lights. Plus, it's cold down here — all the exposed concrete, a hundred years old and showing it. Hurriedly, I check the windows and the outside door, confirming that all entry points are closed and locked before heading back upstairs for a cup of tea with a slug of JD.

I'm safe, for now. But for how long? The vision I had yesterday morning was so immersive. It felt like it was actually happening. And this time I can't blame stress or street drugs.

Street drugs — could I be having some kind of acid-type flashback? I've never done LSD, but sometimes I had to use, take things I couldn't identify, in order to keep up my undercover persona. I just hope I haven't messed myself up permanently.

Too bad you flushed your meds. But you could get more.

I brush aside the voice of temptation. I won't go back to the drugs. I won't.

Killjoy.

4

After two days of kicking around my house and long solitary walks, I'm ready for some human contact. The address on the flyer for the Church of the Spirit turns out to be in an old converted Safeway down by the water. I recognize the signature swoopy roofline, and the shadow of the letters across the front facade. After parking in the lot, I step out of my car amidst the squawk of seagulls and the wash of the waves and the deep rumble of a passing tug. The tide is in, and the river laps just below the edge of the stone-studded bank.

I left my weapon at home, and its absence makes me edgy. Through the big plate glass windows, rows of chairs are visible with their backs to the light, facing a podium. People are already filtering inside, and I square my shoulders and walk through the door. This will be my first large gathering since I left Denver, and even then I wasn't the mingling type. So conflicted — I want the human contact but dread having to run a gamut of false friendliness from some insidious old biddy doing greeter duty at the door. God forbid that I might have to leave my protective shell and act like a normal person.

As usual, my fears fail to manifest. A few folks give me friendly nods but no gushing, oily-handshake salesman materializes, and I commandeer one of the chairs without incident. I keep to an aisle so I can make my escape if necessary, and wait for the service to begin. It's weird to sit in this big open space that dwarfs the congregation. It feels temporary and amateurish.

Despite my reflexive skepticism, part of me is interested in what the message is going to be, and what Victoria Harkness is going to be like, and why I should have had a hallucination of her dying. I look around, observing the milieu like any good cop. Back behind the podium,

21

leaning against the wall, is a series of paintings. Portraits and landscapes, oils and watercolors, and an obvious range of talent or lack thereof. Claire had told me about the tradition of artistic offerings. I wonder if these are past or current examples.

The other congregants are a variety of types. Mostly dressed in jeans, flannel shirts, sweaters, and the like, it doesn't feel like an upscale crowd. The majority are white and female. I spot Claire seated next to a man with thinning dark hair, a pronounced widow's peak and horn-rimmed glasses. She doesn't notice me. At a few minutes before the hour, people stop trickling in. The whole group numbers about fifty. Assorted noises of gathered humanity sound: rustling garments and muffled coughs and sneezes. The lights remain brightly lit, the naked grocery store fluorescent tubes casting an unflattering light on the people below and turning the speckled broadloom carpet a bilious yellow.

I shift in my chair, crossing my legs. Others shift as well. Some glance at phones or watches. The pastor is late.

Minutes tick by. Now people are looking at each other, frowns and shrugs and raised eyebrows expressing ignorance and surprise. At a quarter past the hour, the man sitting next to Claire stands and walks up to the podium.

"Good evening, folks. As you can see, Pastor Harkness isn't here yet. I'm sure there's a reasonable explanation, but until she arrives, let's adjourn to the fellowship hall."

I rise with the others. Outside, night has fallen, and the windows have become almost opaque, throwing back the ghostly reflection of moving people. I feel naked without my gun, and I can't see outside. Someone standing in the parking lot could be watching and I'd never know it.

The people now represent the protection of a crowd, and I hurry to join them.

The fellowship hall is separated from the sanctuary by a partition wall. Some folding tables have been set up with carafes of coffee, tea, and plates of cookies. It has the same broad window wall and high ceilings as the sanctuary.

I normally hate things like this. You know, walking around trying to make small talk with a room full of people who all recognize each other. It's different when I have a role to play. But I also can't bring myself to leave — both the incipient anxiety and the unexplained connection I feel with the absent pastor pull me into the throng like a net of knotted ropes.

I angle my mental antennae and go undercover as a prospective congregant. With a cup of surprisingly good coffee in my hand, I nibble a peanut butter cookie and circulate through the people, listening to snippets of conversation. Most are speculating on Harkness's absence, some advocating sudden illness, a traffic accident, a visit to an ailing follower. I hear anecdotes of the pastor's surprise visits to her flock to help with gardening, child care, or yard sales. No one seems particularly worried, and I labor to adopt that same attitude as I drift through the eddies and currents of the group, avoiding direct contact, moving in and out of clouds of perfume, aftershave, and stale cigarette smoke.

Around the perimeter of the space are more pictures and displays. One table exhorts people to pony up some cash for the fire sprinkler repair fund. Another encourages community service, asking for signups to volunteer at the county animal shelter or pick up trash along the designated 'Spirit Mile' on Highway 101. On a bulletin board with a banner reading 'Support the Creative Spirit,' posters advertise local musicians and theater groups as far south as Cannon Beach. I don't get any sense of political activism or cultish intolerance. Bonus. Maybe it is as open and progressive as advertised. My suspicion drops a few notches, and I'm ready for some light interaction.

Back among the congregants, I gravitate toward a group where the voices sound above the general hum.

"She invited me to come, and now she doesn't want to engage in honest discussion." The speaker is a remarkably handsome Asian man, with a shock of thick black hair and chiseled cheeks and long-lashed dark eyes. He's wearing a white button-down shirt that is currently buttoned *up* to the top with black pants and shoes. He looks more professional than the people surrounding him, more polished. I sidle closer, nibbling on my second cookie.

"Reverend," one of the other men is saying, "you know that's not true. Pastor Harkness is open to hearing whatever anyone has to say —"

"I doubt she wants to listen to me. I don't approve of what she's doing here and she knows it." The reverend has a rich baritone voice that no doubt goes over well in whatever denomination he preaches for.

"It's not any of your business." There's definitely hostility in the tone. "You've got your own flock to attend to, and no right to come here to tell us what to believe."

I now recognize this other man as the fellow who had been sitting next to Claire. The bartender herself joins the small group, and sees me hovering on the edge.

She smiles and speaks to me. "Hello. I'm glad you decided to join us tonight. I'm sorry Pastor Harkness isn't here."

Everyone's attention turns to me, and I paste on a smile. "Yes, I'm disappointed. You talked her up."

"Who is this, Claire?" asks the man in glasses.

I think she might have forgotten my name, so to save her embarrassment I say, "I'm Audrey Lake, newly arrived in Astoria."

"She came in to the Portway last night. Audrey, this is my husband, Daniel."

I put the rest of the cookie in my mouth to free up a hand to shake. Daniel takes it with a perfunctory squeeze and an ingratiating smile. "Daniel Chandler, at your service."

Just a hint of used-car salesman. I kind of don't like him.

"Welcome to Astoria, Ms. Lake," puts in the opposing reverend. "My name is Seth Takahashi. I'm the minister at the Riverside Christian Church, and you'd be welcome in our congregation."

"Stealing souls again, Reverend?" says Daniel.

He may mean it to be a joke, but the remark seems too biting to be simply social patter. Not that I'm especially good at this type of thing myself. Still, the man had been trashing their pastor.

Takahashi says, "I care about people — about everyone here. And about Miss Harkness herself. I simply want to talk, make sure she's aware of the message she's sending. It's just too easy to get off on the wrong track and make a mistake."

I'm no expert, but this sounds exceedingly pushy and overbearing. Claire seems to think so too, rolling her eyes and putting her hands on her hips.

"Mr. Takahashi, please. Enough. You had your chance a couple of weeks ago."

He lifts his hands in surrender. "All right, all right. I give up." There's a bit of an awkward pause, and he says, "Is Jason Morganstern around?"

"Why do you want him?" Claire folds her arms, frowning.

"Just to say hello."

Daniel takes this moment to horn in. "I haven't seen him tonight, either. And I think you've about outstayed your welcome, Reverend."

"I'm telling you, Victoria invited me to come and have an open discussion after the service."

Claire says, "As you can see, she's not here. We should be concerned about her whereabouts, not her theology. Where is she?"

The question is rhetorical, and nobody has an answer.

The coffee hour lasts about thirty minutes. The conversation drifts to other topics, none of which I can contribute to. I'm ready to leave but don't know how to extricate myself from the group. At last, congregants begin to filter out, talking in low tones. Daniel, who turns out to be the bookkeeper for the Church of the Spirit, pecks Claire on the cheek and says he'll be home in a couple of hours, and to keep the home fires burning.

The Reverend Takahashi accompanies me to my car. Not that I need the escort, but he's easy on the eyes. His face is briefly troubled, a frown marring his movie star looks. Then he shakes his head as though to cast off unpleasant thoughts, and smiles down at me.

"I meant it when I welcomed you to town, Audrey. I'm sorry if this has been a less than auspicious beginning. Please come by Riverside Christian this Sunday. I promise the leadership will be there as scheduled."

"Thanks, Mr. Takahashi, but I'm not actually the religious type."

"I hope I didn't put you off earlier. I didn't mean to criticize the Church of the Spirit. Or, I guess I did —" he flashes his smile again, this time with a bit of charming self-deprecation — and continues. "But I shouldn't have done it at such a time, when Victoria wasn't there to answer for herself." He looks back toward the building. "I'm actually amazed at what she's been able to accomplish. This is my first time here, and I'm honestly surprised to see how much support she has. The programs available. It's like a real church."

"What is it that bothers you, Mr. Takahashi?" I'm curious about his reaction, and about the missing pastor herself. To tell the truth, I'm feeling more lucid than I have in days, back to my old inquisitive detective persona. Who needs meds? Especially since I haven't had any more hallucinations.

"Please, call me Seth. Or Reverend Seth, if you want to be formal."

"What bothers you about the church then, Reverend?" Using his first name feels too casual and intimate, and I have the copper's habit of addressing people respectfully. It's always better to start on that footing — it's too hard to go back.

He runs a hand through his hair, a self-tousling maneuver that makes him look like a manga character. We've reached my car and he leans against it. His breath steams in the chill night air.

"There's nothing wrong with it on the surface. I'm sure Victoria is sincere — in fact, I know she is. Her mission is to — and these are her words — 'open the way to the Spirit for everyone'."

"That sounds very democratic."

"It is. And I don't deny that the Holy Spirit *is* available to everyone. But she goes further, insisting that the Spirit uses a person's creative impulse to communicate, and that the best way to access the word of God is to paint pictures, or do sculpture, or produce some kind of art that the Spirit can deliver a message through."

"And you don't agree?"

"It starts a dangerous precedent. It gives people tacit permission to become messengers of God themselves."

"Aren't you one? A 'messenger of God'?" For some reason I feel defensive of Pastor Harkness, and want to needle the Reverend out of his self-complacency. Illogical, I know.

"Yes, but —" He presses his hands to the sides of his head in mock frustration, a gesture that makes him seem boyish and appealing. I'm guessing there are many young women, and even not so young, in his congregation.

"But?"

"There's a lot of unstable individuals out there, and many are attracted to religion. It doesn't take much to encourage a delusional person to believe that he's the pipeline to God, and whatever prejudices and hatreds he feels are mandated by divine decree. Pastor Harkness is encouraging that kind of independent theology." He shakes his head again, and laughs. "You're a good listener. I didn't intend to give you a lecture on worship methodologies. If I haven't frightened you off or bored you to death, please do feel free to come to one of our services. Everyone needs fellowship."

With another nod and a smile, he sets off down the line of cars, and I am left with his final remark ringing hollowly in my ears. He's got some Jekyll and Hydishness going on; but without his presence, the evening becomes cold and empty, and my Garboesque desire for solitude is mixed with a puppyish longing for companionship.

Yeah, that's how they getcha.

5

My cot feels warm and cozy under my unzipped sleeping bag. In Denver, I had gotten so used to traffic and sirens and all the city sounds that they no longer registered. Here in Astoria, a lonely car going by on Marine Drive at the base of the hill is intrusive. The distant barking of a dog penetrates the gentle fog that fills my mind, followed by a snatch of conversation as people walk by on the street. The silence has its own kind of presence.

It's Friday, the last day of the work week. If I had a work week. I should be worried about that but right now I just want to be swaddled in the quiet and sleep. But try as I might, I can't shake the anxiety that has plagued me since my vision on the beach, and the unaccountable absence of Pastor Harkness. Maybe it's my detective's paranoia, always anticipating the worst possible outcome, that makes me suspect something has happened to Victoria Harkness; that she isn't coming back to her church.

Or maybe it's the vision of her death.

But. I don't believe in any kind of foretelling or divination. There's some rational explanation. Just because I can't think of one doesn't mean it's not there.

I've worked with too many obstinate prosecutors to make assumptions without evidence. But I've also been a detective too long to ignore my own hunches. A pastor wouldn't leave her flock for no reason, without letting someone know she'd been delayed and wouldn't be able to conduct the service.

And speaking of anomalies, I've never seen another preacher at a church service that isn't his own. Takahashi doesn't seem like a rabble-rouser, but he'd definitely been on the honk, criticizing Harkness's belief system. Although, to be fair, I have seen direct evidence of what he's worried about: delusional people using God as a scapegoat or an excuse for their own bad behavior. Still, without having heard Pastor Harkness speak, I can't know what exactly she advocates. The promotion of art as a voice for the Holy Spirit seems innocuous in a New-Agey sort of way.

I roll over on my side. Sleep remains elusive and anxiety begins to wrap me in its tentacles. I can't help but think about my recent hallucination, and images from the vision rise in my mind. Once again, I hear footsteps behind me, feel the steel grip of hands on my shoulders and the pain of a blow, the sharp impact of a rock on my skull as I hit the sand, the cold water rushing in, and then blackness…

…I awake in a hospital bed with a saline drip, arms and legs restrained with nylon straps. I struggle against the bonds and an oxygen mask over my face. I'm suffocating. An alarm goes off somewhere. People rush in. Someone presses me down and someone else fills my drip with a sedative that spirals me back down into darkness.

I sit up straight, gasping. The sleeping bag falls away. Tendrils of cool air make their way under the sheet, chilling my skin. A line of moonlight leaks through the metal blinds and slices across the slanted ceiling. The feeling of lingering helplessness, the terror of being confined, sticks to me like a spider's web. I rub my face and rake my fingers through my hair. I haven't dreamed of the hospital before, and much of my time there is hazy. But this seems more like a memory than a nightmare. I rub the scar on my chest. It still hurts, deep down.

Terrific. Just when I think I've successfully eluded the past, it comes right back to haunt me.

That evening I'm at loose ends, so I go back to the Portway. It's a Friday night, so the tavern is full, the tables occupied and noisy with the sound of laughter and clanking cutlery. I take a seat at the end of the bar. Claire is pulling pints and mixing drinks and dispensing menus like an octopus. She barely spares me a nod. I linger over my halibut and chips and a pint of Alaska Amber, waiting until she has a moment, savoring the mixed aromas of burgers and French fries and fish that waft from the kitchen whenever a server strides forth with a tray of steaming plates.

When Claire finally finishes pouring, she comes down to where I sit and leans heavily on the bartop, fanning herself with a damp towel.

"Busy night?" I suggest. Queen of the obvious, that's me.

"Bit more than usual. Nice to see you here again."

"It's close to where I live, plus you have decent food and beer. I'm not working yet, so good cheap eats are priority one."

She nods, and a smile flickers across her face. "Best burgers in town," she says mechanically, but then adds, "Looking for work? Maybe I can help you. I hear a lot about what's going on, what businesses are doing well. And I know a bunch of people. I could at least point you in a direction. What did you do in Colorado?"

I tense. This question always comes up — it's a standard get-acquainted line that everyone asks. I should have rehearsed my answer, but I didn't. Another indication of how far I've fallen off my game. It's too bad, because I like Claire. I've never been ashamed of my career choice, but I also won't blame her if she changes her tune.

"I used to be a cop. A homicide detective with the Denver P.D." I wait for the inevitable recoil. Or the other extreme, the fascinated eyes, the request for anecdotes.

But Claire does neither. She looks at me speculatively, continuing to wipe the already clean bartop. "You said, 'used to be.' Does that mean you're not a cop anymore?"

"Not at the moment." I take a long malty swallow of my beer. "Maybe not ever again."

"Burned out?"

"You could say that."

Maybe I don't want to leave the conversation on that pity-me note, or give her the wrong impression, that my leaving is some political statement. In any case, what I say next is almost as big a surprise to me as it is to her. "I'm going to be a private investigator. Just have to complete the process."

"A private eye? That sounds interesting."

I nod like I know what I'm talking about. "I've got all the qualifications. Lots of experience as a police detective. Solving murders, robberies, missing persons. The works."

Claire nods, looking thoughtful, and moves down the bar to greet some new customers, and I enjoy my meal in peace. It had been easier than I'd hoped. She hadn't asked any awkward questions, and I hadn't had to lie.

Except for making up the whole P. I. thing.

What's to make up? I do have all the experience I need.

Yay, digging up dirt on people's spouses. Chasing down deadbeats. Sounds like a party.

I can work for private individuals. Lawyers.

There's something to look forward to.

I succeed in shutting down that persistent inner voice and work on cleaning up my remaining French fries and draining the last dregs of beer from the glass.

When Claire finishes with her orders, she comes back. "I think things happen for a reason. Do you believe that?"

"Sometimes." Uh-oh. Was I going to get a dose of New Age philosophy?

She leans forward and speaks in an undertone. "Would you consider looking for a missing person? It's not a real case, not yet."

"You mean Pastor Harkness?"

"Yes. I'm worried about her. Daniel — my husband — says it's unreasonable to call the cops. She was an adult, free to go off on her own if she wants to. And it's true she's only been gone for a day. But I can tell you, she would never leave the church. It was — is — her calling. Her sacred role. Something is wrong. I know it. And I can check with Daniel about paying you something. Maybe we can draw on the church's general operating fund." The entry bell rings as a group of three men walk in, fresh off a fishing boat by the state and smell of their clothes.

"Hey Claire, set us up with a round of Buds, will you?" one calls as the three sit down.

"Back in second," she says, as she hurries to the taps.

A job, even before I'd hung out my shingle. Well, why not? It's probably nothing, like most MisPers cases. It feels a little squirrelly to be going in under the radar of the local detectives, but they most likely wouldn't be making much of an effort anyway. I recall my encounter at the police station, Candide's suspicion and Olafson's disdain, and enjoy the thought of putting a dent in their smugness by taking a case away from them. Because a little revenge is balm for the soul.

Not to mention a little money in the pocket. And independence from the Man.

Plus, something to focus on besides my own head trip.

When Claire comes back, wiping her hands, I pay my bill and agree to work for the Church of the Spirit. We set an appointment to meet tomorrow morning so she can give me more information about the missing pastor.

* * *

When I get back to my little yellow house, I unfold my laptop on the card table and bring up the Church of the Spirit website. When I'd been poking around before my visit, I'd noticed an archive of past services, and a link to a radio show Harkness had been featured on. Now I click on the link, turn up the volume, and walk over to stand by the windows. Lights from small fishing boats sprinkle the river, crisscrossing the channel. Something must be out there in droves, tempting the locals to cast their lines and dip their nets.

The sound of the broadcast begins to percolate into my awareness. It's an interview from a weekly program called 'Matters of Faith.' The moderator explains that every week he talks to local religious leaders about their churches. His voice is pleasantly gravelly, and the interview begins with a flourish of organ music.

Moderator: Today we welcome a preacher who's relatively new to the faith community, Pastor Victoria Harkness of the Church of the Spirit. Welcome, Pastor.

VH: Thank you. It's a pleasure to be on your show.

Victoria's voice is a rich contralto. I can imagine her filling her sanctuary with a heartfelt service, the tone of voice as much of an attraction as the content of her message. Outside, the sunset has thinned to a ribbon of orange above the long narrow strip of the Clatsop Spit that splits the river from the sea.

M: Let's dive right in. I understand the Church of the Spirit is non-denominational, is that correct?

VH: Yes. We utilize the Bible in our teachings, but I encourage my congregants to branch out and seek inspiration directly from the Holy Spirit through their own creative works.

M: Interesting. What exactly do you mean by that?

VH: God — or Goddess, or the Great Mystery, however you prefer to think of them, in whatever tradition — is always named as the Creator. In fact, that's how I always refer to the Deity myself. How better to reach a depth of understanding and spirituality than by engaging in the very activity that characterizes the divine?

Ye gods, I think.

M: So you encourage your followers to emulate the Creator?

VH: Well, on a lesser scale, of course. (Laughs). Through whatever artistic medium people are inspired to use — painting, writing, sculpture. Even gardening. My services are characterized by prayers to the Spirit to inspire us with their message, to infuse our works with divine energy and intention and meaning. And I give people the opportunity to offer their works to the Creator by bringing them to the altar. We then display them in the sanctuary and fellowship hall.

M: Your message is certainly unique. I don't think I've heard of anything quite like this.

VH: (laughs). 'There is nothing new under the sun.' Ecclesiastes.

I snort out loud. Ain't that the truth. Besides death and taxes, the other given is the banality and pervasiveness of crime.

M: Moving on, let's take some callers with questions. First on the line is the Reverend Takahashi from the Riverside Christian Church in Astoria. Reverend, you're on.

My ears prick up. So he's had contact with the pastor before. Interesting.

RT: Your sentiments are laudable and heartfelt, Ms. Harkness, but I'm afraid you're misguided. The Holy Spirit isn't the muse. It gives counsel and wisdom, but not art lessons. Your views are not supported by scripture.

VH: On the contrary, First Corinthians, chapter twelve, says true followers will receive messages and miraculous abilities. Who is to say what those abilities might be?

RT: The gifts are listed out: wisdom, knowledge, faith, healing — nowhere does it talk about painting.

VH: Many of the gifts are those of communication: as you said, words of wisdom, words of knowledge, the ability to speak or understand diverse languages. Art is just another language, another means of communication and expression. I see no contradiction, only endless possibilities. Are you, Reverend Takahashi, qualified to dictate the choices and gifts of the divine?

And the point goes to Harkness, notes my inner scorekeeper.

RT: The job of the Holy Spirit is primarily to seal a soul to God, and to communicate God's messages to a believer. It's about faith, not works and self-glorification.

VH: Of course not. But according to First Corinthians, chapter two, no one knows the wisdom of the Creator except the Spirit; it is the Spirit that provides the direct conduit for that wisdom. And how better to express the thoughts of the Creator except through artistic creation? You know yourself how open to misinterpretation words can be. Any good lawyer can tell you that."

The moderator laughs, and I think, she's won him over at least. But Takahashi goes on doggedly.

RT: The only job of the Spirit is to convict a soul to God and the gospel. You make it sound as though it's a personal genie, something outside of the Christian tradition.

VH: On the contrary, I seek to put the spirituality back into religion. I ask for offerings that come from the soul, not from the wallet. The true fruit of the Creator has nothing to do with little green pieces of paper. In the words of the prophet Joel, 'God says, I will pour out my Spirit on all people. Your sons and daughters will prophesy, your young men will see visions, your old men will dream dreams.' And *I* say to everyone who might be listening: follow your dreams that the Spirit has bestowed on you, wherever they may lead. Never apologize for the visions that inspire you; instead, allow them to be your guideposts. Follow the Spirit for they will bring you home.

I feel a rippling chill, a high alert like the distant ringing of a bell. The moderator is speaking but I'm no longer listening. I'd been caught up in the argument, the point and counterpoint of theological logic which I'm admittedly not qualified to judge. Yet now, here was Harkness validating dreams and visions; deliberately seeking out the impossible, the irrational, the spiritual rather than the coldly logical. It felt as though she were shining a light on my own experience.

If I could only talk to her, maybe she could bring some sense to the chaos. She wouldn't think I was crazy. She might even help me make sense of the hallucinations, the visions. She saw they had value — the fruits of the soul.

I tremble and wrap my arms around myself. The power of this woman goes far beyond the actual words spoken. I find myself really wanting to believe her.

I remember a snatch of conversation from Wednesday night between Claire and Takahashi. Claire had said to the reverend that 'he had already had his chance.' I didn't remember the context of her remark, but maybe this broadcast is what she was talking about. To my untutored mind, it seems he had come off the loser.

Where could Harkness be? If she isn't just playing hooky, then what? Something more sinister? I suppose being in the spotlight as a pastor, plus the fact that she's a beautiful woman, it's to be expected that some of the attention she garners wouldn't be positive or healthy. Has she been threatened, or stalked, or just made uncomfortable in some other way? Is she trying to escape from an unpleasant situation? I'll have to ask Claire when we meet. Maybe she'll know if anyone has been after Victoria.

6

Claire and I meet at a coffee shop called Three Beans, two blocks from the Portway and within walking distance of my house. It's late Saturday morning and the place is hopping, hot drink consumption incentivized by the dollops of cold and clammy fog swirling outside. The shop's plate glass windows front onto Marine Drive and the buzz from the traffic is audible, competing with the hiss of the espresso machine and the chatter from the teenagers on the sofas in the corner.

I spot Claire at a table near the window, a heavy white mug and a muffin in front of her. She's wearing a red leather cap and a matching jacket hangs on the back of her chair. The pervasive odor of fresh ground beans tempts me into an Americano with room, and I select a cranberry-orange scone so Claire's muffin won't be lonely. Sitting down so I face the door, we exchange remarks about the unpleasant weather. It's drafty here by the window, so I keep my coat on. My coffee tastes bitter, and I doctor it with a pinch of salt.

Claire opens the conversation. "I've never done this before, so I don't really know where to begin."

"Not to worry, I've done this a lot. I'll start by asking questions, and we can go from there. First, what can you tell me about Thursday, the night Harkness didn't show up at the church?"

"After we closed the church, I checked on her myself, thinking she might be ill. When she didn't answer my text or call, Daniel and I went to her apartment. The car was there, but she was gone. Or at least, no one answered the door."

"Maybe she just went for a walk."

"That's exactly what Daniel said. But why, when she had her service to do? The next day — yesterday — I checked the hospitals before I went to work, but nothing. Now I'm worried."

"You're right to be concerned," I say. "I'm happy to help, but honestly, the police have the resources to do a better search. They can look at phone records and financial records, get a warrant for her apartment, see if she's been active on line."

Claire looks away and takes off her hat, smoothing her close-cropped hair. "Daniel thinks we should give it more time. He's convinced she'll turn up. That we'd be invading her privacy. But yesterday I put my foot down, which is why he agreed to have you to look into it. As a compromise."

Some compromise."When was the last time you saw or talked to her?"

"Me? I'm not sure. It's been over a week, probably. But Daniel sees her on a daily basis. You could ask him."

"He hasn't said?"

"No."

I pause to consider that. I'm getting a bit suspicious of Daniel, frankly. But. He's my client and her husband, so I skip that for now.

"Does she have any family in the area?"

"Not that I know of. But she did live here as a child, so there could be. Her mother lives in Portland."

"Would Victoria have gone to her?"

Claire scoffs. "I doubt it. I'd sooner believe she was trying to escape from her. That woman is a piece of work."

"How so?"

"She's super conservative and smothering. Victoria told me how she was always trying to get her to move back home, drop the church, meet a nice man and get married. I think that's one reason Victoria and I hit it off. I left home as soon as I turned eighteen, jumped on the back of my boyfriend's Harley and headed for Des Moines." Her eyes take on a faraway look. "How I did love riding that motorcycle."

"You from Iowa?"

"Yeah. Went from there to California and wound up here in Oregon."

"So, a transplant like me. If you have her family's contact info, I'd like to talk to them. They might be able to shed some light on her motives, or her location."

"There's just her mother, as far as I know. Daniel will have those details. I'll have him email you." She takes out her phone and thumbs a quick text.

"What about lovers? Friends?"

"I never hear her talk about anyone special. I don't think she's seeing anyone seriously. She does sometimes get close to a congregant, but it never lasts long, not like a relationship-relationship. I think it's just her way of trying to help people. Actually," Claire says slowly, "I think Daniel and I might be her closest friends. Especially after we moved out here. He used to spend quite a bit of time with her after hours, going over the books." She looks down at her empty cup. "I'm getting a refill. You?"

I nod and give her my own mug. While she's gone, I collect my thoughts. Claire's already done some of the preliminary legwork, so it's time to search for Harkness further afield. Assuming Thursday was the day she disappeared, she's had almost two days to get in touch.

When she comes back, I ask, "Would Pastor Harkness have gone off with someone? Is she impulsive, spur-of-the-moment?"

"Nnnooo...I mean, she is open to the moment, but I can't picture her getting into someone's car and driving off without a word."

That's right; her car is still at her home. "Is there anyone you can think of that would have meant her harm? Was she frightened of anyone? What about that other preacher who was looking for her on Thursday? He seemed a little hot under the collar." I tell her about the broadcast I listened to last night.

"I remember when that show aired. The reverend doesn't give up. His heart is in the right place, but he just doesn't get us. Anything outside the mainstream is a cult to him. He's afraid Pastor Harkness is consorting with demons."

"Did he tell you that?"

Claire snorts. "*She* told me. Apparently he told her that by 'opening herself to the spirit' she's actually opening herself to any old entity that wants to come in."

Okay, that sounds creepy and borderline crazy. I don't believe in the supernatural, ghosts or zombies or demons, but is Takahashi some kind of Exorcist-style crusader? The chilly draft seems to intensify, and I take a swig of hot coffee.

"What did she think of that?"

"Pastor Harkness is all about the intention. She says if you are open to evil, then evil can come in. But if you intend to be a channel for goodness and divine energy, that's what will happen."

Except we all know where good intentions lead.

My inner voice seems to have a mind of its own. It's actually beginning to worry me.

Is there a darker side to the church's worship? Something that would justify Takahashi's reaction? I clear my throat. "How did *you* get involved with the Church of the Spirit?"

She sips her own drink. "Remember how I said it was originally in Portland? I used to live there, as well. I heard her broadcast on the radio, and I was interested. Went to hear her speak. Loved the idea of the Spirit speaking through art. I was taking a painting class at the time."

"Did you grow up in the church? Only, her message sounds a little off the beaten path." I raise my hand. "I'm not criticizing, and you don't have to answer if you don't want. I'm just trying to understand the type of person she was, the kind of people she had around her."

Claire answers slowly. "I've always had faith in a higher power, but just got to a point where the dogma didn't do it for me anymore. And I don't want my spiritual life cluttered up with all that secular political crap, you know? And Pastor Harkness doesn't care who you vote for. Her only mission is to help people get in touch with the Spirit. She trusts the Spirit to handle the rest."

Interesting. Whereas the Reverend Takahashi seems to be afraid that letting people communicate freely with the Spirit will lead to all kinds of mayhem. I like the woman Claire is describing. Her organization sounds tolerant and welcoming, centered around positive activity.

"If I'm going to track her down, I'll need all the information you can give me, however trivial. Tell me about the move from Portland. Had Victoria been threatened or been in trouble with authorities? Did someone or something drive her away?"

"Victoria says it was to get closer to the source of the Spirit. She thinks water is an especially spiritual medium, and the confluence of the river and the ocean here make the location cleansing and beneficial." Claire shivers and puts her hat back on.

I didn't miss the slight emphasis on 'says.' "Do you believe her?"

"Yes. At least, I believe that she believes, if you know what I mean. But —"

At that moment, the group of high school students leave their corner, the girls squealing with laughter and the boys jostling each other.

"But?"

Her cup clinks on the table top. "This was a couple of years ago, and I wondered at the time if there was more to it. I mean, moving the church, that's a big deal. It meant losing most of the congregation. She'd have to start from scratch again. Although, I understand about the river. The whole tradition of baptism confirms the importance of water. And I love being so close to the ocean. I grew up in the midwest, like I said — I couldn't have been further from the shore if I'd wanted. But Daniel, he tried to talk her out of it. Tried hard. I mean, the church finances were really going to suffer."

Hmm. At some point I need to talk to her husband. "Was he angry about the move?"

"Not angry, no. He came over here, too, after all. He was just aware of the business side of things."

I'll bet. "How about other people?"

"Clearly, only the most dedicated followed her here. But maybe that was what this was, a winnowing. Separating the wheat from the chaff."

I dredge up some long ago Sunday school lesson. "Sheep. Goats. Like that?"

"Exactly."

We sit in silence for a few moments, and then she says, "Please find her, Audrey. I'm scared. I don't care what Daniel says — something's wrong."

Yeah, and maybe it begins with your husband, I think. Claire has been forthcoming, but I have a lot of unanswered questions. Is there more behind the church moving to Astoria? And what about Daniel Chandler's unaccountable reluctance to go to the police? Does he have something to hide?

Claire leans forward, kneading her hands together. "You've seen cases like this before, you must have. What might make someone want to disappear?"

"There's a lot of reasons. Ruling out foul play, I would say that certain people, for whatever reason, just decide they want a different life. Their problems feel too pressing, or too complicated, and running away seems to be the only way out."

"Dodging the bullet rather than facing up to their issues?" Claire crosses her arms.

"There might be all kinds of reasons that drive people to leave: abusive relationships, bankruptcy, even just a longing for adventure. Or just general overwhelm. In general, men choose to disappear because of financial difficulties, and women —" I stop myself, because I don't want Claire to worry more than she is already.

She won't let me soften the stats. "And women?" she prompts.

"Women tend to vanish because of danger."

She catches her breath. "What kind of danger?"

I shrug, leaning back in my chair. "Abusive partners, obsessive lovers, stalkers. Those are the usual suspects."

"I see. And that's why you've been asking me about her associates." Claire traces the grain of the table top with her index finger.

I nod. "Since I don't have any other leads to follow at the moment, I'm relying on statistics." And those statistics are pretty damn bleak.

7

After leaving Three Beans, I go by the towering Queen Anne where Victoria lives. Each floor of the former house has been converted to a single apartment, four total including the basement. Wooden stairs switchback up the exterior and I hike up to the third floor. The fog is breaking up into scattered rags, and from here I can see the working piers that jut out over the river, the fish processing plants and the timber yard. I catch a glimpse of the Best Western Hotel a couple of blocks away, and feel a knot of tension form under my sternum. Behind that hotel is the little riverside beach where I had the hallucination, where I thought I was being attacked and drowned.

My armpits prickle with a cold sweat, and my tongue sticks to the roof of my suddenly dry mouth. I squeeze the railing at the top of the stairs and will my hands to stop shaking. Just because I'm close to that place doesn't mean I'm going to have another episode. That's not how it works. It's stress, stress and trauma that brings them on.

Yeah, and the fact that you stopped taking your meds has nothing to do with it.

I don't need the drugs. I can do this without help.

What, you think you're still undercover and all on your own?

I don't like how they make me feel.

Oh, and this is so much better? Feeling like the sky is gonna fall, like you're up on the high wire without a net? You used to like that, didn't you? Living on the sharp edge, until it cut you to ribbons.

Shut up, shut up, SHUT UP!

Blessed silence. At least in my head — the traffic on Marine Drive echoes up between the buildings, making a constant background roar. A log truck blasts its horn and the downspout vibrates against the siding. In front of the door is a Welcome mat with a rainbow, and a plant wilting in a bright blue pot. The door itself is solid, no window or peephole. As expected, no one answers my knock. Shaded windows keep me from seeing anything of the interior. I stand in the shelter of the porch roof and count slowly until my breathing calms enough to begin canvassing the neighbors.

The second floor apartment door is answered by an elderly white man leaning on a red chrome walker. I introduce myself and say I'm looking for his upstairs neighbor and wonder if he knows when she went out. He scratches the scruffy whiskers on his chin.

"Usually I can hear her walking around up there, but not today. Are you a friend of hers?"

I hesitate, but disclosing her disappearance might make him more inclined to help. You know, honesty. Sometimes it works. So I tell him.

"Missing? That's concerning," he says.

"You haven't heard anything suspicious upstairs, have you? Like the sound of a person falling?" At this stage, I still can't rule out a medical emergency.

"No, nothing like that."

"Are you here most of the time?"

"Yeah, I'm retired, not much to do besides watch the boob tube and look at the ships come in and read about conspiracies on the internet." He smiles and shakes his head. "You gotta ask yourself why folks believe the things they do. I mean, take these Flat Earthers. I thought we laid that one to rest a few centuries ago, but here there's folks who think the whole space program is nothing but a hoax and we all live under a dome."

Must herd the cat away from the rabbit trail. Even if I agree with him. "Have you heard anyone else upstairs, any voices or arguing?"

"No. Nothing comes to mind."

I think about Claire and Daniel banging on the door. "What about last Thursday night?"

"Thursday? I mighta heard something. Or it coulda just been the TV. I turn it up so I can hear it good. I'm binging Law & Order."

I note the hearing aids. Not a good chance he'd notice a lot of noise. "When was the last time you heard anyone moving around upstairs at all?"

The old man thinks for a minute. "It's not easy to say. You get used to your neighbors' noises and kind of don't notice after awhile, unless something out of the ordinary happens. But it's been some time.

Maybe even two or three days. Maybe longer."

"Listen, Mr. —"

"Bateson. George Bateson."

"Mr. Bateson, is there a property manager or maintenance person I could get in touch with? Someone who could open up the apartment and make sure she isn't hurt or unconscious?"

"Yeah, just a sec." He totters away, and I stand on his doorstep listening to the traffic and the distant guttural bark of sea lions. He has a nice view, at least. In a few minutes he comes back with a business card, spindled and mutilated.

"Here's the property manager."

"What about the other apartments? Do you know anything about your neighbors?"

"The one below me is vacant. Good thing, too. I'm sure I sound like a herd of cattle." He bangs his walker on the floor to demonstrate. "Basement is a young couple, new last month. Don't hardly ever see them. They work all the time."

I thank him for his help, and he thanks me for livening up his day.

"If I do hear someone up there, should I call you? Now you've got me involved, I'll be paying more attention."

"Yes, if you would." I give him my number and we exchange a few more pleasantries — he obviously doesn't get many visitors and is prolonging our interaction — but at last I find my way back to ground level. I knock on the basement apartment, but get no answer.

Back in the parking lot, I check Victoria's car. The green Subaru Forester is at least twenty years old, and a crack scrawls across the windshield. The inside is uncluttered, no coffee cups or clothing or candy wrappers. All the doors are locked. I check the tires for mud or gravel, and the grill for dents or bloodstains, in case Victoria ran over someone and vanished to avoid the rap. The left rear tire is low. Without attention, it'll be flat in another day or two.

Despite the lack of evidence so far, it seems likely there has been something suspicious, if not outright foul play. Most people don't just walk away from their lives and leave everything behind, not without a reason.

Except for you, of course.

The tone of the inner voice is really starting to annoy me.

Did Pastor Harkness have something she wanted, or needed, to get away from? If uprooting her church is any indication, she seems to have a penchant for physically distancing herself from her problems.

Maybe she's now chosen a more permanent form of running away.

Like, being dead? Drowned in the river?

I refuse to take a hallucination seriously. Because that would be crazy. And I'm not.

From the front seat of my car, I call the property manager and leave a message, explaining that there is a concern for one of their tenants' welfare and could someone please come and check. Then I sit there, stewing, squeezing the steering wheel like I'm trying to make a diamond out of a lump of coal. What if Victoria is lying up there in her apartment, unconscious or hurt? What if there's some piece of evidence that might point me in the right direction, something that would save valuable time? Because the clock is ticking with a loud, insistent tone. And for Victoria, it might already be too late.

8

Son of a bitch.

I don't want to go back up to the apartment. I want to go home, get away from the river, have a chance to settle down and do some more research, but I can't stand the thought of Victoria lying there, hurt or worse.

You could call the cops.

Ugh. I really don't want to engage with them. Plus, I don't really trust the police. Not anymore. I'd rather do this myself.

I pull a pair of latex gloves over my sweaty fingers and grab my snap gun from the box under the seat, scrambling up the switchback stairs. Up and up, and I'm panting when I reach the top.

The entry to the apartment is partially shielded by the railing around the top landing. I kneel on the welcome mat and thrust the snap gun into the lock to engage the tumblers. It takes only seconds; the lock is old and easily overcome; the deadbolt isn't fastened, and with a last glance around I open the door and dart inside. I don't give myself a chance to think about the beach, the hallucination, or whether I'm making a really big mistake. Because, if this turns out to be a crime scene, I'll be leaving traces all over it.

Plus, breaking and entering.

Calling out is a non-starter because of neighbor George, so I draw my weapon and walk softly. No lights are on. Venetian blinds shade the windows, casting the apartment into twilight. The front hall leads to a small living area. Sofa, chairs, TV, houseplants. Some decorative fabric squares hanging on the wall. Kitchen is clean, no dishes in the sink, but a sour odor wafts from the trash can. The whole place is stale. I don't linger anywhere, but open doors to find a bedroom with a rumpled bed; a closet full of colorful clothes; a second bedroom set up as an office with a desk and a laptop; a bathroom where the hand soap on the sink is beginning to crack.

Behind me, the refrigerator coughs and hums to life, and I whirl into a half-crouch, weapon at the ready. Almost immediately I realize my mistake and straighten up, taking a moment to steady my nerves with deep, controlled breaths.

Careful. Someone's gonna cite you for hunting appliances out of season.

There's no sign of a struggle, no bloodstains, no mess. I would guess no one's been here for days. I stand silently and listen. Muted traffic noise drifts up from the street, and the laugh track from a muffled television that probably belongs to George rises through the floor. On the move again, I look for a cell phone, or even a land line, but the only electronic item is the laptop in the office. The screen comes to life when I flip it open, requesting a password. I type in 'password' and variations of same. Then I try 'churchofthespirit' and 'spirit' and 'Jesus.' Even 'Godhelpme.' Nothing. I close the computer. There's a pile of paper on the desk and an open notebook. It looks like she was working on a sermon.

You're pushing your luck, Lake.

I know, I know. Just a few more minutes.

I check the closet in the office. Coats and cardboard boxes and an ironing board. Back in the bedroom, I look under the bed. Suitcases. In the living room, there's nothing behind the couch but dust bunnies, and nothing under the cushions but a couple of pennies and a paperclip. Satisfied the place is empty, I return my gun to the holster. Then I see it — in plain sight, such a common thing that it didn't trip my radar. On the dining table is a purse.

In seconds, I've got the zipper pulled back and am looking into the cavity. A green leather wallet takes up most of the space. A quick paw-through reveals pens, Kleenex packet, cough drops and other handbag detritus. No keys. Unsnapping the wallet reveals driver's license, bank cards, a slim wad of cash: several ones and a fifty. I close the billfold and return it to the purse. Wherever she went, she took her keys, but not her wallet. She meant to come back. And since the car is still parked down below, she left on foot.

While my brain is still cataloguing data and drawing conclusions, I hear a noise that sends my heart into a gallop around my rib cage. It's the sound of footsteps on the landing outside and someone rattling the doorknob.

For a nanosecond, I'm paralyzed, standing with the open purse in my hand. Then I drop it with a thump and skitter down the hall to the bedroom. For surveillance purposes, I leave the door open a crack.

"Hello? Maintenance! Anyone here?" The voice is deep, a man's voice. Footsteps. "Hello? We got a call to check on this apartment. Hello?"

A tiny slice of hall and kitchen is visible. A figure crosses the room.

The deep voice calls out again. "Everything okay? Your door was unlocked. I'm gonna check the other rooms, okay? Hello?"

Shit. I dart to the far side of the bed and lie down on the floor. I hear the door to the office open, and then footsteps coming down the hall. From where I'm lying I can see the bottom edge of the door beyond the suitcases. It swings open, and a pair of work boots appears.

"Hello? Anyone here?"

I try to keep myself from breathing, willing him to stay out of the room. A fly buzzes against the window, thumping softly. Seconds stretch like hours. Sweat pours down my face and pools on my lower back. The dusty chemical smell of the carpet fills my nostrils, and moisture springs to my eyes as the sinus cavity prickles. My diaphragm lurches involuntarily. I feel a pain in my chest.

"Hello?"

Must. Not. Sneeze. I hold my breath and press my finger against the trigeminal nerve under my nose, grinding my upper lip against my teeth until the skin splits. The taste of blood is on my tongue. My vision pixilates.

And just like that, I'm back in the Baxter Building. Only now I'm crouched in the dark under a reeking pile of bedding, on top of a mattress crawling with microbes, trying not to sneeze as shots echo against the battered concrete walls. People are screaming, running away, fighting each other with fists and knives.

There's a dead person on the bed beside me. I can't remember who it is or how they got there. I'm too busy trying to hide. From down the corridor I here harsh voices.

"Police! Drop your weapons! Get on your knees! On your knees! Now!"

Gunshots. A thin voice calling, half whispering, half crying. "Zoe, where are you?"

Running footsteps, disappearing in the distance.

The fly buzzes against Victoria's window pane. A horn blasts faintly down on the street. I'm still on the floor behind the bed. Sunlight streams through the window, and I blink the world back into focus. The boots have gone away and the bedroom door is wide open. How much time has passed? I'm shivering, terrified. The memory completely overwhelmed my senses — now I don't know if I'm alone, if the maintenance man has seen me, if the police are on their way.

I am Audrey Lake. I am a police detective. I am in control.

I touch my gun for reassurance.

What the hell just happened to me? It felt like the hallucination on the beach, in all the immersive detail, as though I had been transported somewhere else. But unlike the beach experience, I know without doubt that the incident at the Baxter Building really occurred. Much of my experience during that last undercover assignment is hazy. I flinch away from that experience, more than happy to let it sink into oblivion.

I force myself to my feet. My knees tremble, and I lean on the bed for support. The bedspread puckers under my hand and I have to smooth it away. Must get out. Leave no trace. Peek around the jamb and listen before moving into the hallway. Pause to listen again, make sure I'm alone. The only sound is the roar of blood in my ears.

Inside the purse on the dining table, the green leather wallet is gaping open. The long compartment that should hold cash is empty. The maintenance man has robbed Victoria.

A flood of anger leaves me breathless, undermined by a sneaking surge of shame. If I hadn't left the purse unzipped, with the wallet clearly visible, would he have dared?

And now, a conundrum. Do I return the purse back to its original condition, wallet closed and compartment zipped? Or do I leave it where it is? After an agony of indecision, I leave it as it is. At the end of the day I'm still a cop. I'm unable to erase the evidence of a crime.

Skip the moralizing, Lake. You don't have a get-out-of-jail-free card.

Again, I freeze. The voice, the flashback. The tone and character are the same. It's Zoe, from the Baxter Building, back from the dead. I have well and truly lost it.

Chill. Finish your biz and get out.

I start moving, if only to get away from the insistent voice. The laptop in the office beckons, but I resist taking it. I also want to go through all the papers, but my nerve has departed with the maintenance man. I really just want to get out, get away from the poisonous memories and crawling fear. At least Victoria's not here, waiting for someone to help her. I leave the apartment and lock the door, shutting it hard behind me.

9

After my little bout of breaking and entering, it's a relief to get back to the comfort of my empty house. A quick perimeter walk to make sure all the doors and windows are still locked helps settle my nerves, and I relax into the camp chair to check my email. Daniel has provided contact information for Victoria's mother, whose name is Elizabeth Harkness. She apparently likes being a queen, and named her daughter to follow in her footsteps.

Since Victoria isn't in her apartment, her car, or her place of work, the last arrow in my quiver is her mother. If the pastor isn't with her family, I'll have to think of a different tack.

I'm still jittery, so before the call I prepare my pistol cleaning apparatus, laying out the rod, brush, patches, and solvent. It's a Zen-like activity that always calms me. I open the window to provide some ventilation before turning on the speakerphone and tapping in the number from Daniel's email. The phone rings three times before a woman answers in a cultured voice.

"This is Ms. Elizabeth Harkness. To whom am I speaking?"

"Hello, my name is Audrey Lake. May I speak with Victoria?" I remove the magazine from my gun and place it on the table, then open the chamber and peer down the barrel to make sure the Glock is empty.

"What's that noise?"

Oops. "Nothing. Is Victoria there, Ms. Harkness? Can I speak with her, please?" I begin to strip the gun, breaking it down to its component parts.

"Who did you say you were?" A small dog yaps in the background.

"Audrey Lake."

"Your name means nothing to me."

Big surprise. "Can I please speak with your daughter?" I begin pushing a solvent-soaked patch through the barrel with the rod. It emerges almost as clean as when it went in. I haven't been firing my weapon lately, something I'll have to rectify soon with some target practice. I've probably already lost my edge.

"She isn't here. Why do you think she might be?" Ms. Harkness's voice is brittle and clipped.

Her tone seems off. I do a quick auger with the bore brush before pushing through a dry patch. "I haven't been able to reach her at home. Or at work. I thought she might be with you."

"Listen to me. I don't know who you are or what your game is, but it's obvious to me you don't know Victoria. I'm hanging up now."

"Wait." Her defensiveness is inexplicable. Why isn't she more concerned? I pick up the phone and switch off the speaker. "Please, wait. I'm a private investigator hired to find your daughter. Are you saying she's not with you?"

"Who hired you?"

I don't know the proper etiquette regarding client confidentiality, so the journalist's approach seems safest. "I'm not at liberty to say. But I can confirm that your daughter is missing, Ms. Harkness. Do you know where she is?"

"Are you working for that heathenish organization she calls a church?"

Whoa. No love lost there, apparently. "A friend of hers approached me." Claire said she was a friend. I'm not lying. "Are you saying that Victoria isn't with you?"

Her voice lowers; it sounds husky now. "I haven't seen or spoken to my daughter for over three years."

My turn to pause. "I see." I take a turn around the room, rolling the gun barrel in my palm. Sometimes I think better on my feet. "Do you know where she might be? Is there any other family? A sibling? Her father?"

Ms. Harkness's reply drips with venom. "Her father is the last person she would go to."

"Look, Ms. Harkness. I'm trying to find your daughter. A little help would be nice."

Setting the phone back down, I re-activate the speaker, giving her time to assimilate the information and adjust her attitude. After a pause long enough to enable me to run the lubricating mop through the gun barrel, Elizabeth Harkness says, "I don't know who you are, but I'm coming out to that riverside rat hole, and so help me God, no one had better stand in my way." The call ends, and my ear fills with the sound of dead air.

What a bitch.

I push aside Zoe's opinion. Maybe if I ignore her long enough she'll go away.

The key to a successful interview is not becoming emotionally involved, but I'm shaking with the effort of not reacting. Channeling away the anger, I use a gun brush to apply a light coat of lubricant to all the moving parts of the Glock. The familiar acrid smell and the resulting smoothness of the action satisfy my internal power receptors — I have a working, dependable weapon ready to hand. As I burnish the reassembled pieces with the luster cloth, I'm once again in command of myself and my unruly emotions.

There's something going on with this case that I don't understand. But whatever the cracks and crevices in the family dynamic, there's now no obvious place to look for Victoria. I mentally review the timeline. According to Claire, the church moved to Astoria two years ago. Victoria hasn't spoken to her mother for three. So, although Ms. Harkness obviously doesn't think highly of the town, their estrangement wasn't caused by the move. It also didn't sound as though Victoria's mother knew about her disappearance, or where she might be now. Nor did she seem overly concerned. Unless it was fear coming out as anger.

I know something about that.

When I was a detective at the Denver Police Department, the Major Crimes Unit handled missing persons, so I've had my share of looking for the lost. Hundreds of thousands of people are reported missing every year, but the vast majority turn up safe within a few hours or days. Unfortunately, those that don't are often victims of crimes like kidnapping and murder. Hence the involvement of the MCU.

What the general public doesn't seem to get is that it's not a crime to disappear, to leave your world behind and start a new life. After all, I'm doing that myself. You can even argue that historically, these are the kinds of individuals who built our country. So unless there's compelling evidence to the contrary, the police have to assume a missing adult is acting by choice. And most of the time, they're right.

The gun-cleaning apparatus goes back into its box. I pull the trigger a few times, dry-firing to make sure everything is working. Then I begin thumbing bullets into the magazine. Up to now, I have found no evidence of a crime committed against Victoria Harkness. Just the fact that she left her home on foot without her purse, but with her keys and phone.

And a frightening hallucination.

If Victoria's disappearance is voluntary, she may have been fleeing a stalker or obsessional congregant. Although the purse left in her apartment makes me infer she left with the intention of returning, it's possible she may have felt so threatened she didn't dare go home. This scenario feels more plausible than the pastor avoiding unpaid debts or overdrawn credit cards, although I can't rule it out. I don't know her money situation and have no right of access. This is where the resources of the police beat those of a lone investigator. My only resources are wits and experience.

The alternatives to voluntary leaving are foul play or an unforeseen accident. Movies and novels notwithstanding, very few people wander off with amnesia. Something prevented Victoria from coming home. And when I think of the darkened Riverwalk, the lonely beach, and the rolling chop of night-black water, the conviction grows: she was alone, vulnerable, unable to defend herself. Something terrible has happened. I don't need a vision to tell me that.

I've done what I can. So, I call Claire. Leave a voicemail. Tell her to consider talking to the cops.

Time to give my brain a rest. I turn on all the lights and secure the loaded gun in my shoulder holster. Then I defrost a frozen pizza and spend the rest of the evening listening to the radio and researching how to become a private investigator in the state of Oregon.

10

Monday morning I'm up early, after spending all night flipping from side to side like a fish on a riverbank, and getting all snarled in my blankets as a result. The past and the present have tangled themselves in the wrinkles of my brain. Dreams and thoughts and memories are all interwoven into a net, and I'm the unlucky salmon caught in the strands.

I make my way down the suicide stairs to the kitchen. I call them that because the risers are steep and the treads shallow, the railing is low and the window on the landing is placed exactly so that if I slip and fall, I'll crash through the glass and bleed to death from all the lacerations.

I drag the card table and camp chair over near the windows that look over the Columbia. A tugboat chugs up the channel, pulling a barge heaped with gravel. I feel a kinship with the tiny boat and its heavy load. Whitecaps appear and disappear as the wind stirs the chop. For now, the rising sun illuminates the streets, but purple-bellied clouds stack themselves up near the mouth of the river, promising future overcast.

March. What are you gonna do? If I was still in Colorado, it might be sunny or snowing or blowing this time of year, or doing it all at once. I feel a pang of homesickness for the Centennial State's vibrant climate, which despite the wild springtime still remains largely sundrenched and inviting. I miss the sunlit days, the lapis blue sky with its untamed cloudscape, the horizon edged by sawtooth mountains.

Resolutely, I grind nostalgia to powder under a metaphorical heel. No going back, remember?

Last night, I discovered the licensing process for private investigators is mostly a matter of filling out forms and sending some money to the state board. Once they approve the application, I have to take the P. I. Proficiency Exam. I definitely have the work experience, but the necessity for three letters of reference gives me a hollow feeling in my chest. The detectives in my unit at DPD had either witnessed my breakdown or heard about it, and might not be inclined to say nice things about me. Cops are leery of mental illness. They see too much of the down side, people having freak-outs in the street with kitchen knives. I'd have to think carefully about who I asked for a reference.

Knock, knock, Lake. What about your MisPers? Today is day four.

I know, I know. I need to talk to Claire again, and Daniel, and Seth Takahashi.

In fact, maybe *I* should call the police.

You can't trust them. You know how they are. First thing, they'll check up on you. Find out you're an unreliable witness.

Plus, the police will want to know all kinds of things that I won't be able to tell them. I don't have a picture, I don't know her habits. I've only seen her on video snippets posted on the website. And the thing is, I know she's dead. She isn't lost or trapped somewhere. Her life isn't depending on being found.

The best person to make the call would be Claire. Or Daniel. I've made my plea. The Astoria Police Department isn't the DPD, but they can still get a warrant for phone and financial records. I wish I was still a cop.

Stop right there. No, I don't. The overbearing authority of the Man; the paperwork; the testosterone-fueled hierarchy. I don't miss any of it.

I run my fingers through my hair in frustration, then go out to check the mail, and get a breath of fresh air. I keep hold of my coffee, comforted by the warmth and familiar bitterness.

An older white woman walks down the street toward me, tugged by a smooth-haired gray and white dog. My muscles tense. Pit bull mix. Owners swear by the breed, but I've had too many run-ins with pit bulls trained into aggressiveness by drug thugs and other criminal types to treat the animals lightly.

"Hello," the woman says, smiling. "You must be our new neighbor. Link said he'd met you. I'm Phoebe. And this is Delilah."

Link. The judge. The man who brought me cookies and flowers. Belatedly, I realize I haven't combed my hair and am still in the rumpled sweats I threw on when I got out of bed. Oh, well. At least there's nowhere to go but up. And her husband has seen me worse. One good thing: this time I'm unarmed.

"Hi. I'm Audrey." I gingerly dangle a hand for the excited Delilah to smell, and she leaves a smudge with her cold wet nose and gives it a hearty lick, tail circling like an industrial fan. Despite my wariness, the friendly canine makes me smile.

Phoebe is in her sixties, her graying hair cut into a fashionable shoulder-length wedge. Though lines web the corners of her eyes and mouth, her cheeks look as soft and smooth as a piece of fine linen. Intelligence gleams in her gray eyes, and I remember she's a psychologist of some kind. More dangerous in her way than Delilah. If the dog attacks, at least I'll see it coming, and the wounds will only be physical.

She glances at the cup in my hand. "I see you've already got coffee, but why don't you come in for a bite? Link was baking scones when I set off on Delilah's constitutional. They should be ready by now."

Constitutional. Ye gods. But despite my inner hermit, I feel the need to connect with someone, to send the shadows back into their corners. I have to be friendly some time.

Plus, baked goods.

"Okay," I say.

Like mine, the Rutherford house is on the downhill side of the street and accessible by a dozen concrete steps, but that's where the similarity ends. Oh, it has some of the same Craftsman details — covered porch and knee braces under the eaves — but it's twice as big, with leaded glass transoms and cedar shingles. The forest green door has a geometric stained glass window, and a wind chime of dangling wood and metal hangs between the porch supports.

Inside, the hardwood floor gleams with a high sheen, covered in the middle with an intricate Persian rug. The rug in turn is partially covered by a fuzzy gray Persian cat. It looks up as Delilah romps in and stalks away in a disgusted huff.

I like the cat.

"Link, we've got company," Phoebe calls, and leads me into the kitchen.

"Good morning, Audrey," says the judge with a smile. "Glad you could join us." He hands me a plate.

I've already sampled the warm spicy aroma that wafts from the oven with my nose. Now my taste buds get some action. The scone is deep brown, sweet and gingery, with stripes of white icing that literally melt in my mouth. So much better than stale doughnuts or store-bought cookies.

I nod and smile around my mouthful. It's nice, talking to normal, friendly people. Relaxing. It makes me feel like an actual part of the human race. But small talk has never been my strong suit, and the case is at the forefront of my mind. Maybe Phoebe can cast some light on the more abstract, troubling aspects that have been chasing themselves around in my head.

Are you nuts? Oh wait, of course you are.

Chill. I'm not going to talk about myself. Not too much, anyway.

They ask me about my aunt and my family and past life. I tell them about my mother the architect, my father the cop. I explain that the house I've inherited belonged to my mother's sister. But I don't want to talk about my professional past, so I switch the focus.

"Phoebe, Link told me you're a therapist."

"Here and there. I'm a psychologist, half-retired, but still see some of my long-term clients."

I swallow past the sudden tightness in my throat. "Could I consult you — professionally?"

The judge coughs. "Looks like I'd better make myself scarce."

"Oh, not for myself." Let's step on that idea before anyone gets the wrong impression. "I mean, I need some background for a job I'm doing."

"What kind of job?" Phoebe asks.

"I used to be a cop, and I've taken on a private investigation."

Link says, "Now I really had better leave. This sounds like a potential *ex parte* contact, and the last thing I want is to pick up any bias about a potential case." He grabs his coffee and beats a retreat.

Great, I've already driven one neighbor out of the room, even if he's got a valid excuse. "Phoebe? Do you mind?"

"What is it you need? I can't comment on my patients, you know."

"I get that. I don't want to ask about a specific person." At least, not yet. "I want to get your insight about cults. Leaders, followers, like that."

She cocks her head. "Now I'm definitely intrigued. Okay, as long as general information is all you're after, let's go downstairs to my office and talk."

Just what I asked for. And also what I dread the most. I swallow past the tightness in my throat.

* * *

Phoebe directs me to the outside stairs which lead down to another exterior door, the gateway to her office. It's furnished with a leather-and-chrome lounge chair — the modern version of the head-shrinker couch, I guess — two comfortable armchairs, and an old-fashioned desk with a laptop and an ergonomic stool. The paint is a soothing cerulean blue, the carpet a deep-napped gray. Sunlight streaming through a window makes a bright rhombus on the floor.

The therapist points me to one armchair and sits behind her desk. "Now, ask your questions."

I lean forward and steeple my hands. "What kind of person would join, or lead, a cult?"

Phoebe takes a handful of paperclips from her desk drawer and begins to construct a chain, linking them together. "I've never actually met anyone who was a cult leader, but some of the markers are pretty well known. Mind you, this is based mostly on testimony from cult followers. Not too many leaders want to be psychoanalyzed. In fact, they tend to reject any kind of close scrutiny."

"I understand." Nod, nod. Actually, this conversation feels good, two professionals exchanging information. I've consulted with experts galore in the course of my career, and now I'm back on familiar ground, investigating the possibilities. I uncross my legs and lean forward again.

Phoebe continues, adding a few links to her growing chain. "Your average cult leader tends to exhibit symptoms of a narcissistic personality disorder. They want adulation, control, power — and many are charismatic and know how to manipulate their followers into submission. Some are delusional, others are simply sociopathic. They often have a didactic dogma about life or religion that purports to be 'the answer.' Many will exploit their followers for money and sex." She pauses, perhaps to gather her thoughts. Based on what I know so far about Victoria Harkness and her church, this doesn't sound like a match.

Phoebe is speaking again, "You have to understand that this is at best a gross generalization. For example, I don't think Marshall Applewhite — one of the founders of Heaven's Gate — had sex with his followers. But, he did insist on celibacy, and he and some of his male congregants had themselves surgically castrated. So we're still talking about sexual control. I would say the prime motivator for cult leaders is power, which is maintained by domination, manipulation, and aggression, and often justified by personal delusions of grandeur." Once again she pauses. "What is it you are trying to figure out? Has someone gone off to join a cult?"

"Not exactly." I wonder how much to tell her. "I'm trying to track down a missing person, who has associations with a religious group. I'm trying to get a handle on whether the disappearance is voluntary, and if so, where this person might go and what actions they might take."

Thought you'd decided it wasn't *voluntary. Because, you know, the purse. No phone or keys.*

It's important to explore all the loose ends. Assumptions are dangerous.

You just don't want her to be dead.

So sue me.

Untouched by my inner dialogue, Phoebe says, "People don't usually vanish after joining a group; they want to remain where they can access it, get that validation. Again, Heaven's Gate was an exception — the founders and their followers did seem to disappear for a while but were later discovered to be living a transient lifestyle, off the grid. That was before they settled in California and committed mass suicide."

"This person is the leader of the group. And the group is still around."

"Then it makes even less sense. As I said, cult leaders crave adulation. They want to surround themselves with people who support their grandiosity. They can't do that by leaving their followers behind."

I shake my head. "After hearing this, I don't think the group qualifies as a cult. It seems benign, if unorthodox."

"Then maybe your missing person is just trying to escape the pressure. People often have unrealistic expectations of their spiritual leaders, and are offended and outraged when they prove to be all too human."

Yes. Escape the pressure. Leave everything behind to become someone else. Or maybe to escape the person you had become.

We talk about what might be early indications and warning signs of an emerging cult, but I think this is a dead end. None of it seems to connect to the pastor's disappearance.

Someone knocks on the door of the office. Link's voice comes through, slightly muffled by the barrier. "Are you ladies done?"

Phoebe glances at me before rising to open the door. "I think so. Is something the matter?"

He seems distracted, frowning. "I heard something on the scanner."

"What's that?"

"They've just found a body in the river. Down by the Cannery Pier Hotel."

My attention narrows to a laser focus. Link's troubled face fills my vision.

"No! Do they know who it is?" Phoebe flicks her dismayed gaze to me. She suspects, as I do, and the possibility distresses her. Not just the cool, clinical psychologist, then. I like her better for it.

"It's a woman. At this point, no one knows her identity."

But I'm afraid that I know, and my chest seems to fill with icy water.

I make my excuses to the Rutherfords, jump in my car and rush down to the docks. All the time my heart is on overdrive, and my muscles clamp my bones like steel shackles. I'm like the tin man of Oz before the oil can.

The Cannery Pier Hotel is three stories, barn red with beige accents and a standing seam metal roof. It has a kind of industrial chic. The building and parking lot are actually located beyond the bank on the river itself, supported on a forest of pilings and accessible by a built up causeway on a foundation of boulders, almost like a jetty. A small crowd mills about on the macadam of the causeway. Some have sought refuge under the carport that shelters a small fishing boat — a bow picker, according to the informative placard. Two men in wetsuits are debriefing with the square bulk of Detective Olafson and a gawky blonde woman sporting a sheriff's badge. An ambulance is parked nearby, and the attendants are unloading a gurney.

Some uniformed patrol officers are starting to shoo people away. I've made it just in time.

I give the law enforcement a wide berth and join the group beside the bow picker on display. A female reporter and a male photographer, both with lanyards from the *Astorian* newspaper are talking to a young couple who are as pale as the sheets that drape the gurney.

"I still can't believe it's a body," the man is saying. "I thought it was a mannequin."

"Until the seagull landed on it, and started pecking." The woman closes her eyes and presses a hand to her mouth.

The reporter turns to the photographer. "See if you can get a picture of the remains. I know the pilings might be in the way. Do your best. Also, take some general shots. And when the divers go in, get some images of the recovery."

The photographer nods and goes to the edge of the parking lot. He kneels and begins clicking away.

The reporter notices me. "Are you with the police?"

"Not exactly. But I'm involved in an investigation that might tie into this incident."

"How so?"

"I'm afraid I can't comment at this time. Don't interrupt your interview on my account."

She frowns, but apparently doesn't want to leave the couple until she's wrung them dry of details. Meanwhile, I'm watching the men in wetsuits. They've picked their way over the boulders that edge the causeway, and wade in among the pilings. And now, I can see what they are heading for. A bundle of clothes, floating. A mass of long dark hair that resembles a clot of seaweed. It does look unreal, like an inflatable doll or an oversized puppet. But I've encountered enough corpses to know one when I see it.

As the men in the water secure the body between them and work to bring it to shore, I feel the now-familiar frisson, and know without a sliver of doubt that the remains must be those of Victoria Harkness.

That evening, the local radio news has more details. Standing at the windows of my empty house, looking out over the river as a squall spits rain against the roof and siding and tangles the branches of the tree next door, I listen with a kind of resigned anxiety.

"Earlier today, a vacationing couple staying at the Cannery Pier Hotel spotted human remains floating face-down in one of the piling fields along the shore. The pilings are all that is left of the huge cannery industry that once thrived along the Columbia before the devastating 1922 fire.

"The remains were recovered by the Clatsop County Sheriff's search and rescue team, but there was no hope of resuscitation or rescue. According to the EMT's, the body is that of a white woman who has most likely been dead for several days.

"The remains have now been identified as Victoria Harkness, pastor of the Church of the Spirit, a local religious group. Anyone with any information should contact the police. At this time, the cause of death is unknown. A candlelight vigil will be held Tuesday evening at 7:00

p.m, at the Church of the Spirit, and the community is invited to attend."

When the broadcaster goes on to other stories, I click off the radio and lean against the card table, resting my head in my hands. The emotions, the sense of loss and anger, wash over me. I don't understand my own feelings. Who is Victoria to me? I've never even met the woman. But I feel guilty for failing to find her. And a new sense of outrage when I think of the theft that occurred while I was in her apartment. And wonder about how her identity became public knowledge so quickly.

I call Claire; what else can I do? The case is over, and yet she may not know it. The ringing buzzes in my ear as I pace through the empty rooms. At last I hear her voice.

"Claire, it's Audrey. Have you been watching the news?"

"Yes. Oh my God, I still can't believe she's dead." She sounds stunned. "The police called the church earlier, and Daniel talked to them then." Her voice is shaking. "There's going to be an investigation."

"That sounds right. They'll have to determine how she died."

"No, an investigation of the church. Her mother is pushing it, says we knew Victoria was missing and should have reported it. She wants to sue us."

Elizabeth Harkness found that out from me. I feel a cold runnel of dread.

Claire's voice is firmer. "Audrey, please, I want you to stay on the case." Pause. "I got your message last night. Daniel was still hesitant about bringing in the police, but it looks like that's out of our hands."

I'm confused. "Why do you want me to stay on? I mean, I will if you want me to, but there's not much left for me to do, now that she's been found. Whatever happened, the cops will take care of it."

"Pastor Harkness's mother thinks we — the church — had something to do with it. Please, Audrey. I don't know how she knows what she knows, but it was she who identified the body. She says she filed a missing persons report this morning — that's how the police were able to identify the body so quickly."

"Okay. Well then, I did some investigation yesterday after our conversation at Three Beans, so I'll write up a report and email it to you."

"Thank you."

I put the phone down and stare out the window. The darkness is punctuated by street lights and headlights along Marine, and a few boats on the river. I climb the suicide stairs to my cot. Leaning up against a wall with a blanket over my lap, I begin to write up my findings. It's thin — just what I found out from neighbor George and Elizabeth Harkness. Putting my illegal activity down in writing seems to be a bad idea, even if my intentions were good, so I don't. And what about the theft? If I report that to the police, I have to admit to being in the apartment. And I also can't talk about my vision of the murder without sounding like a lunatic. All the unmentionables are like an iceberg, barely submerged beneath the surface and just waiting to sink the ship.

If Victoria's mother is blaming the church, I have some responsibility for that. I'm the one who told her Victoria was missing. If she came over from Portland to talk to the police, and found out there was no official inquiry, I can see how that would upset her.

But. I recommended to Claire that she file a report and she didn't want to.

But. I could have filed one myself, after I realized that something was amiss.

But. Then I would have to admit I was in her apartment.

Around and around.

Regardless, it's too late for that now.

Wouldn't be the first time you crossed the line, though. Remember the Baxter Building? You were one of the regulars.

That was different. I was undercover. I had a legend to maintain.

Which one? The one about you being a criminal, or the one about you being a cop?

I'm awake for a long time, listening to the wind and staring into the dark.

11

Despite my many and varied reservations, I decide to attend the Tuesday evening candlelight vigil. The church sanctuary is crowded. A table with small white candles in cardboard holders and a larger, central lit taper has a sign that invites us to add our soul magic to Victoria's. I decline to participate, but many do, lighting a candle from the bigger flame and cradling it in cupped hands. Mostly, the group is somber, talking quietly in small groups, hugging or holding hands. Interestingly, no one is dressed in black, or very formally. Sweaters and shirts and blouses, khakis and clean blue jeans. Moisture-slicked raincoats.

A harpist plays in the background, a mournful Celtic air. Canvases and scraps of paper with drawings and paintings of all media and ability cover the walls. Scattered across the front where they are visible through the windows are sculptures, many abstract or of found materials. There are even some books written by congregants: self-published poetry and memoir. More spirit offerings.

I'm here because I feel like I need to be. Because despite the fact that I didn't know Victoria Harkness, I recognized her. And witnessed her murder. That is arguably the most intimate thing I've ever experienced. With anyone. Since I'm still investigating, I'll observe all I can. Just being alert to mood and listening to conversation may provide a lead when more direct inquiry fails.

Daniel Chandler stands at the podium and taps the mic. "Welcome, all. Please, be seated."

I commandeer a chair in the back. He waits while everyone finds a place and all the coughs and whispers have settled into silence.

"Surrounded by the offerings of Spirit, we gather to honor the memory of our beloved founder, Victoria Harkness." His voice roughens, and he pauses. He bows his head for a few seconds and says, "I'm sorry, I can't do it. Anyone else who would like to say a few words, please come up to the mic."

There's some shuffling of feet, then a young man walks up to the podium. He tugs the mic down to his mouth. He's unshaven, with a thick mop of dirty blond hair.

"Victoria changed my life," he says. His voice booms and the speakers squeal with feedback.

Chandler steps in, clears his throat. "State your name, please. We're making a recording of the proceedings, for anyone who wants it." He points to the video camera positioned in the aisle.

A glare flashes across the young man's face, but he says, "My name is Jason. I —"

"Sorry, last name too?"

"Morganstern." He pauses. "Can I talk now?"

"Of course." Chandler gives a wide gesture of permission and backs away.

"I started coming to the church when it first got here. I was going to another one, but this one seemed better. Victoria really saw me. She showed me I could be a real artist. And she helped me when I was looking for work." Jason drops his gaze down to the top of the podium, and almost whispers. "I loved her."

"Thank you, Jason. We all did." Chandler ushers Morganstern away. A flash of belligerence twists the young man's mouth, but he relinquishes the mic.

I wonder if Claire's husband is going to be that rude to everyone.

"Who's next?" Says Chandler. "Come up when you're ready."

The harpist twingles in the background, running her fingers up and down the strings. A couple of other people say they'd found their true calling through Victoria. Then another man stands. He has thick shoulder-length brown hair styled in an artfully disheveled wave. His eyes are dark and deep set. He, too, is unshaven, but his stubble looks decorative, whereas Jason's looked merely unkempt.

Behind the podium, the man surveys the crowd. He's in his thirties, white, confident in his handsomeness and presence.

"My name is Eric North. I've known Victoria, off and on, for most of my life." He smiles, gaze panning the crowd. "When I first saw her, she was climbing a tree in the yard next door. I was an artist even back then, sketching all the time, and I caught her image on paper..." the rich voice goes on, describing their friendship. How he'd always been drawing and painting, and how he hoped he'd inspired Victoria in some small way in her universal message of allowing the Spirit to speak through art.

Nothing like a little self-stroking at someone else's wake.

I consider sharing how seeing her picture on a flyer in a tavern sparked a connection that made me want to hear her message, but I don't. It sounds too touchy-feely-culty.

Plus, public speaking.

When no one else comes forward, Daniel Chandler, self-control restored, launches into a narrative, relating how he and his wife Claire had served the church in Portland, and followed Victoria to Astoria and continued to serve here. Chandler has a pleasant voice — I can see him as preacher, or a used car salesman. I shift, wishing that the folding chair had more lumbar support. I don't know what I thought I was going to gain by coming here, but now I'm bored, strangely let down and ready to go home. Standing unobtrusively, I ease toward the door. And there, standing near the entrance, are Detectives Olafson and Candide.

My mouth drops open. Unattractive, I know. For a split second, I think they're here for me. For breaking into Victoria's apartment. For impersonating a private investigator. For all the things I've done and wished I hadn't.

Get a grip, Lake. It's not always about you.

Just then, Daniel announces, "We're now going to have a prayer vigil where her body was found. Officers of the APD will escort us and manage traffic, and stand by while we send our prayers over the water."

I feel equal parts relief and dismay. Because now I'm going to have to go through the entire ceremony. Anything else will look suspicious.

Plus, I'm damned if I'll let those two scare me away.

The detectives lead us outside. It's brisk — my phone says forty-six degrees — but at least it's not raining anymore. A sunset blaze of hot orange and yellow illuminates the western horizon as indigo suffuses the east. Olafson takes the lead. The mourners become a straggling line of singles and couples, and their candles flicker like stars in the twilight, illuminating faces but leaving eyes in shadow. Patrol officers are stationed outside, directing traffic as the candle bearers cross Marine Drive and then head west along the sidewalk.

Jane Candide takes the drag position at the rear. I stay near the middle, not wanting to encounter either of them and risk a confrontation. I am, however, keeping my eyes and ears open. The question of what happened to Victoria Harkness still burns; maybe even stronger now that I know for sure she's dead, robbed of all options and choices. Life has meaning, and therefore, so does death. Even if we can't suss it out completely.

People in the procession are mostly quiet. Some are crying, some holding hands or with arms around each other. No one laughs, and conversation is sporadic and soft-spoken. One or two individuals within earshot are murmuring rhythmically, perhaps praying.

We cross the street again where it turns north beyond the roundabout, and proceed in a snaking, glowing line to the Riverwalk. The framework of the Megler Bridge makes a dark lattice across the sky. Just beyond the bridge is the tiny beach, tainted now by my hallucination. I clench my hands into fists, concealed in the pockets of my coat.

The procession turns and walks along the gravel causeway to the parking lot of the Cannery Pier Hotel. The hotel is illuminated by the white blaze of LED lights. The carport sheltering the bow picker is an angled silhouette. Detective Olafson leads the coiling line of mourners to the edge of the lot nearest the bridge.

When all have gathered, Olafson clears his throat, and gestures with his arm. "She was found here, below us, floating in the water. The hotel has generously allowed you to have this ceremony in their parking lot, but asks that you don't linger too long. Therefore, if you could pass by, say your prayer or respects, and then head for your shuttle, it will take you back to the church." He points to a sky-blue bus parked in front of the hotel. It has 'Church of the Spirit' emblazoned on the side in a curvilinear font.

Daniel Chandler looks up from where he is setting up the video camera. "The bus is for anyone who wants a ride back. We thought it might rain..." there's a scattering of faded laughter "...and that the procession would break up here." He finishes what he's doing, and steps away from the camera, bending his head and murmurs a prayer, or maybe he's just rehearsing his lines. He takes a breath and says, "Victoria Harkness loved all waters, but especially this river. She saw it as analogous to the current of life that flows to us from the Sprit. Thus, I say to you, O Great River, nestle her soul in your waters. Nurture her in your bosom, and convey her to the divine home that awaits us all."

I try not to roll my eyes. That would be disrespectful. And it's just a reflex anyway, indicative of my discomfort with anything spiritual. The truth is that I don't know how to mourn for someone I never met. Instead, I look out over the water and wish Victoria Harkness Godspeed to whatever her next destination might be. If there is a destination beyond the present reality.

I step back to watch, envying the congregants their faith. If nothing else it gives them something to look forward to. The mourners fall into procession, looking out over the river, some of them casting flowers into the water. One person, the young guy — Jason Morganstern — who spoke first at the memorial, throws in his candle. Olafson steps in and grabs his arm.

"None of that. You don't want to start a fire."

"It's water, ain't it?" Jason tries to shake loose, but the detective holds him firmly.

I move forward. To support Olafson? To defend Morganstern? I don't really know. Call it copper's reaction, heading toward the trouble instead of away from it.

The detective's voice takes on a steel sternness. "The pilings below are wood. And as you may know, Astoria has an unfortunate history with fire."

"So? I ain't from here," growls Morganstern. "Let me go."

Olafson maintains his hold for a few seconds more, to make his point, then releases the man after a little shake, and gestures toward the bus. Face crumpled with anger, and maybe sadness, Morganstern spits on the asphalt and walks away, straightening his shirt. Everyone else seems to be ignoring the altercation; more people move forward, hands cupped around their candles. Olafson speaks to some, nodding, acknowledging the people he knows. It's evidence of how long he's lived here, how embedded in the community he is. And how much of an outsider I am.

A woman's voice comes from behind me. "I didn't expect to see you here." I turn, too quickly, and Claire Chandler steps back. Her eyebrow goes up. "Did I startle you?"

"A little. Do you know that guy?"

"Detective Olafson?" She shakes her head. "Not well. He was there when they recovered the body. I'm not happy about the police being here. It's so intrusive. They should let us mourn her in our own way. But with Elizabeth Harkness involved, that's too much to hope for." Her eyes glisten with moisture. "I suppose — I suppose the church is done with. I don't see how it can go on without her."

"Surely you can get another pastor?" An image of Seth Takahashi surfaces briefly in my mind, like a cryptic message in a Magic 8-ball. "Or your husband. He seems to be stepping up to the role."

"Oh, *Daniel*," she momentarily closes her eyes, and shakes her head in negation. "It wouldn't be the same. She had a light. I don't know who will be able to take her place." Claire brushes her eyes with the back of her hand. "Please. Figure out what happened to her. Daniel may want to keep the police at arm's length, but I won't let this lie. She was my friend, and if someone hurt her, I want to get to the bottom of it." With a firm nod, she turns and walks toward the waiting bus.

I rub the back of my neck. I don't have the resources to work the case properly. I'm off my game. And I don't know the territory. At all. Olafson was right — knowing the people, the politics, the community — it's the bedrock of policework.

But. I've been a cop for a long time. And whatever I experienced — hallucination, vision, faux acid trip — I saw Victoria murdered. Beyond saw — I was there, in a way I can't explain. I may not be able to paint a picture, but I can offer this: the hope of justice.

When I turn back to the river, my gaze intersects with that of Detective Candide. The set of her jaw speaks volumes: get off our turf.

In answer, I lift my chin and meet her eyes squarely, delivering my own subliminal message. Back off, lady. You don't scare me.

Claire wants me to keep investigating, so I ride the bus back to the church and drink tea and mingle with the congregation, listening and gathering information about Victoria Harkness, sometimes guiding the conversation to when people had last seen the pastor. I hear anecdotes about how she had helped people; stories of creative talents discovered and tended with her encouragement; memories of times that she dropped in to help with a gardening project. But people didn't generally seem to just hang out with her. The most recent sighting I note is a couple of weekends ago, so several days before she missed her Thursday night service.

At the minimum, she'd been missing four days before her body was found. At the maximum, over a week — say, ten days.

I'm not the only one on the stalk. Olafson and Candide have set up a table in the corner and are systematically interviewing people. But most folks don't like to talk to cops, even if it's for a good cause. Probably I'm gleaning more than they are. Olafson gives me the stink eye once, but otherwise ignores me. By eavesdropping on people after they leave the interview table, I learn that the detectives are mostly trying to establish a time of death. They don't appear to be asking for alibis, or treating her death as anything more than a tragedy to be investigated. They just want to know when she was last seen.

After gleaning what I can, I leave before they decide to call me over. I had walked down from my house to the church, and I decide to walk back. Without saying anything to anyone, I cross the parking lot and head for home. I shiver and check the temp on my phone again: down to forty-two degrees, but it feels a lot colder, the damp wind from the river biting through my jacket. I bury my hands in the pockets and wish I had worn a hat.

I wonder if making a video of the ceremony had been all Chandler's idea, or if Olafson had suggested it. It's a good idea. Despite my antipathy, I'm impressed. It's surprising how often a murderer attends the victim's funeral. The recording might pick up something useful.

But. It's not necessarily a murder.

Sure about that?

Oh hell. I'm not sure of anything. Just that I feel a connection to the dead woman and that I had a strange vision of her death on the little riverside beach. And a weird flashback when I was hiding in Harkness's apartment. I'm fusing everything together. Creating links where there are none. In a word, craziness.

But maybe I am still crazy. Insane people always think they are rational, don't they?

I cross Marine above the roundabout and proceed to Florence, paved with old concrete and heading straight up the hillside. I feel the pull of the ascent in my knees and calves.

Daniel Chandler is a dark horse. Claire keeps telling me he didn't want to go to the police. I smell a fish, and it isn't the mudflats. There's something going on there.

At the dogleg, I turn left up the even steeper Agate Street, puffing a little. When I reach the intersection with Alameda, I stop to catch my breath and look out over the big river. The New Youngs Bay bridge glitters with headlights, the prongs of the drawbridge blinking with red warning beacons. A smudge of faded sunset still remains in the west over the scattered lights of Warrenton. It's pitch black, and here among the houses, street lamps are few and far between.

"It's nice out here, isn't it?"

I turn at the unexpected voice, half-reaching for my gun — that's twice in one evening someone has sneaked up on me — and behold Phoebe with Delilah tugging at the end of a green leash.

"I come out here every night, rain or shine, unless it's really storming. Wouldn't want Delilah to blow away! It's the best view in town."

I agree with a nod.

"You looked like you were thinking hard."

Delilah twines her leash around our ankles as she looks for a perfect spot to do her business.

"I'm trying to decide what to do about something." The words pop out involuntarily.

"Your investigation?"

"Yes."

"It's not always clear, is it?" Without looking, Phoebe unwinds Delilah as though she has done it a thousand times before, and expects to do it a thousand more.

"No. It's not."

She continues in a musing tone, "I always ask myself, 'what's the worst that can happen, if I do X?' and then, 'what's the worst that can happen, if I don't do X?' That usually helps to crystallize the problem. Sometimes the barrier isn't what to do, but just giving ourselves that initial push."

The worst that can happen? I could wind up in the psych ward again. Or, a murder might remain unsolved, a killer allowed to go free to enact violence on someone else.

Phoebe's voice is warm but impersonal, calming. "Sometimes there's another alternative, one that only becomes apparent when we make a choice and move to a new perspective. Like this place here. We have a wonderful view from our house, but neither bridge is visible. If I didn't know better, I might believe that the river was uncrossed and uncrossable. But here, I can see the bridge to Warrenton. And when I walk the other direction, I can see the Megler Bridge over to Washington. I'm not marooned after all."

What I wouldn't give to not be marooned, looking out from my island at the endless unfriendly sea. I'm confused again, conflating my own situation with the case at hand. I can't seem to separate the threads into their discrete patterns. Victoria's disappearance; my own voluntary retreat from everything familiar; secrets hidden under the veneer of normality.

Put a sock in it, Lake. Crying in the dark don't make things any better.

Yeah, I get it. The only way I'm going to discover my way out of this darksome place is to blunder around until I find the light switch, or the door.

Phoebe and I walk back together along Alameda and up our own Rhododendron. As I stop at the top of the stairs that lead down to my front porch, I say: "You must be a heck of a shrink, Phoebe."

She smiles, reaching down to pat Delilah. "Thank you. I like to think so."

12

The next morning, Detective Olafson calls. He offers to meet me for breakfast at the Pig 'N Pancake.

So, I'm not going to be able to avoid talking to the police. I know how this works. If I don't agree to this friendly meeting, on neutral ground, I will eventually receive a summons to the station. Or he might show up at my house. I'd given him my contact details when I'd gone in to apply for a consultancy; at this point, I'd prefer to keep him at a distance.

His summons doesn't give me time to do my usual perimeter check, so I'm nervous already as I walk down toward the restaurant, bundling my jacket around me. What do they know? What has Claire told them? Only that the church hired me as an investigator after the pastor disappeared. They can't possibly know I broke in to the apartment. They might fault me for not making a missing persons report, but the church has a bigger onus there than I do.

Yes. Good. I've succeeded in reassuring myself. I can enjoy the feeling of the intermittent sun on my face as clouds dart across the sky, ignore the bite of the clammy air gusting off the water.

The Pig'N'Pancake is a family-style restaurant located near the five-way intersection of Columbia Avenue, Marine Drive, and Bond Street. When I enter the restaurant, I take a quick look around to see if he's brought backup, and spot Olafson himself raising a hand from a corner booth. He's already nursing a cup of coffee and a plate of bacon and eggs with a raft of hash browns. I order the short stack and a glass of orange juice. We make small talk until the waiter brings my dishes, and refills our coffee cups, and I make sure there's no one close enough to hear our conversation.

Olafson gets down to business. "So. Audrey. I understand from Daniel Chandler at the Church of the Spirit that you have been doing some work for them." He folds a slice of bacon into a square and pushes it into his mouth. Crunch, crunch.

Here we go. I swallow my mouthful of pancake. "That's right."

Still chewing, he says, "Is that why you were down at the docks Sunday night?"

"Yes." There's no point in lying. "I saw the Sheriff there. Is the county taking over?" I ask mostly to keep this from being a one-sided interview.

"Nope. But search and rescue comes under their purview. Ruby was there as a professional courtesy."

He's let me know he's on a first-name basis with the Sheriff. That they are, in fact, in cahoots. In case I was thinking of peddling my consultancy to the higher-ups.

"Since any investigation will now fall to the police, I'd like you to ease the transition by telling us what you've discovered." He shovels in a forkful of hash browns yellowed with egg yolk.

So, first you diss me, and now you want my help. Please. "The Church is paying my bills, so I only give information to them. What they choose to do with it afterward is up to them."

"Chandler cleared it with me, said you'd help in any way you could."

Does he think I'm a complete idiot, to fall for such transparent trickery? "Whatever he told you, he hasn't said anything to me. Until I hear differently, the confidentiality policy still stands." I'm trying to sound nonchalantly confident; in reality, anxiety is creating a big hollow in my abdomen.

Olafson drops his chin in warning. "Don't get off on the wrong foot here, Audrey. Cooperating with us is in everyone's best interest. Including Victoria Harkness."

"Have you got the post-mortem back yet?"

"You know I'm not gonna answer that."

I shrug. "So the information flow is pretty one-sided."

Olafson snorts in disgust. "You were a cop, Audrey. You know the drill. I can't comment on a current investigation. It's your duty to reveal what you know."

I lean forward. "Look, Steve, I'd like to help. Truly. But I won't reveal information that belongs to my client. You need a court order. If you want my help, maybe you should hire me yourself. As a consulting detective. Then my experience would be at your disposal." I fork in some more pancake.

"Is that what this is about? Maybe your old precinct had different standards, but the APD doesn't pay people for information."

The heat from my irritation rises from my chest to my cheeks, and I have to swallow twice before I can speak in a normal tone. Male cops get to show anger, but female cops don't. Because any kind of emotional display will be seen as weakness. I had that experience drilled into me from day one on the force.

"You're insinuating that anyone outside your own little pocket is corrupt or incompetent. You just can't stomach that I might have more experience than you."

"Don't assume that you got the chops to insert yourself into an investigation, just because you're some big city cop on vacation." He's frowning now, shifting his coffee cup from hand to hand.

I can't help pushing him. "How many murders do you get? One a decade? If I were you, I'd be pulling in all the help I could get." Fork. Pancakes. Orange juice.

"There's no evidence that Victoria's death is murder. Accident is more likely. We don't make assumptions until the evidence is in. Regardless of what you are accustomed to do."

That finally gets me. He's made it personal. And just to show how far from normalcy and good judgment I've drifted, I say, "Well, I predict: drowning, after assault, by person or persons unknown. You've got a killer on your hands, Steve. Better get cracking." I throw down my napkin and clank my cup on the table, sloshing the dregs to the lip.

His face is red as the ketchup bottle. "And how do you know that, Ms. Lake? An eyewitness? Security footage? Or just delusional thinking on your part?"

"Find your own evidence — you've already dissed any contribution from me." But my screen of outrage is only to hide my sudden terror: I've referred to my hallucination as though it were real. Rationality is going out the window, and I need to end the interview before I discredit myself further.

As I struggle out of the too-soft booth divan, Olafson drops his voice, lowering the volume but upping the menace. "Tell me, Ms. Lake, do your clients know about your — medical issues?"

The blood seems to congeal in my veins.

He presses his advantage, his tone like some old school headmaster.

"You're not a well person, Ms. Lake. You should stay home. Get plenty of rest. Don't try to pick up where you left off. Because it's not going to work."

He's articulated my deepest fears as though he were ordering a second breakfast off the laminated menu.

"We'll see about that," is all I can think of to say. And then I leave before I put a fork in his eye.

The P&P is only a block from the Riverwalk, so to calm my nerves I stand on the boardwalk, staring over the water, taking deep breaths to steady my heart.

I can't blame the detective completely for my reaction. He's only tapped into the substrata of resentment that bubbles beneath the surface. My father was a detective, too. He idolized law enforcement and the military, and when my brother Dean entered the Marines, Dad couldn't have been prouder. Seeking that same level of approval, I got a degree in criminal justice and went through the Denver police academy, taking my place on the thin blue line.

But following so closely in his footsteps meant he never stopped criticizing my performance, or comparing me to other cops. My colleagues took their cue from him. Instead of enjoying a cloak of protection from the status of my father, it was open season for hazing and derision. It wasn't until his early retirement after being wounded on the job, and my own receipt of a gold detective shield that I was marginally accepted. And even then, I still had to endure the sexism of the other detectives. To be fair, not all of them were like that. But enough.

Suck it up, Lake. Everyone has a sad story. Don't choose victimhood.

No. I'm not a victim. But Zoe's intrusive voice still makes me doubt my sanity. With a shudder, I realize once again I'm not far from where I had the hallucination. Granted, Astoria is a small town but I always seem to end up here. I've been skirting around deciding if the vision is real — real in the sense of accurate, a true portrayal of an actual event: like a memory. But in my foolish tirade against Olafson, I've brought it into the open.

When I interviewed witnesses, I sometimes found it helpful to introduce a smell, a sound, get them to think about a sensory experience associated with the thing they were trying to remember. I'd even take them back to the original place if that was possible. Maybe if I return to the beach, I can re-invoke the vision, and get some more detail. My knees feel weak at the thought. Deliberately try to induce a moment of psychosis, when I'd been fighting so hard to keep that under control?

Yes. I have to grapple with this — better to do it alone, where no one can see me fail, or worse, call the authorities. So. I walk toward the little crescent of sand. Seagulls squawk, and I hear the whisper of traffic on Marine Drive.

The wind off the water skirls around my thighs and slips down the collar of my coat. I shiver. The dampness reaches into my bones, chilling me from the inside out. To my left, the steel skeleton of the Megler Bridge arcs high across the water. I pull up the hood on my jacket and hear the patter of rain on the fabric, see the black stippling appear on the sidewalk and pepper the river. I close my eyes and try to empty my mind of other thoughts, and step down onto the sand. The packed grains give way beneath my feet, and I wander down to the water's edge. When I look back over my shoulder, I see my own clear prints embedded on the surface.

Don't be an idiot, Lake. You can't make it happen. Not like streaming on demand.

All right then, maybe I can *let* it happen. Deep slow breaths. Thinking about nothing in particular, just letting my senses inform me about the place. The wind. The sloshing wavelets. Damp fingers of fog. Traffic rumbling high above.

Then: fear. Darkness. Slap of running feet. Hands on my arms, my shoulders.

I struggle to stay above the surface of the sensations and waves of emotion, closing my eyes in tightened concentration even as my heart hammers and sweat slicks my palms.

A ringing blow to my cheek. I fall, knees and elbows into the wet sand. A feeling of dislocation — I'm on the ground, but also standing. The me on the ground looks over her shoulder, puts up a hand. No!

A harsh voice cuts through the night, full of pain and anger. "It was just a game! You see that, don't you?"

A smeared face, a hulking shadow, fear, betrayal — I'd trusted him...

Him.

He grabs my shoulders, slaps me again. My vision tunnels. I fall, hit my head. Kick out, feebly. He pushes me, pulls me, into the river. "I can't let you spread your lies, Victoria. I won't let you wreck my life." He holds me down. I bat at his arms, try to scratch. Fail. Cold water.

Filling my chest. Down down down...

A foghorn blasts from a freighter nosing under the high span of the bridge. I come back to myself, blinking, gasping for air. Heart is racing like a hummingbird's, and cold sweat bathes my chest and back. The vision is so real. The same as before, or almost. This time I hadn't been so caught up, so taken unawares. I learned something important. The attacker was a man. Someone known, someone trusted. And now I know for certain whose death — whose murder I've just experienced. He said her name out loud.

Victoria.

The certainty settles around my heart like hoarfrost. And yet, I've known it all along.

As I'm walking home it starts to rain. Typical. I don't want to think about what I just experienced. So I think about the meeting at the restaurant, the argument, and losing my temper.

Yeah, way to annoy the locals, Lake. Don't think you'll be getting a job anytime soon.

But he'd been the one, threatening me with what he knows. That's blackmail. Typical small-town good-ol'-boy.

Now who's biased?

Oh, shut up.

He knows. The bastard knows I'd been in the psyche ward. Someone at the station must have talked. Who was it? Who outed me? Olafson must have called in, checking my references, or just curious — the sin and virtue of every good detective. It would be too much to hope that he keep any revelations to himself. And this is a small town. Word will get around. I'll be unemployable. A pariah. My fury ignites anew.

Wow. Paranoid much?

Okay. So thinking about the meeting isn't an exercise in calm. But neither is the other thing. My hallucinations — or visions — are real. They reflect a real thing that happened. The whole idea makes my brain lock up. Because if I can witness to something that already happened, be present in the past, that means — I don't even know what that means. Just that my whole idea of the universe has been flipped upside down.

A convulsive shiver racks my whole body, like I've poked an electric eel.

Maybe you projected Victoria into your craziness.

Zoe, back for another low blow. But I can't shake my certainty. Whatever its source, whatever has suddenly made me able to sense an event outside my personal experience, now I have something concrete to investigate.

Refill your prescription, Lake. You're talking to yourself a lot.

No. I stopped taking my meds when I'd emptied the bottle into the toilet. No more lint padding between me and the world. I'll just have to endure Zoe's commentary as I sort through events. Because I am going to move forward with the investigation. Claire trusts me, and Victoria seems to be calling from beyond, demanding justice. Or something.

Or is that my own delusion?

Regardless, as I'd challenged Olafson, it's time to get cracking. The attacker in my vision is a man. That lines up with homicide stats. I can start narrowing down the search without going too far out on a limb. Figure out who were the men in her life, who she was seeing. The church rolls are the obvious place to start, but I also need to know about family, lovers current and past, friends. According to the vision, this wasn't a random killing, not some roving serial killer. And statistics bear this out as well: women are most often killed by people they know. I can justify taking this line. In all likelihood, Victoria had not just known her killer, but trusted him. Or at least, enough to meet him on a deserted beach.

Deserted. Yes, maybe, in the sense that no one else had been there. But it isn't exactly isolated. There's a hotel within a hundred yards. A busy street within a block. Pedestrians, out for a stroll along the Riverwalk. Someone must have seen something. That's where the police should come in, questioning, searching, armed with the authority of their calling. Me, no one is going to answer my nosy questions. And I simply don't have the resources to go after all the people who had been staying at the hotel, who might have been looking out their window at an opportune time, even if I could talk the hotel management into letting me see their records.

The body was found in the pilings of the Cannery Pier Hotel. Olafson and Candide would probably concentrate their efforts around that area. Only I know the location of the actual murder, the beach behind the Holiday Inn. I need to tip them off, so they can widen their search for possible witnesses.

Yeah, Olafson is gonna be eager to hear your recommendations.

Dammit. There must be a hotline, or some procedure. We'd relied a lot on anonymous tips at the DPD. Meanwhile, I'll follow up with Daniel Chandler, and get a list of male members of the congregation. And find out whether he really wanted me to share info with the APD.

When I get home, I put the teakettle on for tea and shuck out of my wet clothing. No time like the present to call the cop shop. I turn the caller ID function off in my phone settings, engage the record function and punch in the numbers for the general station line. A perky female voice picks up.

"Astoria Police Department. Is this an emergency?"

"Uh — no. I wanted to give you some information. Regarding an ongoing investigation."

"I see. Can I have your name?"

"No. I'd prefer to remain anonymous."

Pause. "I see. I'll put you through to one of the detectives."

"Wait — " but she's put me on hold. I almost hang up. I don't want to talk to Steve again. But who else is going to do this footwork? I won't tell them who I am, just that I have a tip and —

A voice breaks into my thoughts. "Detective Candide speaking."

I try to drop my voice below its normal register. Clear my throat. "I have some information on the killing of Victoria Harkness."

"Who's calling, please?"

Ignore. "You should look into the Holiday Inn. Someone staying there might have seen something."

"In the hotel?"

"Outside, by the river. Check the rooms that overlook the water. The murder happened on the beach."

"How do you know this? Who are you?"

I hang up, and stop the recording. I don't want to give Candide any more time to recognize my voice, or put two and two together. She won't ignore the tip. I hope. And if anyone gives me static later about withholding information to the police, I've got the recording to back me up.

Heart's thumping like a drummer on crack, so I walk around each floor of my house: basement, main, and second. By the time I finish checking the perimeter, my anxiety has abated somewhat. The fort is secure. Civic responsibility has been addressed. Now the hunt can truly begin.

13

First stop is the Church of the Spirit, and the police-averse bookkeeper, Daniel Chandler. I find his office. It smells like fast food and furniture polish. It's small and cramped, with sagging bookcases, faux wood desk, and acoustical tile ceiling. One of the tiles has a telltale brown splotch: water intrusion.

Daniel himself looks exhausted, with bags under his eyes and lines etched in his cheeks. Strands of his thinning hair stick out all over, as though he's been running his hands through it. Despite the signs of emotional upset, he's not bad looking, in a kind of professorial, intellectual way.

"I just had a little confab with Detective Olafson of the Astoria police." Pause to see if this has any effect on the man. It doesn't, so I continue. "He told me that you said I could tell him about anything I discover in the course of my investigation. Is that true?"

"I haven't spoken with anyone from the APD."

I'm not surprised to learn the detective lied to me. Typical cop trick. "Good." I nod. "Do you have a church directory? I'm going to need a list of all the members and their phone numbers."

He leans back, rubbing his forehead. "Audrey, can you explain why you're still involved? I appreciate it, naturally, and support Claire's decision, but I honestly don't understand why the investigation is still active — either with you, or the cops. Vicky's not missing anymore. She's...dead. And we're not exactly swimming in money."

I clock the slight hesitation before he states the word 'dead.'

His face reddens. "It's such a terrible accident."

Uninvited, I sit down in his visitor's chair anyway. "Mr. Chandler, two things. First, I hear Ms. Harkness wants to sue you, which is going

79

to cost more than my bill. Second, I'm not sure Victoria's death was an accident."

"What? Why not? Surely you don't think she killed herself? She would never leave the church. It was her child — her greatest achievement."

"At the very least it is a suspicious death. Maybe even a homicide." For sure it's a homicide, but hallucinations are not evidence.

His mouth drops open, then shut, then open again. So textbook, it's almost comical. "That's ridiculous." He glares. "That's preposterous. What — why —"

I explain my reasoning, citing the presence of the detectives at the vigil. "Did you record the vigil at their request, or was it your own idea?"

"Mine. But they said they might want to watch it later."

"See? They want to screen it for suspects. Or suspicious activity. Didn't they talk to you first?"

"Yes, but they said it was just routine."

"Mr. Chandler, regardless of what the police think, or do, we've got to move forward. The more time passes, the more difficult the investigation becomes." I bait a little trap, because I don't trust him. "The cops are going to come sniffing around, unless I can hand them a solution."

He shifts the position of his stapler by two degrees. "I see."

"I've got a lot of experience in solving homicides. More than anyone in this town." Which may or may not be a good thing, from his point of view.

"Well. Carry on, then. I'd like to minimize the intrusion as much as possible. And I don't want the media to inflate her death into a circus. The scandal would break her heart."

"Great. Now, I want a list of the members of the congregation."

"I just said I want to limit any intrusion, not abet in an invasion of privacy. No one in the church would harm her, or anyone!"

"All the better to rule them out early, then. If this turns out to be a murder investigation. Don't worry, I'll be polite and discreet. Also, did Victoria have a husband? A boyfriend? A girlfriend?"

Chandler's face flushes. "A — a girlfriend? Certainly not! And she wasn't married. Or seeing anyone else. As far as I know. And I think she would have told me."

"What makes you think that?" Was Daniel a confidante, or just an employee? Plus, he said anyone *else*.

"We were close. I've known her for years."

"How close?"

He jumps to his feet. "What are you insinuating? Whose side are you on?"

"Whoa." I hold up my hands. "I'm just trying to understand Victoria's milieu, her life and the people around her." I wait until he sits down, then ask, "What is your role in the church affairs?"

His head jerks up. "There are no 'affairs,' Audrey."

"I meant, your role in the administration."

"As I said earlier, I do the books, keep track of donations, revenues, and expenditures." His voice is testy now, annoyed.

"Do people pay to be members?"

"There's no fee. People give tithes, or make other donations. Vicky sometimes got paid for public speaking at other venues. And she had her own money, which she used to cover the rent on this building, for instance. Some of our members are recognized artists, and their spirit offerings are sold to interested collectors."

"Do you get a lot of spirit offerings?"

"Let me show you."

Chandler takes me to the worship hall. When he clicks on the lights, I see the walls covered with paintings and collages and lithographs. I'd noticed this before, but only peripherally. Now I pay attention.

He says, "It varies. Usually Vicky decided what she wanted to display. She judged the pieces on individual merit but also on the donor, whether or not they could benefit emotionally or psychologically from seeing their work displayed." He clicks off the light, and we go into the adjoining fellowship hall. "More here, as you can see." Pictures and photographs arranged haphazardly, and a lovely full-length portrait of Harkness. She's shown as an angel, floating on the water with wings spread. A piling field stretches away, and the Megler Bridge soars overhead.

I shiver. This image is too much like the riverside beach to ignore. "Who did this one?"

"Eric North. He gave this to us months ago. North is a local painter of some renown. He spoke at the memorial service — tall, brown hair, good looking. At least my wife seems to think so," Daniel says dryly.

"I remember."

"Ever since childhood, Vicky had a special connection to the Columbia River. It's one of the reasons she moved the church here. She always said that water, especially moving water, had a spiritual component. The veins of Gaia, she called it. We sometimes had services on the shore, or down on the beach by the jetty, where the river empties into the Pacific Ocean." He clicks off the light.

More than ever, I feel the killer must be connected to the church. Putting her body into the river was almost an act of grace. North's painting could even have given the murderer the idea.

I assume we're going back to the office, but instead Chandler takes me to a storeroom. A single bulb illuminates more canvases, wood carvings, pottery, and metal sculptures. I point to one piece which features several broken machine parts welded together haphazardly. "Is this an offering too?"

Chandler grimaces. "Yes. Young Jason Morganstern. Not much talent there, I'm afraid, although I think North was mentoring him some." He runs a hand through his hair and rubs the back of his neck. "I simply don't know what to do with all this. A lot of rubbish, most of it." He closes the door and we return to the office.

He plops back down in his chair and sags back, squeezing his eyes shut. "I'm just the bookkeeper, but there's no other employees to see to things. I'm the only one with access. I'm trying my best to handle all the details, but I don't know what's to become of the church."

"I'm sorry, Mr. Chandler. Truly. I never met Victoria, but I can tell she was someone special. Exactly how long had you known her? You said a long time."

"Eight years. She was so beautiful, so dedicated. I still can't believe someone would want to kill her. You must be mistaken."

"I know. It's an ugly, ugly thing. But you can help me. Please, give me the list of church members with their phone numbers, and if you can think of anything, no matter how small, that seems suspicious or strange, please tell me." I crack a smile. "You'll probably have to go over all this again for the Astoria cops, if they're doing their job. So you might as well have it ready."

He blanches. "I was hoping that you'd be able to keep them away."

"You won't have any choice. It's a suspicious death." Here's the avoidance, first hand, that Claire had described to me. Maybe now I can get some answers. "The cops are going to want to know why you didn't file a missing person report."

"I suppose because I thought she'd turn up. I thought maybe she'd gone off on a retreat or something, to work on her book."

This is the first I've heard about a book. "Without telling anyone?" I raise my most skeptical eyebrow. "Come on, Mr. Chandler. It looks strange."

"Whose side are you on?"

That's the second time he's said that. "I'm just trying to find out the truth. If you don't want to talk to me, fine, but the police won't back off. If you want them out of your hair, the best thing to do is be honest with them. And me. If I can get a head start, maybe we can wrap this up before they make this even more unpleasant for everybody." I recall my breakfast with Detective Olafson. "Do you want me to share information with the police? Or run it by you first?"

He rubs his forehead again. I'm beginning to think he's giving himself a permanent groove.

"I don't want Vicky's legacy to be tarnished. Tell me what you find before the APD."

"Will do. Pay my bills and answer my questions, and you'll be the first to know about anything." Loyalty oath with built-in back door in case he stiffs me. Good enough. To get him into information provider mode, I ask him about the book he mentioned earlier. He tells me Victoria was working on a manuscript about utilizing artistic creation to recover from trauma and abuse. The book had exercises and rituals that she thought would promote healing and forgiveness. Daniel was going to handle the publication and printing detail, if and when it ever got that far.

I'm not sure what I think about this type of thing, but I suppose every half-baked guru can self-publish a manifesto these days. And she might have her own experiences to cauterize.

"Was Victoria an abused child?" I think of her icy mother. It wouldn't surprise me.

He frowns. "It feels wrong to talk about her private life, things she told me in confidence."

I lean on the desk. "Mr. Chandler. She's dead. Someone killed her. Her privacy is of secondary consideration now."

"You're the only one saying it's a homicide." He folded his arms.

I try another tack. "Did anyone else know about the book?"

"I'm not sure. She was hosting a group for abuse survivors, working out the rituals and exercises and things, seeing what helped. Some of those people might know. She also had some services about abuse, and finding love and light through 'cleansing your wounds.' I can't remember if she talked about her book then."

It seems like Claire would have said something. Is this just another example of Daniel keeping things close to the vest? Or are there other things he isn't telling me?

I stand and go over to his shelves, checking out the books and objects. This is mostly to make him nervous, but also to get a sense of him. The books are business related. Accounting techniques, opportunities for women-owned companies, specific practices for non-profits and religious organizations. A few DIY topics, like selling on E-bay and starting up freelance businesses. Even reading the titles causes my eyes to glaze.

"When was the last time you saw or spoke to Victoria? Did you see her the day of the service? The one I attended?"

"Not that day, but the day before, on Wednesday morning. We had a ten o'clock meeting. She came into the office and we discussed church finances. It ended at around ten forty-five."

"How did she seem?"

"Normal." He takes off his glasses and polishes them on his sleeve. "Believe me, I'd no idea —" He pinches the bridge of his nose. "No idea it would be the last time I saw Vicky alive."

"I know." I try not to be brusque, but I really want to get a move on. I prod him for the list of congregants.

"What are you going to do with it?"

"I'm going to shake the trees and see what falls out."

He grumbles, but hits a few keys and puts the information on a flash drive. It's a little old-school, but I see he's got a handful of them scattered across his desk.

"We don't have formal membership. These are the folks who have asked to be on our newsletter mailing list."

"Perfect." I pocket the drive and fake leave, turning just as I reach the doorway. "One more thing...who stands to benefit from Pastor Harkness's death?"

His answer surprises me. "The church, I suppose. There's a key person life insurance policy for a hundred thousand dollars that was supposed to cover the expenses of finding a new pastor if the unthinkable ever happened. We had a salesman in about a month ago. Vicky swallowed his pitch, hook, line, and sinker. She even bought a policy for me. Since I don't have any other benefits."

"And now that the unthinkable has happened?"

"I just don't know. We'll look for a new pastor of course. But Vicky herself was the main draw. Everyone is going to miss her. So much."

He's not looking at me when he says this last, but I can see his face is red.

I wait until I'm out the door and away from his line of sight before thumbing off the voice recorder on my phone. It never hurts to have a record. What I've just done is illegal in Oregon. But. I don't have a photographic memory, and I'm not planning on using this for evidence.

Plus, As Victoria Harkness herself apparently believed, you never know when you'll need a little insurance. Detectives are a suspicious lot, and client or no, I'm not convinced that Daniel Chandler is as squeaky clean as he lets on. It wouldn't surprise me in the least to learn that he and Harkness were having an affair.

So. Shaking the trees.

Daniel's list of newsletter recipients totals fifty-three. The majority are women; only nineteen are male.

I spend the rest of the day on the phone. I explain I've been hired by the church to collect information to help with the police investigation into Harkness's death. Just a little fudge, to beef up my bona fides. I ask about their movements, when they'd last seen the pastor, how well they'd known her, and if they have any ideas as to what had happened. Almost everyone assumes it was an accident, and I don't disillusion them.

People are stunned; a few sound heartbroken. Some are matter-of-fact: these things happen. I learn that no one saw her after Wednesday: that makes Daniel Chandler the last one to see her alive, always an interesting position.

The trouble is that I don't know exactly when the killing took place, so I can't really press for alibis. My vision seemed to be at night, but which one? I'm forced to ask general questions and listen to whether someone seems to know more than he should, or is otherwise 'off.' I hear about jobs and dinner dates and television shows. I hear about political conspiracies and am urged, jokingly, by a fellow impressed with his own sense of humor, to follow up on jealous wives.

"Why jealous wives?" I ask, antennae alerted.

"Well, you know," my informant replies, "Pastor Harkness was beautiful. Any man would be attracted like a moth to one of those killer bug lights."

"Are you saying she had intimate relationships with members of her congregation?" My conversation with Phoebe rears up in my memory, and her descriptions of sexual control being a prime identifier of cults.

"Don't put words in my mouth."

"What are you implying, then?"

"It's just that, to watch her on stage, to listen to her speak, was mesmerizing. You couldn't help but be attracted."

"Did anyone go beyond attraction? Did you?"

A guffaw. "Not me — my wife stands too handy with a frying pan. But some of the younger guys, maybe. Guys like the welder or the painter. I mean the real painter, North, the guy who did the big picture hanging in the fellowship hall."

"Why them in particular?"

"They stood right up at the service and said they loved her. Or try that other preacher, the one who thinks we're all going to hell." A chuckle. "He looks like the type who might go off the deep end. Too buttoned up and serious."

I thank my informant and go over my notes. Eric North isn't on my list, but I had seen him at the vigil. And he presented the organization with such a nice piece of art. He's on my radar for follow-up.

When it gets too late to make phone calls, I watch the copy of the video Daniel filmed on the night of the vigil. I'm able to cross-reference the names of the congregation with the faces of the mourners. Nothing stands out to me except Jason Morganstern, the belligerent young man who'd thrown his candle in the water. He hasn't answered his phone, so I'm no further with him. The only one who has any apparent motive is the preacher, Seth Takahashi, and he wasn't at the memorial service. Murder seems to be a pretty harsh response to a religious difference, although there have been plenty of precedents down through the years.

With a sigh, I rub my eyes and resolve to talk to Claire and Daniel again. I must tread lightly with my clients. It wouldn't be the first time the people who seem most eager to solve the crime turn out to be the perpetrators. But the moon is setting across the bay, and it's long past the witching hour. I've done a good day's work — I have some leads to follow and no one mentioned the police so I know I'm ahead of any investigation from the APD.

Plus, Olafson hasn't come to arrest me for breaking and entering.

I've only got one more thing to do, and I spend a couple of hours doing it. There's a room in the basement which has been finished, unlike the rest of the lowest story. It has a window, a closet, and a locking door. I pull down the shade and turn the space into an incident room, complete with maps, pictures, and post-it notes.

In the morning, I'll be ready to roll.

14

"I want to talk to you about Victoria Harkness," I say to Reverend Takahashi.

It had taken a good part of the morning to find him, with the help of the friendly lady at the church administrative office. I'd finally tracked him down to a shelter for transient men in a repurposed rambling bungalow on Bond Street.

"It'll have to wait, Audrey. I've got a ministry to attend to here."

"I'll just follow along and hold your coat." I don't want him to get away from me, and he seems to have a full schedule. Besides, this will give me an opportunity to observe him in his element.

He looks at me oddly but doesn't argue. We go inside to the common room, where a few men have gathered. Two sit on a rust-colored corduroy sofa with armrests dotted with cigarette burns. One slouches, arms and legs crossed, in a hard-backed rocker. Takahashi nods to the men and sets up a few folding chairs.

It's been a week since I visited the Church of the Spirit and met the preacher for the first time. The Chandlers had challenged his presence then, and he'd said Pastor Harkness had invited him to come to that evening's service. I want to find out more about that, and I don't intend to allow Takahashi to evade my questions with any slick preacher-ese. If I have to sit through a sermon or a prayer meeting, so be it.

More men enter slowly, by ones and twos, heralded by quiet conversation. Two are commenting on the Episcopal Church dinner they went to last night. Another breaks into their discussion and says the best place to get a hot meal is at McDonald's: if you wait near the drive-through menu board, someone will eventually order something for you.

"You gotta do it right. Standing at the end of the drive-through is no good. People have already placed their orders. But if they want to help, they'll generally say, and then you can go around to the pick-up. Sometimes they even ask you what you want."

"But there's that sign, says it's illegal to give food away from a car."

"Just go stand on the sidewalk, off the property. Public way. You got the right to be there."

The gathering tops out at nine. My own chair is tucked unobtrusively into a back corner, where I can view everyone in the room. The Reverend himself is also seated in a folding chair, the focus of a ragged parabola of haunted eyes. The men look cynical, bored, calculating — anything but devout. I wonder why they're even here. But Takahashi doesn't seem to be bothered by the lack of enthusiasm.

He starts off with a casual wave. "Hi guys. As some of you know, I'm Seth Takahashi, pastor for Riverside Christian Church. But you don't have to call me 'father' or 'reverend,' just 'Seth' will do fine."

I notice he still wears his shirt buttoned to the top. But the black trousers and shiny shoes he wore a week ago have been replaced by blue jeans and hiking boots. Dressed as I am in a navy blazer and white blouse, I'm a tad formal for the surroundings.

"I hear last Thursday Father O'Callaghan from the Catholic church was here. He's a good guy. Could talk the birds out of the trees if he wanted to." The men chuckle. One rolls his eyes. "Before we get started, I'm going to say the Lord's Prayer. Join in if you want."

Takahashi bows his head. His voice is smooth and compelling. A couple of the men say it with him, and I find myself echoing the familiar words. It's been a long time since I've been to church, or believed in anything but what I can see and hear for myself, but I still remember that iconic prayer.

After the final 'Amen,' he leans forward, elbows on knees. "This is how the early Christian church was born, just groups of disciples — friends — meeting in someone's house. Just interested folks, like yourselves, stopping in for fellowship and conversation." He makes eye contact with each of the men. "If you can imagine, there would be some guy, a visitor like me, or maybe the householder himself. He'd say, 'Hey, I heard about this teacher named Jesus. He said we're all forgiven for everything we've ever done.' And then someone else might say, 'Yeah, the Romans killed him. Guess they weren't really the forgiving type.'"

A couple of the men snort with laughter. Takahashi smiles, as though joining in the amusement. His smile is a flash of light that seems to illuminate the room. He goes on speaking, still very colloquially, delivering the standard message of sin and redemption. But as he gives it, I can feel his sincerity. It isn't the holier-than-thou, glorify-the-lord and by association, glorify-me kind of preaching which has become so common on TV and radio, celebrity pastors in their fancy suits and megachurch millions. It's one man, who cares about these others. The emotional message is clear. The verbal content is almost a sideline.

Bemused, I sit quietly in my corner. Occasionally Seth's gaze meets my own, but never lingers. Meanwhile, I do my own observation of the group. They all seem to be paying attention. One man with a scraggly beard even has a spiral notebook on his knees, and is scribbling across the page with a well-chewed pencil. He glances up, sees me looking, and drops his eyes. His shoulders hunch a little, but he keeps writing. When he sneaks another look, I nod, and wonder if he's clocked me as a cop.

"You know, Seth," another man in a stained green sweatshirt remarks, "I see what you're saying. But I don't think God has much love for me. He never helps me out of this shithole of a life."

Takahashi nods, his expression serious. "I know it can seem like that. And we all wonder about our own circumstances." He points out the window. "Why does that guy have so much money?" He points in the other direction. "Why does this guy over here have a trophy wife and a big mansion and gets to be president besides?" He shakes his head. "Yeah, it's pretty inexplicable. But here's the thing," he leans forward, and drops his voice as though revealing a secret. His audience has to lean forward as well.

"None of that stuff really matters, not in the big picture. It's who you are, not what you have, that counts. Even your past doesn't matter. Even if you've done some crappy things, Jesus will still forgive you. But you have to be real with Him, too — you have to commit to Him, if you want Him to commit to you. That's what love is." He holds their gazes for a few seconds longer, then deliberately breaks the spell by slapping his thighs and standing.

As the meeting breaks up and the men mill around, talking amongst themselves and with the preacher, I'm left to consider what I've observed. Takahashi seems sincere, although there is an element of calculation to his performance. But that might be just the result of lots of experience with public speaking, and interacting with an audience. I have to respect his ability to engage with these men, without coming across as patronizing. They're probably even more cynical about life than I am.

Truthfully, I'm struggling to maintain the appropriate level of suspicion and skepticism. He seems like a genuinely nice guy. Even if I personally don't buy the 'change your life by choosing Jesus' routine.

I rub the scar under my clavicle, make sure it still hurts. It reminds me never to let down my guard.

In any case, I'll be interested to see what kind of performance Takahashi puts on when I ask him about Victoria.

When we leave the shelter, we walk along the narrow lane of Bond Street. Seth has slipped on a blue down jacket, and jams his hands into the pockets.

"Can I talk to you about Victoria Harkness now?" I ask.

"I don't understand your interest, Audrey. Her death is a tragedy. I suppose she fell off one of the piers and the river swept her away. It's happened before." He walks ahead, scanning the street, friendliness fallen away.

"I've been hired by the church to look into her death, and I'm interviewing everyone who interacted with her recently." I'm forced to drop behind him as he swerves to avoid an abandoned bicycle fallen across the sidewalk. Annoyed, I say, "I heard a radio broadcast with an argument between the two of you."

He gives me a sharp glance before puffing out his cheeks in a sigh. "I regret that. It wasn't a good way to approach her. But she wouldn't talk with me, wouldn't see reason, and I was — and am — worried about her congregation. Whether she meant to or not, she was starting a cult."

His response jolts me. "Why do you think that? Did she try to indoctrinate you?"

Like preacher man was doing just now at the shelter?

He skirts a battered red truck parked overlapping the sidewalk, forcing me to drop behind again. "Her so-called church uses some of the trappings of Christianity, but in reality it's nothing like. It's really all about her, Victoria Harkness. Listen, in this business of saving souls, you can't let people confuse the messenger with the message. When people start following because of the personality of the preacher, and not because of the truth of the gospel, that's when it gets dangerous.

That's when bad things happen."

"Like what?"

"Like Waco. Like the spaceship comet people. Like the Manson family."

"Oh, come on. Surely you don't equate Victoria Harkness with Charles Manson."

"Not like him, no. But maybe like the spaceship comet people." He snaps his fingers. "Heaven's Gate. And Marshall Applewhite. That guy couldn't admit he was wrong, and he led his followers to their deaths."

I recall Phoebe had also spoken about Applewhite. "Did you think that's what she was doing?"

"Well, no, but she had people believing they could put their own spin into the Bible. I mean, it says what it says, but she thought you could interpret it in your own way. Like art." He turns to face me. "The signs were there. She already relocated her church, and a bunch of people followed her. Gave up their livelihoods. Gave up their homes. Trusting in her to be their savior. Don't you see?"

I want to believe that his almost-rudeness, his lapse into unfriendliness, can be ascribed to his passion and heartfelt concern. But I don't think Victoria was encouraging people to actually worship her. So I say, "Isn't that what Jesus did?"

"Yes, but that was Jesus. He actually *was* the message. But no one else gets to take that role, and when they do, it dilutes the whole thing. Then when people encounter the *real* Word of God, instead of what some charismatic leader has thrown at them, they dismiss it, not knowing that *no one else but Jesus* can claim to speak for God."

Give me a break. None of these holy rollers ever see their own hypocrisy.

I hadn't intended to get into a religious debate with this man, and it feels like I'm floundering in the deep end without my water wings. "What do you think should be done with people like that?"

"They need to be stopped, before they do incalculable damage, which is why I called the radio show." We have reached Seth's car, and he punches the fob and climbs inside. "I've got to go."

"Wait. Do you think someone stopped Victoria?"

He starts the engine, and I have to strain to hear him. "I think maybe God stopped her. God or someone acting as His instrument." He begins to reverse. The car has been boxed in by two large pickups, and he's going to have a hard time getting out.

Seth's remark gives me the chills. It makes him seem cold and judgmental, not at all like the friendly, sincere helper I'd seen at the shelter. Even if he's innocent, his ability to lay the blame at God's feet seems unhealthy, at best. At worst, he has just expressed a motive for murder.

While I've been standing on the sidewalk thinking, Takahashi has been maneuvering his vehicle in a twenty-point turn. Now he lowers his window. "If you really want to know why I began opposing Victoria, stop by my office in a day or two and we'll talk further."

"You have another reason?"

His hand tightens on the steering wheel. "She misled one of my flock."

I jog alongside as he pulls out into the street. "Who?"

"A young man named Jason Morganstern."

I stop dead, and watch as the preacher drives away. I've shaken the tree, and instead of an apple, I've gotten a mango. An unexpected fruit.

And I'll have to be satisfied with that for now, since I completely forgot to ask him about the last time he saw Pastor Harkness.

15

The inside of the Bowerstein Boatworks warehouse echoes with clanking, shouts, and engine buzz. Forklifts dart about with sheets of fiberglass, crates and engine parts. Four boats are up on blocks, and workmen cluster around them. The sharp metallic scent of hot metal mixes with the acrid stench of burning plastic.

I'm here to speak to Jason Morganstern, who is employed here as a welder. I'd gotten that bit of info from Daniel Chandler. The main office of Bowerstein is in a metal building owned by the Port of Astoria, and the receptionist had directed me here, to this warehouse turned workshop. Apparently, they don't care about someone wandering around their job site, which suits me fine. I want to learn about Morganstern's movements in the last few days, and follow up on Takahashi's reference to Jason as a former member of the Methodist Church. I don't know if that has anything to do with Victoria Harkness's death, but at least I'm uncovering some connections between the people who may be involved. Still, I caution myself to take things slowly.

I walk toward the telltale spray of sparks and a single figure beneath a welder's mask. I wait until he reaches the end of his seam, being careful not to look at the blaze of the arc. He lifts his mask and wipes his forehead, and I wave a hand to get his attention.

"Jason Morganstern?" I recognize him from the memorial service.

He nods, eyes darting and wary. His dirty blond hair is damp with sweat, tousled from the mask, and rings of moisture darken the armpits of his flannel shirt.

"Who're you?"

"My name is Audrey Lake. I'm here to ask you some questions

about an ongoing investigation."

"I'm working."

"This will only take a few minutes."

He lays down his torch and put his mask beside it. He jerks a thumb and leads me outside.

"Quieter out here. What's this about? Are you doing a report? Because all that about taking tools, it isn't true. I didn't take a welder off premises. I don't know who did." He folds his arms.

"That seems clear enough. Except, it's not why I'm here. I've been hired by the Church of the Spirit to look into Victoria Harkness's death. I'm calling all the members of the congregation, but you didn't answer your phone."

Morganstern doesn't say anything, just stands there, frowning, with his arms crossed.

I decide to shake his complacency. "Where were you when Victoria Harkness died?"

A multitude of micro-expressions flit across his face, like a school of minnows in a pond. His voice hoarsens. "Here, in the shop."

"How do you know for sure? There's been no time of death established."

"You trying to trap me?"

"Just asking questions. How do you know when she died?"

"I don't. But I been in the shop twelve, fourteen hours a day for the past couple of weeks. Salmon season coming up. Lots of boats to fix."

"I see." I give him ten seconds to elaborate, then I ask. "How did you become involved with the Church of the Spirit?" During the next few laborious minutes of conversation I'm able to elicit a few facts, that he joined the organization soon after it relocated to Astoria, after being a member of Riverside Christian for ten years. He'd been going through a rough patch, and Pastor Harkness had helped him find a job, and encouraged him to express himself creatively. She'd even gotten a real artist, Eric North, to help him get started. No one else, it seems, has ever done that.

I ask, "Do you know anyone who would want to harm her?"

He clenches his fists. "No one. I thought she just fell in the water."

There's a long pause, during which I study him. A lean and hungry white guy, forearms corded with wiry muscle. He's younger than me; I guess early thirties. His faded flannel shirt is stained and frayed, his jeans the same, showing evidence of prior contact with engine oil and sparks from the welding rod. He looks strong enough to hold someone under the water.

He shows his first sign of aggression, stepping toward me. "Did someone hurt her?"

I get a waft of musky sweat. "That's what I'm trying to find out."

"Then why are you accusing me?" His forehead knots, and his fists tighten. "I loved her. I would have protected her. But she just laughed." He glowers from under the fall of his bangs. "But I'd kill anyone else who'd hurt her. Are you saying that's what happened?"

I take an involuntary step back. "Did you offer to protect her? When was this? When did you last see her?"

It's too many questions at once. As he pauses to sort them out, an angry voice comes from the warehouse.

"Morganstern!" A burly brown man starts walking toward us. "What the hell are you doing out here? Get back to work!"

Jason looks at me with reproach before spitting on the ground and heading back inside. He dons his heavy gloves and mask and picks up his torch without speaking to the foreman, or whoever the authority figure is, who stands waiting for him to resume, hands on hips. His scowling attitude toward Jason gives me the impression that Morganstern isn't an ideal employee. When the foreman comes toward me, probably to order me off the premises, I beat him to the punch.

"Are you in charge here? My name is Audrey Lake. I've been hired to investigate a crime. What can you tell me about missing tools?" A bona fide reason for being here.

He blinks, and scratches his head. "The only tools that can't be accounted for are a welding torch and goggles."

"When did they disappear?"

"Couple of weeks now." He nods toward the main building. "Report's in the office."

I nod. "Who's in charge of equipment?"

He straightens up. "I am." He tops me by a good eight inches.

I ignore the loom. "How are the torches secured when not in use?"

"All the tools are kept locked in the shed. It's unlocked when the workday begins and the men are issued the tools they need for the day's work. I review the sign-out sheet at the end of each day. The torch was signed out, but not returned. It's not in the shed, or anywhere I can find it."

"Who had it last?"

The foreman's voice is a growl. "Morganstern."

"I see. What's the value of a welding torch? I mean, could someone sell it or what?"

"Not that much." The foreman snorts. "I mean, some guys will take anything. Someone probably has a home project going on and they don't want to spring for their own welder." He shakes his head. "Go back to the front office and talk to the owner. I gotta get back to work."

I nod, and set off briskly for the office. But I don't go in — instead, I circle around the building and back to the parking lot, amazed and a teensy bit smug by how far an official manner and a tailored blazer can take you. But really, I haven't gotten much that's useful. No indication that Morganstern is anything other than a possibly light-fingered employee. He doesn't seem particularly smart, but it would be idiocy to sign out a piece of equipment and then just keep it, with the paper trail pointing straight to him. And even if he did take the torch, so what? Maybe he was using it to make a metal sculpture to impress her.

But. It wouldn't be the first time a man has murdered a woman he says he loves.

My next stop is the studio of Eric North above an art supply store on Marine Drive. He's not on Daniel's list, but he spoke at the service so I figure he's fair game. I knock on the door and enter at his gruff acknowledgement. Tall windows admit a cool and clear north light. Canvases populate the perimeter, some half-finished, some with only pencil sketches, some drying on their easels. The smell of mineral spirits and oil paints makes an almost physical curtain between myself and the artist.

"Who are you?" he says, eyebrows raised. "I was expecting someone else."

He's extraordinarily good looking. Yeah, I know — another one. But unlike Seth Takahashi, Eric's appeal lies in his rough untidiness, and an energy that leaps from his face and hands. His eyes are large and deep, their brown depths a place where a woman could get lost, or at the very least, get compliant. He's dressed in paint-stained sweats, a torn t-shirt under an unbuttoned denim shirt. The cuffs are rolled up to his elbows, and his forearms flex under a light pelt of dark hair that matches the three-day stubble on his chin. His dark brows knit into a frown.

I've been glowered at by too many perps to let him cow me that easily. "My name is Audrey Lake. I've been hired by the Chandlers to investigate the death of Victoria Harkness."

"What does that have to do with me?"

"It has to do with everyone in the congregation of the Church of the Spirit."

"Well, Audrey, I'm not a member."

"You spoke at the service. You painted one of the pictures in the sanctuary."

"I did those things for Victoria, not for her church."

"Is there a difference, then?"

He scoffs. "I knew V. back when she was a little kid. I don't associate her with spiritual salvation. She lived next door to us. She's younger than me. I used to draw her."

"How much younger?"

"Five years. Although she was always old for her age."

"What does that mean?" It sounds creepy.

"It means that she was precocious, mature." His need to define his terms is irritating. He adds a daub of color to the canvas he's working on. "The first time I saw her, I was sketching in the back yard. Birds, flowers, that kind of thing. I heard someone calling, saying 'hey boy' and I looked around. I saw V. up in the tree, looking down on me. The light was behind her. She looked like — I don't know, like a fairy. Like an angel. That's when I knew I wanted to paint. I couldn't capture the light — her light — in pencil. I had to have color, a medium whose opacity I could control in order to get the effect I wanted."

His scornful tone puts me in my place as someone too ignorant to understand painting. People like this are annoying, but they can't seem to stop talking. Especially about themselves.

So I egg him on. "You had a pretty close relationship with her?" It's a suggestive question, designed to elicit a reaction. He'll want to set me straight.

Eric cracks his neck. The sound makes me wince, and he smiles. "I'd hardly call it a relationship. She was too young to be a real friend. But sometimes she would model for me."

"What, stand there and let you draw her?"

"Nothing so formal. I'd watch her playing with dolls or Legos or digging in the dirt and sketch whatever she was doing. I learned a lot that way, about movement and grace and the human body."

Again, my creep meter pings. "And her parents were okay with that?"

"Her parents were too busy climbing their status ladder to worry about it."

"So, what happened to your relationship?"

"You're not listening. Nothing happened — there was no relationship. The Harknesses moved away when I was a senior in high school. I think V. was thirteen or so. Just beginning to be a little woman. Who knows? If they'd stayed, maybe I'd have dated her in a few years. As it was, she was still like my kid sister."

Little woman. Asshole.

For once I agree with Zoe. "Were you surprised when she came back to town?"

"Maybe she was trying to get back to her roots."

"I wasn't asking you why she came, only your reaction to it."

"A lot of people move away and come back. I wasn't expecting her, no, but it didn't surprise me unduly either."

"How did you reconnect?"

He shrugs, a movement that starts in his shoulders and ripples down to his wrists. Before the 'little woman' comment I'd have been impressed. Now I just want to pistol whip him. "She came to a show of mine. She came up and introduced herself, but I'd have remembered her without that."

"Did she invite you to the church? Call on you later for old times sake? I'm trying to get a picture of her routine, her life, the people she knew and associated with."

"I don't know anything about her life. I went to a service or two, just to be friendly, but I didn't really believe in her message."

"Why not? It seems like she thought artistic expression was a direct message from God."

"She didn't have any discrimination. To her, some hunk of metal welded together, some childlike watercolor, had as much meaning as the work of a dedicated artist, someone like me who has actually gone to school, and studied abroad. It belittles everything I've striven to accomplish with my life."

"I can see why you'd think that. But you donated a painting."

"I did that as kind of a thank-you for being my muse. For old times' sake."

"Did you still consider her your muse?"

"Not now, obviously. I've moved on in the past twenty years. I don't even see why you're pursuing this — Daniel must be an idiot, if he's the one who hired you. Her suicide is a tragedy, and I'm sorry about it. But I've got my own work to do, pictures to finish for a gallery showing in a month. So, I've really got to get back to work."

Gee, so much for sorrow at the passing of his muse. "Why do you think her death is a suicide?"

"Isn't it?"

"No official cause has been announced." That I knew of.

"Well, what else? You'd have to be pretty stupid to walk off the end of a pier by accident."

"Did she have a reason to commit suicide, do you think?"

"Well, her church was failing. It owed a lot of money. Her mother hated her. She couldn't maintain a relationship. Take your pick."

I haven't heard about any of that. Wouldn't Daniel have told me about financial problems, if there were any? Although he had mentioned selling some of the art. "You seem to know a lot about her life."

"She came by to visit every now and then."

"Sounds like she confided in you." I amble among the easels, looking at the pictures. See views of the river, women in various poses, street scenes.

"What can I say? Women often unburden themselves to me."

Okay, I really don't like him. His looks have definitely lost their power.

"Sounds like you were willing to do her favors."

"What's that supposed to mean?"

"She asked you to help mentor a young artist, Jason Morganstern."

He snorts. "Jason isn't an artist, he's an idiot. But since you ask, yes, I did help him some, tried to get him to think of imagining a particular sculptural form as a goal to work for, rather than just sticking parts of things together."

"I thought you were a painter, not a sculptor."

"I'm a man of broad horizons. As it happens, I've been branching out a little, and trying new forms of expression."

Ye gods. "One more question then. How would you feel if Daniel Chandler sold some of the artwork, including your piece, to pay the church's bills?"

"He can't do that. It's not why I gave V. the picture."

"Well, he seems to think he can."

I feel smug and satisfied as I leave the studio, having succeeded in pissing him off.

To complete my day of tree-shaking, I stop by the Portway to talk to Claire, let her know what I have been up to, and get her to weigh in with ideas and suspicions. The bell on the door announces my entrance, and Claire comes out of the back. Breakfast was a long time ago, so I order a root beer and basket of fries, and lean my elbows on the bar.

"So Claire," I begin, "level with me. Who do you think killed Victoria Harkness?"

She flinches, and doesn't look at me. "Is it a done deal? I mean, do we know for sure she was murdered?" She twists the bar cloth in her hands.

I hesitate. The cops haven't been forthcoming with any conclusions, but I know. "That's the assumption I'm working on, until we learn differently. Unless you think she killed herself."

"No. I don't." Claire leans forward and puts her face in her hands.

"Are you sure? Has it ever come up in any of her sermons? Did she ever talk about it with you? I understand her childhood was less than ideal." I sip my soda and munch a couple of fries. I'm reaching for that conclusion, but based on Daniel's description of her book and my own experience with her mother, it's not much of a stretch.

"She believed that trauma could be processed and healed through art. I don't think she would take her own life. It would devastate her congregation. And believe me, that would matter to her."

"Okay, not suicide." Although it was interesting that self-harm had been North's first assumption. "But it also seems to be a strange sort of accident for someone to have."

Claire raises her head. "If it's not an accident, I won't waste your time saying no one would have wanted to hurt her, because someone obviously did."

Bravo, I think.

"That being said, I don't have much in the way of ideas. The only person I know who has a visible problem with her is that preacher, Takahashi."

"Do you know him at all?"

"I've talked to him, briefly. He was upset with Pastor Harkness for stealing one of his sheep."

"Is it that big of a deal? I mean, people switch churches all the time. I would think."

She nods. "Churches are like any institution, they can get stale. Victoria's message was fresh and exciting. It resonated with people."

"I agree." I eat some more fries. The salty starchy goodness is extremely satisfying. "What about the lost sheep, Jason Morganstern?"

"What about him?"

"I don't know. He seemed a little...belligerent...at the vigil. He's not very friendly in general."

"He's been with the church a couple of years, almost since we came here. I think Pastor Harkness helped him find a job. He was a little smitten with her, but so are most of the guys." Claire frowns. "You know, she had a real gift, a real message. I think it bothered her when her followers were...attracted to her, you know? At least, that's the feeling I got."

"We should all have that problem."

"I know, right?"

"Did he ever seem threatening?"

"Jason?" Claire frowns as she wipes down the taps. "I wouldn't have said so, but then I only have ever seen him in the context of the congregation. He might have tried to contact her privately. Daniel might know."

"When I talked to him, he indicated he had offered Victoria protection. Do you know what from?"

"Protection? I can't imagine why. I mean, protection from him, maybe, but —"

"Why do you say that? I thought he wasn't threatening."

"Not threatening, but he was kind of persistent. Look, Audrey, I'm not privy to all of Pastor Harkness's personal life. But she worked closely with Daniel and so I got to know her, too. She mentioned that Jason kept asking her out. To repay her for her kindness, he said. But she didn't want repayment; as far as she was concerned, helping people was all part of the job. She laughed about it, but she had a hard time discouraging him."

Jason had those anger flashes while talking to me, and moments of aggression. How would he have handled it if Victoria had rejected him? Lots of guys can't stand that. It enrages them, and they have to get back at the woman, sometimes by killing her. I've seen it happen.

And speaking of men: "What about Eric North?"

"He knew her from when she lived here before. Did you see that nice painting he gave to the church? He obviously thought highly of Pastor Harkness."

I finish my snack and drain the last of my root beer. I'm not sure what all to tell Claire, and truthfully, I'm not sure what the result of my tree-shaking is. I've learned some things, have some leads, but no evidence or smoking gun. Still, part of this maneuver is a waiting game. The fruit doesn't always fall right away.

"Audrey, are you sure this was a murder?"

I take a deep breath. Calm. "Yes, Claire. I am. The evidence in her apartment, that she left her purse and billfold behind, that her car is still in the parking lot. It looks like she went for a walk and never made it home. You've said yourself that she wasn't suicidal. And neither of us think she just fell off a pier into the river."

"Maybe it was just a random stranger. There's lots of transients and tourists in town."

"Maybe, but why? She didn't have any money with her — no purse, right? No one wanted her car. Why would someone just attack her for no reason?"

Claire takes my dishes away. She replenishes her supply of glasses and wipes the taps again.

"Audrey?" Her voice has taken on a serious edge.

"Yes?"

"How do you know she left her bag in the apartment?"

I feel the ground give way beneath me. A high-pitched hum vibrates the crystalline silence. It's hard for me to think.

"Audrey?"

Claire's voice seems far away. I'm back in Harkness's bedroom, lying beside the bed, staring at the booted feet in the doorway. Hearing the buzz of the fly in the window and the rush of blood in my ears. Feeling the rough nap of the carpet beneath my cheek.

"Audrey? Are you all right?"

I don't want to know what happens next. I just know somewhere, sometime, I've made a terrible mistake.

"Audrey!"

A hand clamps on my forearm, followed by a quick, vigorous shake. I blink, look around, feel the hard edge of the bar under my elbows, smell the deep fat fryer in the back.

"What's going on?" Claire's face is close, her eyes wide. I notice she has a mole above the peak of her right eyebrow. It's her hand on my arm.

I sit up straight. "Nothing. Sorry. Just — zoned out for minute. I haven't been sleeping well lately. I'd better get home. I'll be in touch."

She lets go, but still looks concerned about me. Hell, I'm concerned about me. But it's bad form to reveal your craziness to a client. I give her a jaunty wave, the kind that says 'everything's great here in la-la land' before heading out the door. I almost collide with an elderly couple dressed in matching sweatshirts but, after exchanging apologies, make it safely to my car.

I'm halfway home before I realize I walked out without paying for my meal.

16

My phone is ringing. I'm thrashing around on my cot, patting the floor, looking for where I left it. Finally, my hand closes around the cool black rectangle. The name on the lock screen is Elizabeth Harkness.

"Hello?" I'm still groggy, but make an effort not to sound like I'm still in bed at nine in the morning. I wonder why she's calling. She wasn't friendly the last time we talked, and seems to be estranged from Victoria.

"Is this Ms. Audrey Lake?"

"Speaking." Sort of.

"I wish to make an appointment to talk to you about my daughter."

Now I'm awake. "Where and when?"

"Say, in an hour. At Victoria's apartment." Pause. "I assume you know where it is."

I have some trepidation about returning to Victoria's apartment. It's been five days since her body was pulled from the Columbia River; a week since Claire Chandler engaged me to investigate her disappearance. My last visit wasn't exactly a jaunt in the park, but if Elizabeth Harkness is here, that means it's not considered a crime scene, and *that* means no one has looked for forensic evidence. And now I'll be legitimately shedding my own fibers and whatnot. In case anyone asks.

After negotiating the calf-wrenching access stairs, I knock on the door, noting the tiny scratches I left on the knob the last time I was here. Ms. Harkness herself answers: a tall white woman with silvering dark hair wearing a rose-colored cashmere sweater. Around her neck is small silver cross. On her wrist is a delicate silver watch. Or maybe it's white gold. Or platinum. I'm surprised to see her. For some reason I expected her to bring a butler.

"Are you Audrey Lake?"

"I am. And you must be Victoria's mother."

She opens the door wider to let me in, and I enter the apartment for the second time. It's the same, and yet different. Ms. Harkness's own handbag is on the table, a pale pink Fendi clutch, along with a steaming cup of tea. Nothing has been disarranged, but her presence has filled the small space. Victoria is no longer here.

"Would you like a beverage? Tea, or coffee?"

"No, thanks." I don't know if she brought her own, but it feels wrong to drink Victoria's.

"Let's get down to business, then. If you'll come with me to the bedroom, I'm packing up her things." She takes the cup and leads the way.

The bedroom, where I'd had my flashback and a close encounter with the carpet. She's put the suitcase that was under the bed on top of the mattress, and it already contains a few items, folded with retail neatness.

She says, "The rent is only paid through the end of the month, and the landlord wants all her things removed. This isn't how I want to remember her, but needs must." She takes another blouse from a hanger in the closet and lays it on the bed in preparation to folding. "I'll come straight to the point. What have you discovered in your investigation of my daughter?"

I can see Ms. Harkness chairing a board meeting or a citizen's committee with authority and precision. I lean against the doorjamb and take out my notebook. "Have you spoken to the police?"

"I have, and was very disappointed to learn that there was no missing persons report, although you led me to believe you were actively investigating her disappearance. Now that she is dead, I want some answers." Her voice shakes ever so slightly, and I'm suddenly in sympathy with her. This tiny break in her tight control reveals the grieving mother beneath the sophisticated facade.

"What have the police told you, Ms. Harkness?"

"Are you not in communication with them yourself?"

"Bear with me, please. I'll answer your questions as best I can, but it will be helpful if I can understand what you know already."

"All right." She places the blouse into the suitcase and walks back to the closet. "I understand that Victoria did not appear for a church service she had scheduled for Thursday of last week. The first I heard of this was your call to me on Sunday, which alarmed me." She glances at me, her expression reproachful.

I oblige her by squirming a little.

She continues. "When I came over here the next day to talk to the police, I discovered no one had filed a missing person's report. The police had no idea she was gone. Until the call about her — her body came through." Elizabeth's voice has risen, and her eyes are swimming with tears. She looks away, into the depths of the closet.

The door casing is hard against my spine. "I'm so sorry you had to learn about it like that."

"The M.E. says it was most likely an accident, that there are no signs of foul play. That Victoria drowned after falling into the water." She fingers the bright fabric of a floral skirt, and carefully removes it from the hanger. "Now, Ms. Lake, I would appreciate it if you would explain your role in all this."

I don't hesitate. Unlike my conversation with Olafson, I feel like this woman has a need to know that goes beyond the legal niceties. I only wish there was more to tell her. I explain that I was hired by the Church of the Spirit to look into Victoria's disappearance. That I don't know why they hadn't contacted the police, except that they didn't think it was necessary. But that at least they hired me. And now the hard part. I clear my throat.

"Ms. Harkness, I am not convinced your daughter's death was accidental."

Her face is finally bereft of its frozen mask. The lines deepen, the lips tremble, just for a moment before the facade is restored. And I get it. She's probably afraid to crack, afraid that if she relinquishes her armor she'll dissolve; that without self-imposed walls to contain her she'll lose herself completely.

Projecting a bit, aren't you?

When she speaks her voice is barely above a whisper. "Why do you think that?"

I hesitate. "At the moment, I have no hard evidence. But I have been a detective for a long time. This — event — just doesn't feel right. Listen, I see that you've been given access to this apartment and presumably all her things." I wait for Ms. Harkness's nod before continuing. "Therefore, it's not being treated as a crime scene. Did you find her handbag here? Her keys and I.D.?"

Objection! Leading the witness.

I'm treading on thin ice here, but I want to establish a basis for my earlier observations.

"The police gave me her keys. They were in her pocket. Her purse was here. With her wallet. They did check for fingerprints on it and laptop, and a few other places."

My stomach drops when she mentions fingerprinting, but remind myself that I was wearing gloves when I was last here.

Resuming the thread, I ask, "Phone?"

"No phone."

Probably at the bottom of the river. But. "Did you find a suicide note?"

Her mouth twists as her cheeks redden, but she holds it together. "No. The police walked through with me, but we found no note. No evidence of violence. Hence the verdict of 'accident.' Now, tell me why you think it might be something else."

"I've talked to her associates. No one thinks it was a suicide." Except for Eric North. I'll ask about him later. "You can never completely rule out accident, but to me it just doesn't sound likely, unless she was intoxicated when she went out. There's railings and fences everywhere along the boardwalk, so it's not easy just to fall in the water." I'd found no signs of alcohol in the apartment when I'd gone through the cupboards, not even beer, so I didn't think she was a habitual drinker. "So, ruling those out, we must consider foul play. Whether or not there's evidence."

"You mean murder." She closes her eyes. Mascara is smudged beneath her lashes. The fabric of the skirt she's folding bunches in her hands. "How do I know you're not just dragging this out, in order to collect a paycheck?"

"That," I say through gritted teeth. "Is out of line." How dare she? When was the last time she risked her life in the line of duty? Put herself into danger for a person she didn't know?

Easy there, Lake. Don't attack the witness.

I simmer down with an effort. "Think of it, Ms. Harkness. She had her keys. She left her wallet. She meant to come back. She may have been meeting someone. Or it may have been a chance encounter. I know this is painful, but I need to know everything you can tell me about your daughter. It will help my investigation."

"Everything?" Ms. Harkness laughs mirthlessly. "I've known my daughter for thirty-two years. I can tell you lots about her childhood. But now? I'm sure I'm the last person to know anything useful."

"Let's talk about this church Victoria founded."

Ms. Harkness's shoulders straighten. She lays the skirt in the suitcase. "I don't understand how my daughter could have gotten so far off the path. I could only hope one day she'd find her way back. But now..." She touches the silver cross pendant. "It started about ten years ago, after she left Reed College. She had been majoring in art but didn't complete her thesis project. She joined a Bible study group, but soon was inviting friends from Reed over to 'pick it apart' — her words, not mine. Eventually she stopped going to church. And then she started having discussion groups at one of those New Age bookstores. And, aided and abetted by these other so-called 'spiritual seekers' she started her own on-line video channel, which then grew into a, a movement." She twists the chain of her pendant in her hand. "I could not, can not, support what she was doing — what she did. I asked her to move out of my house, and never to speak of this — this sham she was perpetuating."

I wonder how an art school drop-out managed to support all these activities, and I ask, albeit more diplomatically. I learn about the trust fund set up by her grandfather, Ms. Harknesses' own father, for each of his grandchildren when he passed away. Victoria and her cousins could access the interest, but not the principal, until they were forty years old, the idea being they would be set for life but unable to squander their resources in a misspent youth.

Nice. Nothing like second generation entitlement.

"I see. And who gets that money now?"

"The contents of the trust will be disbursed among the remaining accounts."

"Where are her cousins?"

She stares at me. "Back East. One's in London. Why?"

"Ms. Harkness, is there anyone you can think of who might want to harm Victoria? Ex-boyfriends, jealous classmates, anyone?"

"I couldn't get her to settle down to a proper relationship. They never lasted more than a few weeks. She was a pretty girl and there was always someone in the wings." She abandons her folding and walks to the window, looking out.

I notice a dead fly on the sill. The light outside is cool and white.

She says, her voice muffled, "I just wanted her to have stability, a house, a family. I didn't even object to her being an artist, if that's what she wanted."

I take a few steps into the room, around the bed. "So, no exes, is that what you're saying? What about slighted friends, enemies, other family members?"

She turns around. "Ms. Lake, I appreciate your efforts, but I don't feel up to talking any more today."

I'm surprised and put off by her abruptness. She's been fairly cooperative. But maybe she's just getting emotional. I can understand, but some questions need answers. "Just one more thing. What about Eric North?"

She looks confused. "The neighbors were named North. When we lived here in Astoria. Is he connected to them?"

"Yes."

"I barely remember him. I believe he was older, a teenager. Why are you asking?"

"He's still in town, and I believe he and your daughter had… renewed their acquaintance."

"Tell me she wasn't seeing him romantically." Her voice is colored with disdain.

"Not as far as I know." I think about the painting. "He might have admired her, though."

She nods, once. "Everyone admired my daughter."

"What do you remember about Eric?"

"Nothing. Other than the fact his father was a fish-packer and his mother was a secretary. Now. Forgive me for being rude, but please leave. I have a great deal to do."

"Okay, Ms. Harkness. Thanks for your time." I make a show of putting away my notebook. "If you find anything useful on her laptop, please give me a call."

"It has a password."

So she's looked. "You might want to see if someone can help you retrieve the data. It could throw some light on your daughter's state of mind, and how she spent her final days. Plus, I've heard she was writing a book."

She stares, fingering her necklace. "A novel, you mean?"

"No," I look back at her blandly. "Nonfiction. Perhaps a memoir of sorts."

Ms. Harkness doesn't like that. I can see it in her eyes.

17

My next stop is the Riverside Christian Church where the Reverend Seth Takahashi is ensconced. Yesterday, he'd seemed sincere in his desire to help and protect people, if a bit misguided; he'd teased me with the mention of Jason Morganstern. Would he still be willing to talk today?

I called to set up the appointment, so he's expecting me. The receptionist ushers me in to his office. He's sitting behind a scarred desk, the kind of faux-wood furniture available from big box stores. His desk has knife-edged stacks of papers, a couple of pictures facing away from me, a computer monitor and a telephone. A yellowing spider plant dangles its progeny from the window sill. One plantlet has already detached itself, made the leap, and reposes in a browning clump on the carpet.

"Hello, Audrey," he says. His movie-star smile appears on cue. "Sit down. Would you like some tea, or coffee?"

I wonder why hospitality always seems to begin with a beverage offer. "No, thanks. I just want to talk to you about Victoria Harkness."

His smile vanishes. "I thought we covered that yesterday. Is there more tragedy to report?"

"How do you feel about her death?"

"Sad, of course. It's always sad when someone dies before their time."

Poke. "I thought you would be relieved that she can no longer delude vulnerable souls."

He winces. "Ouch. Well, I probably deserved that. But it's not my habit to dance on anyone's grave. I'd rather she'd been able to use her gift for the furtherance of the gospel."

"I think she thought she was."

"You know my views on that. But I was very sorry to learn about her death. I had hoped she and I could come to an agreement, not a parting of the ways." Seth leans back in his chair, his hands folded in his lap. His expression is troubled. "I liked her, you know. She was bright, thoughtful. I loved her passion — she was really dedicated to her church. Even if we didn't agree, I think she was sincere. But it's just those qualities which can be dangerous when applied wrongly."

"You said yesterday that she had 'misled one of your flock.' Can you tell me more about that?"

He sighs, leaning forward on his elbows. "There's a young man who used to attend my services regularly. He was troubled and vulnerable, hadn't had an easy life. But he was coming to know God. I had high hopes for him. At least, until he began going to the Church of the Spirit."

"This is Jason Morganstern?"

"Yes."

"I saw him at the candlelight vigil Tuesday night. He seemed upset."

"I'm not surprised. I'll reach out to him. Maybe he's ready to come back. It's not unusual for people to investigate other denominations." He jots a note on a yellow post-it.

"You said he was troubled. What does that mean?"

Takahashi hesitates. "I don't like to breach someone's privacy, but I suppose it's part of his police record. He's done some petty crime, engaged in minor violence. He had some inappropriate attitudes about women."

"What do you mean?"

"He tended to either idealize them or demonize them. Put them on a pedestal, and then when they weren't perfect, turn them into monsters."

An alarm bell is clanging in my mind. "What's that about, do you think?"

Takahashi shifts in his chair, adjusting his collar. "He had a disturbing relationship with his mother. I'm not prepared to say anything further about that. But it colored his outlook. I actually thought he might become attracted to Catholicism, and their sanctification of the Mother of Christ, and I wanted to steer him away from that. He needed help, and I worked with him quite a bit when he joined my church. I was getting him to see that his criminal actions weren't justified, despite his anger toward society. He still needed forgiveness, and to repent if he wanted to get closer to God and have Jesus be a presence in his life. He wanted to blame other people for his lot in life, but we can never control what others do. I was trying to show him that "society" isn't some abstract entity bent on holding him down, but just a group of individuals, like himself, all trying to succeed in life as best they can."

"So, empathy." What a novel concept.

He smiles. "Exactly. Thinking of others before self. And that is where Victoria Harkness's teachings were so corrosive. She has her congregants thinking of themselves before others. Self-development, self-actualization, all the seductive buzzwords that make people believe they are growing and changing but in reality are just teaching people to coddle their own egos." He slaps the desktop. "I wish I could make people understand how dangerous that kind of thinking is. It's got to be stopped."

Whoa. He's gone from concerned mentor to judgmental overlord in about two seconds.

This is exactly my problem with organized religion. Who is Takahashi to decide how others should conduct their spiritual lives? He's pretty locked into his own track. But is he also a fanatic, willing to kill for his beliefs?

"So Reverend, how far would you go to protect someone's soul?"

He laughs and leans back, once again the friendly reverend. He picks up an old-fashioned letter opener on his desk, turns it in his hands. "What is this, a job interview? Well, Jesus said, 'Greater love hath no man than he who lays down his life for his friends.' I'd like to say I'd go that far, but I suppose none of us knows until we're in the situation. How about you, Audrey? How far would you go to protect someone? Would you take the proverbial bullet?"

The room brightens. The letter opener flashes in the sunlight.

I've never taken a bullet, but I have taken a blade.

In the street outside the church, a car backfires. It sounds like a shot.

Distant shouts. "Police! Don't move!" Gunfire pops on the floor below.

I feel the cold slide of steel beneath my skin. The warm spill of blood as it cascades over my breast and side. Sonny's own blood coats his teeth as he smiles down at me.

"Pig," he whispers. "I got you." His breath is raw and rancid, his eyes veined with red.

The wound under my collarbone throbs, in tune to the beat of my heart.

"No!" I grip the arms of the chair, drenched with sweat. The scar on my chest feels hot and burning.

"Audrey! What's wrong?" Seth's voice is urgent. His hand is warm on my shoulder, on my forearm.

I blink, and my vision clears. I'm in Seth's office. The preacher kneels beside me. His eyes are wide and worried, and his voice is steady and soothing.

"It's all right. You're safe."

He's too close. The letter opener is still in his hand. I push him, hard. "Get away!" I struggle to my feet, kicking the chair aside. The residual heat of his hands is imprinted on my skin.

Takahashi falls back, catches himself with one arm. He lets me retreat, then stands with animal grace. He says carefully, "What's wrong? You suddenly just froze. And your eyes — you looked like some of the men at the shelter."

"I'm fine. Really. Just a headache." I'm in control. I'm not crazy. And even if I am, I really don't want him to know.

He raises his eyebrows skeptically. "Okay. But I'd like you to rest here for a few minutes. Can I get you an aspirin? Do you need a doctor?"

"No. Thanks. I just need to get home." Mercifully my knees hold rock steady. I don't want him to see how shaken I am. I don't want to showcase my vulnerability. There are things I still didn't know, but I can't continue the investigation at the moment. My questions will have to wait.

I drive home in a state, binding my emotions with the knobby iron claw of self-control.

For the second time in less than a week, a flashback has left me sick and shaken. Fear takes up residence in my abdominal cavity and purrs softly in its lair. What the hell is wrong with me? Why can't I get over that undercover assignment in Denver? Is it just a product of too many late nights, too much stress, too much bad food and coffee and irregular hours? I'd been embedded in the Baxter Building for months, posing as one of the squatters: a used-up ex-prossie who'd taken up residence on the eighth floor. In reality I'd been collecting names and dates and observing drops and deals. Hardened as I was to vice and violence, the situation sickened me. Prostitutes of both sexes, some young enough to be in grade school. Drug pushers ditto, johns and pimps and users all mixing in a fetid stew.

When the raid came, it was meant to be a clean-up, a sweep of the dregs that feasted upon themselves in an endless cycle of predator and prey. But somehow Sonny had gotten wind of it, tumbled to my identity, and tried to kill me.

I'd just been down to see one of the dealers, and had been forced by circumstances to take some coke. I'd been amped, alert, ultra-confident. I'd failed to lock my door. And ironically, it was my drug-induced state of hyper-alertness that made me aware of Sonny when he broke into my room.

Maybe it was also the drugs, or the emotional overload, or maybe just simple blood loss, that had led to the vision I'd had on the abandoned mattress in the closet, waiting for the raid to finish.

But I wouldn't think of that.

Maybe you need your meds, Lake. Just sayin'.

No. No drugs. Not ever again.

My empty house with its echoing rooms does nothing to alleviate my anxiety. I do a perimeter check, open all the shades so the sunlight can illuminate the rooms, and fill the electric kettle with water, waiting impatiently for it to boil so I can make myself a cup of tea. It's after noon. I'm hungry, but my gut is too tense to eat.

I try sitting on my camp chair, but finally pace across the room to stand by the windows overlooking the river. The water is speckled with whitecaps, and full of sailboats. My inner vision swoops back to Denver and the raid on the Baxter Building. That was the first time the hallucinations had really broken my life. There had been one or two before that, maybe, when I was younger, much milder and easier to understand. I'd seen an image of my brother after he'd died by his own hand. I'd glimpsed him in my peripheral vision, standing in a corner, looking pale and sad. The grief counselor said such sightings were perfectly normal. I begged to differ, but I just wanted to get through the process, so I didn't argue with anything she said.

The vision at the Baxter Building had been disturbing precisely because I couldn't understand why I should be hallucinating police officers and criminals joining forces. Was it because I myself had been playing a role for so long? Was it just because the building was so awful, squatters on every floor, children and feral animals and desperate doped out men and women? No — I swallowed. It was because my vision had shown some of the very same men I worked beside taking part in the degradation of the people who lived there. True enough that those people had made their own series of bad choices, but the cops were supposed to be above all that. Knights in the front line of defense, not aiders and abettors of evil.

For weeks I'd lived the life of a strung-out crim, sleeping on a rickety bed in an abandoned room on the top floor, hoping that the stairs would be a deterrent to the lowlives down below. The days were hazy, an endless succession of deceit and self-harm. I couldn't always keep away from the activities of the other dwellers; to maintain my legend I had to participate. But I'd been able to get the names of the players, clock their comings and goings.

And here I am, still running from that darkness within myself. The empty house is proof enough of my failure to recover my sense of self, to move forward with my life. Something broke back in Denver. To much had happened in a short time. I told myself I could handle it all — of course I could. Until the day of the raid when I'd ended up in the psych ward.

I just want it all to be over. To get beyond the relentless haunting of my past. The investigation gets shelved for today. Tea cup in the sink, and I head out to walk the streets, to work myself to a state of exhaustion.

18

It's afternoon. I'm in a better frame of mind, physically fatigued and ready to write up my notes. I still don't have much to go on, but I have a broader understanding of the people involved, and can look at the case with a clearer eye. Without having to muck about in my own past.

I'd left my phone at home on the card table, and when I get in the door it's ringing. For some reason I feel a stab of nervousness, in case someone from Colorado has tracked me down; but since I don't recognize the number, and it's an Oregon prefix, I pick it up.

"Audrey Lake speaking."

"It's Coralee. From Riverside Christian Church. Something bad has happened!" She has a catch in her voice — I can hear it behind the effort to keep it steady.

It takes a moment to click. Coralee. The receptionist. "What? Are you okay?"

"Yes, I'm fine. But Reverend Takahashi's not. He's been arrested."

"What? When?" Shock stiffens my spine. I just talked to the guy a couple of hours ago.

"Just now. Please, I know you're an investigator. Help him!"

"Are you sure he's arrested? Were you there when he was taken? Did they have a warrant? Read him his rights?"

"Yes, I was here. I heard everything. They said they wanted to ask him some questions, and then they took him away!"

"Okay, in general, the police will read him his rights if they are arresting him. So they probably just want to talk. Did they say what they wanted him for?"

"They said it's about Victoria Harkness's murder! Please, go down there and tell them that he couldn't be involved."

"Ma'am, I'm sorry, I can't interfere in a police investigation."

Hypocrite.

"But aren't you working with the police? I thought, when you said you were an investigator, that —"

"Listen. The police don't arrest innocent people. If he hasn't done anything wrong, he's got nothing to worry about. He's probably just a person of interest."

"You mean a suspect? Oh my God! I've got to organize a prayer chain! I've got to —"

"Ma'am, please. Slow down." I take a breath. "If he's innocent, he'll be back soon. If you tell people now, they may be worried without cause."

There's a long pause. I wonder if she's told some people already.

When she answers, her voice is small. "I just want to help him."

"Then just sit tight. Worst case scenario, he's going to need a lawyer. If the church retains one, you could have that contact information ready if the Reverend needs to call an attorney. But most likely, he won't."

The call ends. I see again Takahashi's compassionate face, the buttoned up shirt. But also the gleaming letter opener. Had the threat he posed been real, or was I just being overwrought? When I was talking to him, he didn't seem worried. Or guilty. But I don't have any access to the police, or any forensics, or even the autopsy. What do they know that I don't? I hear again the slap of Takahashi's hand on the desktop, insisting that Victoria had to be stopped. Is he more dangerous than I realize? Or are the police keeping tabs on my movements, and my visit somehow precipitated his arrest? The only way I'm going to learn is by going directly to the source. But visiting the police station is the last thing I want to do.

As it happens, I don't have to figure out how to approach the APD. A black SUV with the word POLICE stenciled on the side rolls up to the curb. I watch through the front windows as Detective Candide slams the door, adjusts her shoulder holster, and stomps down the concrete steps that lead to my front porch. Her boots echo hollowly on the planks. Her knock sounds just shy of a SWAT assault.

Here we go. I stand in the doorway, as nonchalantly as I can manage. "Detective Candide, this is an unexpected pleasure."

"You." Her voice is cold, but I can hear the tremor of anger behind it, and in the tension across her jaw.

"Can I help you, Detective?"

"You and I are going to talk. Now. So either let me in or get in the car and we'll go down to the station."

I think about that. I don't particularly want her to see the inside of my house, the lonely card table and camp chair. And if I go to the station I might get a chance to see Takahashi, or find out how their investigation is proceeding. Plus, points for cooperation.

"The station it is, then," I say and step out onto the porch with her, locking the door behind me. I've surprised her, and she scowls. But she stomps back up the steps and opens the rear door. I oblige by getting inside, and she commandeers the driver's seat.

We are quiet on the way across town. Conversation seems to be a no-go, and I don't want to give Candide the power to ignore me. The back of the car is spic and span—no trash, no scuff marks on the back of the front seats, no slits in the upholstery. The grill between the front and back is black and shiny. Nice. The SUV still has that new car smell, and I inhale appreciatively. My own car is well beyond its salad days; it's about ready for the compost heap.

Candide regards me in the mirror before turning her attention to the road. In a few minutes, we pull up in the parking lot of the station, and she ushers me in the back door.

The interview room is typical, made to be intimidating and uncomfortable. But I know the drill, and sit back in the folding chair with my legs crossed. I consider waving at the one-way mirror, but decide that wouldn't go down well. Candide sits across from me, notebook at the ready, pen beating a tattoo on the worn formica of the table.

She begins without preliminaries. "Why did you interview the Reverend Seth Takahashi?"

Here we go. Maybe I can learn something here. A little quid pro quo. "I'm talking to him in connection with the murder of Victoria Harkness. Why did you arrest him?"

She blinks. "He's not arrested."

"That's not what I heard."

"Then your sources are unreliable. And you have no business interfering in an ongoing investigation. So, again, why were you talking to him?"

"I was hired by the Church of the Spirit to find out what happened to their founder. Seth Takahashi had expressed some adverse sentiments to Harkness's teaching. I was following up. Like you, apparently."

"You're interfering. Who knows what damage you've done, what misinformation you've spread. This is an ongoing police investigation, and you are muddying the waters. I can charge you with obstruction of justice."

I snort in disbelief. Her tactics are beyond heavy-handed. Is this her own call, or Olafson's? Regardless, I know the law. So I say, "I've offered him neither payment or engaged in threats of force. I have not encouraged him to lie or to commit a crime. I've simply asked him questions. Ergo, I have done nothing wrong. You're free to do the same."

"Our work is not your business. I want you to stay away from potential witnesses or informants. You could contaminate or prejudice testimony, and I won't stand for it."

"Come on, Detective. Freedom of speech, and all that. You've detained Takahashi, so you must have something to link him to the crime. What is it?"

She glares. "None of your business."

"You got more out of him than I did, if he admitted something to you. So you can't be overly bothered by my visit with him. Or maybe you have some evidence." I lean forward, hands clasped. "We shouldn't be antagonists, we should be allies. After all, we're all on the same side. Trying to put the bad guys away."

She takes a deep breath, as though to steady her temper. "Why do you think her death isn't an accident?"

"Why do you think it was?"

"I'm asking the questions. Why are you investigating?"

"Because I've been hired by the Church of the Spirit to do so."

"If they have some reason to believe it, they need to talk to us."

"Have *you* gone to *them*?"

There's a pause, then Candide says again, "None of your business."

"Never mind — I know you haven't, because Claire or Daniel would have told me so."

"Who else have you been talking to?"

"Her mother. People who knew her. Following standard operating procedure."

"What have you found out?"

"I don't have to answer, not without a court order. The information belongs to my client."

"You were a cop. Once. If you know something, you have a duty to tell us. Or risk being an accessory."

"Do you want a catalogue of unimportant factoids? Because that's what I've got. Stop trying to threaten me with fake charges. I know the law. Better than you, apparently."

She doesn't answer, just looks at me. We engage in a silent battle of wills, neither willing to give an inch.

The door to the interview room opens, letting in a gush of fresh air. Steve Olafson fills the frame, his sleeves rolled up to expose his thick forearms.

"That'll be all, Jane. I'm taking over."

Face white, Detective Candide gathers her things and stalks out the door without a backward glance.

Ouch. It may be SOP to change out interrogators, keeping them fresh as the perp gets worn down, but it seems a little soon for that. I don't blame Jane for being annoyed.

Olafson takes Candide's place at the table. "Ms. Lake, you are in some trouble."

I lean forward and interlace my fingers. "Detective, I'm on a job, hired by the Church of the Spirit. If I find anything out I think you can use, I'll share it with you. If you're afraid I'll mess up some angle of yours, all you've got to do is share your plans with me."

He takes a long time looking at me, tapping his fingers on the table. "You got a P. I. license?"

My anxiety goes up a notch, but I keep it under wraps. "I'm not a private investigator. I'm a consultant."

"Don't split hairs with me, Ms. Lake. I've got my own investigation going on. On you. I've got some feelers out, and soon I'll know just why you left Denver. But what I do know doesn't make you look good."

"I've got nothing to hide." But I could hear the hollowness is my own voice, and I know he hears it too.

"Nice try. But your reputation precedes you, Lake. See, I've already been warned about you." He drops his voice, until it's so low I can barely hear it, but the venom is there in spades. "There's nothing I hate worse than a dirty cop."

"What?" It's so not what I expect him to say. I'm shocked. And furious. I jump to my feet. "I've never been dirty. Not ever. And if anyone says different, it's a lie."

"You may have squirmed away from Denver just in time, but if you think your big city corruption is going to fly here, think again." He sits back and resumes his normal voice. "I know all about how you alerted your criminal friends to a police raid, and good men were hurt because of you. I'll be watching you, Lake. Now get out, before I lose my temper."

19

When I leave the police station, I feel both shaken and stirred. I try to talk myself down as I set off on the long walk home. At least the station is only a couple of blocks from the Riverwalk, so my journey will at least be scenic. This portion of the trail is paved with asphalt. An occasional thorn-studded blackberry branch reaches out to snag my trousers, so I'm distracted for a bit from the thoughts and fears hammering behind my eyes.

How much do you think Olafson knows?

Whatever it is, it isn't true. I've never been dirty.

Gotten close to the edge a time or two, though, yeah?

I was undercover, dammit!

Olafson said he'd been warned. That means someone in Denver told him about me. I clench my fists, uselessly. Who was it, and what did they say? Not my handler, no way. Someone on the strike team? But my undercover identity shouldn't've been known to anyone. Still, office gossip. War stories. Word gets around, even when it shouldn't.

Worst case scenario, what if Olafson discovered that I was in a psych hospital? I could certainly kiss any work opportunity with the police department goodbye. But really, I've already done that. And it's not like he can arrest me for anything. Whatever he says, I'm still a good cop. I am.

But he accused me of being dirty, of leaking information. The implication being: for money. He must be referring to the raid on the Baxter Building. But I didn't say anything to anyone.

Sonny knew you were a cop.

Yeah, he did — I thought I'd given myself away somehow. Gangsters have a nose for law enforcement.

What if someone at the department squealed?

It's true that three officers were hurt. That the element of surprise hadn't been as decisive as they'd planned. That the leader of the Black Dogs — Sonny's gang — had been missing, when we thought — when I'd thought — that all the main players would be present. But if Sonny knew ahead of time, why did he stick around?

To kill me?

I'm spinning. Thoughts and what-if's are ricocheting around my head like a pinball. I try to get a grip, bring some order to the chaos. That was all in the past and a thousand miles away. It can't affect me here. Olafson is just trying to intimidate me.

Sounds like it's working.

I stop to look out over the river. Half a dozen freighters are anchored in the channel, waiting for berth openings in Portland or further upstream. The shiny black head of a sea lion bobs out among the waves. It looks at me for a long time before dipping back beneath the surface and arching away like a sleek brown torpedo.

The lumpy spine of hills on the Washington side of the river has square brown patches where clearcutting has shaved away the trees. The landscape here is so different from Colorado. Back there, I'd never seen a river the size of the Columbia, big enough to accommodate ocean-going ships. And the air is so much more humid. Even now, the clouds bellying up at the mouth of the river promise more rain, a soft spring shower to gift the ever-present greenery with moisture.

I like this little town at the confluence of river and sea. It's authentic and real, and I want to be a part of it. I want to stay. I won't let Olafson or anyone else push me out.

I don't want to be part of a hierarchical organization any more. Toe the line, take orders, worry about how my colleagues will see me, or how some reporter will portray my actions to a condemning public. But most of all, I don't want my actions to endanger someone else, again. By working alone, I can mitigate that danger. If I am going insane, at least I won't take anyone else down with me.

Whatever happens, I have to follow my own certainties. Even when I'd been a detective I'd been prone to the odd hunch, just like any good cop. Sometimes impressions and instinct are all you have. That, and perseverance. Just keep digging until something turns up.

Or until you pop out on the other side of the planet.

By this time, I've reached the Maritime Museum, with its curving roof reminiscent of an ocean wave. The asphalt path gives way to boardwalk, thick wood planks like the ones on the docks and wharfs. The trolley tracks become inset, the grooves ready to turn an unwary ankle. In the process of watching my step, my subconscious, left alone, relaxes. There's nothing I can do about what people say in Denver. There's nothing I can do about Olafson's suspicions, or Candide's attitude. I've done nothing wrong. So what if they say I'm crazy? There are worse things to be known for.

Yeah, like being dirty. Don't forget that.

I've never been dirty!

Okay, deep breaths. Stop talking back to the voice in your head. Think about the present.

I'm still no closer to determining who killed Victoria Harkness. I think of the men I've interviewed: Jason Morganstern, Eric North, and Seth Takahashi. Takahashi is on the APD radar already — I wish I could have gleaned something at the station. Is he the one? He has the best — the only — motivation I can determine, but it's a big step to take for a man of God, crusades and terrorism notwithstanding.

In my experience, the worst criminals have egos to gratify and a basic selfishness that allows them to cross the line into taking someone else's life to better their own. And they aren't necessarily all that smart, or imaginative. Usually they just can't think of a better way to solve their problems other than the short-term method of killing whoever stands in their path.

But Victoria isn't a typical murder victim. There doesn't seem to be anything for anyone to gain. Her trust fund reverts to her cousins. Takahashi might gain some new parishioners, and quash a dangerous religious offshoot. Morganstern I'm not sure of. He'd been attracted to her, no doubt about that, but had that attraction morphed into obsession? Takahashi told me Jason had inappropriate attitudes toward women, but he didn't sound obsessed when I talked to him yesterday. He didn't seem smart enough, or controlled enough, to conceal his feelings to such an extent. I suppose he might have killed her in a fit of jealousy or frustration.

And Eric North? He has the ego, but what's the motive? He's a successful artist, a local celebrity in some ways. Still, he's the only one who'd known her before — is there something in that I can follow up on? She'd been a child, thirteen or so when they moved away. Maybe one of her teachers would remember her. I make a mental note to check the local school district. Dig, dig, dig.

I also can't forget Daniel Chandler. He's known Victoria for a long time. He's paying my bills, but he seems slick to me. More like a salesman than a bookkeeper. Plus, there's a big wad of insurance money coming to the church, and he's got the keys to the checking account.

Claire Chandler, on the other hand, seems honest. No facade, nothing that trips any alarms. Except for the fact that she's married to Daniel and lets him call the shots. Doesn't show very good judgment on her part. Still, she wouldn't be the first woman to let some guy delude her.

Near the end of my long walk toward home, I look in on the church. The hot spots on my heels and toes are turning into incipient blisters. But the repurposed grocery store gleams in the late afternoon light, at least until a cloud passes in front of the sun. A slate-colored Toyota Highlander is alone in the parking lot. I peer through the window, see leather seats, faux woodgrain dash. Nice. I walk inside the unlocked door. Shake my head. Church people are way too trusting.

My footsteps scuff in the large carpeted sanctuary, echo against the industrial linoleum in the big fellowship hall. The storefront windows let in a lot of light, and I slow down and have a look at the hanging art. My first tour with Daniel had been a quick pass-through. Now I take my time. The pictures are an eclectic mix of style, size, and media. Photographs. Etchings. String art. Paintings — oil, water color. A paint-by-number of horses grazing in a field. The only thing lacking is a black velvet Elvis. Or dogs playing poker.

What I mean is, the lot is strictly amateur. Oh, some are better than others. Some are pretty good, still lifes of fruit or flowers rendered with skill. Some pieces are abstract, with splashes of exuberant color and no apparent subject. But Jackson Pollock they aren't. That's why the painting by Eric North stood out. Past tense. Where it had been hanging is now an empty space. I remember it as having a muted palette, grays and tans and slate blues and sage greens. Victoria Harkness, standing with the river behind her and the Megler Bridge soaring overhead. When I saw it at the memorial service, I was struck by the similarity to the scene of my vision, and wondered then what the connection might be. But now it's gone.

Glancing around, I see other blank spots, places where pictures are missing. Gift rescinders reclaiming their own? For the most part, Chandler is probably happy to see them go. Unless he's the one harvesting the crop. I ponder that thought for a minute, then shrug and head for the office, intending to ask him.

Daniel Chandler is seated behind his desk, peering at a spreadsheet. The reflected light from the computer monitor makes him look sallow and unhealthy. I rap on the doorjamb to get his attention. He jerks his head up, then relaxes when he recognizes me, lifting a hand to remove his glasses and rub his eyes.

"Audrey. I didn't expect to see you. Are you reporting in?"

I'm not, but now I feel like I have to. I give him a rundown of who I've interviewed. I don't tell him about my run-in with the cops.

I wind up with, "Anything more you think I should know?" I clocked the slight emphasis on 'you' when he greeted me earlier, and wonder if he's expecting someone. Plus, the unlocked door.

"How do I know what's important?" He cracks his knuckles, proceeds to tell me about how much Victoria inspired people, what a good speaker she was. Her physical beauty. All the stuff I keep hearing.

"What about her family?"

"She didn't have any siblings, and I never heard her mention her father. Her mother is one of those society women, always on the hunt for the next rung in the ladder. Vicky didn't really get on with her. She said her mother was disappointed in her daughter's choice of vocation. Not enough lucre in it. Or real religion."

He laughs nervously. I'm not sure why. Then I think about the missing pictures in the fellowship hall, and ask him if he's taken them.

"Guilty as charged. Right now the church is drowning in bills. Rent on this behemoth. Utilities. Vicky used to supplement with her own money, but now of course that's impossible. So, I've been selling a few of the better ones to raise operational capital."

"Is that legal?"

"They belong to the church. Assets. If we go into receivership, they'll be seized anyway."

"What about her key-person insurance?"

He looks, very briefly, annoyed. "American Life is dragging their feet. You know what insurance companies are like. In the end, we'll probably have to close the church." He shakes his head and rubs his eyes again, rumpling the already-rumpled eyebrows. "That'll be hard for Claire."

"But not for you?"

"No, it'll be hard for me too — but there's been financial hardship for a long time now. It's not like I haven't seen it coming — the curse of being the bookkeeper. One of the reasons we came out here was to cut operating expenses. But unfortunately it also lost the church's most generous members and patrons. I went around and around with Vicky about her decision to come to Astoria, but she was absolutely immovable. Said she had to return to the river. Which is nonsense — Portland has a river, too. Two of them — the Columbia, and the Willamette."

"What about her book, the one you told me about? Maybe you could publish it posthumously, with some of her talks. As a memorial."

"Don't think I haven't thought of that. But I've only seen a rough draft. And it's pretty personal. I'm not sure anyone else could complete it. Or that it would even make much money." He looks at his watch, glances over my shoulder to the doorway and back at me. "Listen, I'm pretty busy here. Can we talk later?"

Remembering the laptop in the apartment, I think the book is probably on the hard drive. Wish I'd snagged it when I had a chance. Any amount of information might be hidden there. Too late now. Or is it? Maybe her mother will let me try to access the contents.

Belatedly, I think he seems a little agitated, but I'm not letting him go just yet. I nail down another item of curiosity. "Did Victoria do any art herself?"

"Not like the congregants, no. Her offering, she always said, was her heart and soul to her people."

Careful. You're gonna get a cavity from all this sweetness.

"What about you?" I ask. "Any of those pieces out there yours? Or Claire's?"

He shakes his head, cracking his knuckles again and shifting in his chair. "Not me — I don't tap into the Spirit, or at least not the right one. Claire is doing some sewing thing. Little quilted squares. I think Vicky might have taken them home. She liked them."

I remember seeing some fabric pieces hanging in Harkness's apartment. But his response feels weird to me. I mean, he doesn't seem, I don't know, devoted. He seems flippant. And taking down the spirit offerings and selling them feels disrespectful, a betrayal of the original givers' intent. But probably not illegal.

"Are you not a believer in the Divinity of Art?" I offer in a tone that is slightly amused, slightly sarcastic, but not so much that he can take offense, in case he is some kind of devotee.

"Just never had the bent for it. But I loved to hear Vicky talk, and inspire other people to access their creative gifts."

Sounds like a racket to me.

"How'd you wind up as bookkeeper anyway? Answer an ad? Or were you already in the congregation?"

He sighs. "I'd done some book work for another church, so I knew the ropes. And they needed someone, so I spoke up."

"So you were already in the congregation?"

"Not an official member, no. But I was in the faith community, so I was aware of her, and became a member when she hired me."

"I see." I pause, wondering what is niggling at me. He just feels so networky and insincere. Plus nervous. But. I suppose church workers have to make a living. "What was the other place you worked for?"

There's a beat, two, which sets my antennae quivering. How hard is it to reel off your former employers? But then he says, "Beaverton Foursquare." And glances at his watch again.

"Is there a problem, Mr. Chandler? You seem edgy."

"No, no problem. Just—"

"Busy. I know." I nod, no wiser. He's hiding something, but I can't think of anything more to ask him. And my feet hurt, a headache is starting, and there's still several blocks to walk home, all uphill. So I tell him goodbye.

As a parting shot, he says, "We really need some results on this, Audrey. Otherwise I might not be able to pay you."

That remark leaves a bad taste in my mouth. Because it's manipulative. And because his concerns about money seem to override his concerns about Victoria. And justice. And the moral arc of the universe. I'm fuming as I make my way home.

Could Daniel be the killer? He'd certainly know the victim's habits, and be trusted by her. He'd definitely have opportunity. But why? There was no benefit that I could see. In fact, her death had hurt him. He had more work in the short term and no job in the long.

Except, the coming insurance payout. How much access would he have?

20

It's Saturday. Five a.m. The weekend, for whatever that's worth. Unable to sleep, I'm lying on my camp cot, looking up at the overhead light and imagining pictures in the ceiling drywall. Guns. Knives. A dog. A bonfire. I think about what I need to do today: follow up on Chandler's employment history. Call the life insurance company and try to spoof some information about Victoria and Daniel's policies.

My cell rings, and I have to roll over and reach for where it lies on the floor with the cord curled around it like a noodle. I lean too far and tip the cot over and bang my nose on the floor.

"Son of a bitch!" I press my hands to my face as the call goes to voicemail. I get up, dress, and make coffee before listening to the message.

"Audrey, it's Claire. Please call. It's Dan — he's been — he's been kuh-killed."

The final word, killed, is almost lost in a guttural sob. I only understand because it's a word I've heard a lot, in a variety of tones and accents. I put aside my surprise and dismay: those emotions won't be helpful. Instead, I call back immediately. She's at home, and I get directions, pour the coffee into a thermos and show up at her door. Inside, we sit on a black leather sofa that has a matching recliner. House plants crowd the corners and the coffee table has an artful stack of photography books. A giant TV covers most of one wall; a freestanding Tiffany floor lamp glows in the corner. The image of middle-class prosperity.

But. First things first.

I get a mug from the kitchen — note the soapstone countertops and white-painted cabinetry — pour out some coffee, add cream. Notice the tremor in my hand.

"Drink this, Claire. That's right. Now. Tell me what happened."

Her voice is tight, controlled, but breaks forth occasionally into an emotionally charged stutter. "He didn't come home last night. He often works late, so, I was annoyed but not worried. I went to bed at midnight. But he wasn't back this morning. I called his phone, cell and office, but no answer. Went by the church, but it was locked. His car was still in the lot. I don't have keys so I banged on the door, yelled. Then I called the police."

"Deep breaths, Claire." Wait while she complies. If ever I need evidence of who was behind the initial delay of investigating Victoria's disappearance, I have it here. Claire would have called the cops if not deterred by Daniel.

Although, I guess he is her husband and not just her friend. Still.

A steel-and-crystal clock ticks from the wall. Claire glances at the face and together we watch the creep of the minute hand.

"They came while I was banging the door again. Of course, they thought I was a burglar — 'til I said I was the one who called. My husband, inside. No answer. They got the door open, went in, 'Police!' One kept his eye on me, tried to keep me back. As if! But I was too worried to care. I pushed in, following, went right to Dan's office. He was —" she breaks off, gulping air like a climber on Everest.

I picture it, the desk, the computer, the piled papers. "He was…?"

"He was leaning back in his chair, all the way, his face all bloody, his head — oh God — his head —" her voice rises, a near shriek. "So awful. What kind of monster would do such a thing?"

Anxiety clamps around my body like a coffin. I was just there yesterday evening, talking to him. Just a few hours ago. I shudder. Was the killer in building, lurking? Waiting until I left? I take a breath of my own, try not to think about how I was the last person to see him alive. Except the murderer.

And maybe the murderer saw me.

I force myself to calmness, take refuge in the routine search for information. It's the best way to help my friend.

I take her hands. "It's okay, Claire, you're all right. I'm going to help you. Find some answers. Let's go back to the parking lot. Outside. You saw his car, right? What kind is it?"

"Toyota Highlander. Grayish blue. Or bluish gray."

The same thing I saw yesterday. "Were there any other cars in the lot?"

"No. Just his. And mine." She's stopped stammering, is holding tight to my hands.

"What do you drive?"

"Little white pickup. Ford Ranger."

These questions are largely to get her to steady down, recounting information she's sure of. But the discrepancy in their vehicles is telling. We're talking a twenty thousand dollar price difference. Daniel didn't stint himself. Where did the money come from? My dislike of the man is growing, posthumously. Remembering how I had been able to just walk inside the previous day, I say, "Is the church usually kept locked?"

"Victoria liked to leave it open if she was working there, so people could come in to see her. But if Dan was alone with the money, I'm sure he'd lock up. Especially at night."

"What money?"

"Collection money. For the various fundraisers and service offerings."

I remember some of the requests from my first visit to the church. He'd been alone with the money yesterday, I assume. But it couldn't have amounted to more than a few hundred dollars, if that. Probably much less — there'd been no service in which to pass the plate. I recall my meeting with him, his words: Audrey, I didn't expect to see you. A slight emphasis on the 'you'."

"Would he have been meeting anyone?"

There's a long pause. When Claire answers, her voice is choked, not with grief but with anger. Or maybe both.

"What. Do. You. Mean. Meeting with someone? Like, an affair, do you mean? Do you mean, cheating on me? With *another* woman? Who do you mean, exactly?"

I pull my hand away, surprised by her outburst. And I clock the way she says 'another.' Not like 'other than herself.' No, like 'other than the one she already knew about.' I don't know where to go with this. Claire is hurt, distraught. I don't want to hurt her more. But this sounds like it might be important. I soldier on, trying to be gentle while stepping on the petals of her heart with clodhopper boots.

"Why don't you tell me about the affairs, Claire."

I'm taking advantage of a vulnerable witness, and I know it. Her guard is down, the bars are off the doors, the train has been derailed from its safe and preplanned tracks. But. It's necessary — there's no time for niceties. People are dying. At least, that's what I tell myself.

And she tells me what I suspect already: Daniel has never been faithful, but he always comes back. He loves her. He does. But he can't help himself. I learn about the married secretary at his previous job, the one that made him leave Beaverton Foursquare; the choir director at Pacific Universalist before that. Claire hoped it would get better after the move to Astoria. And it was better, for a while. But there was someone. She thinks it started six months after they came here. And she thinks it stopped about the time that Victoria went missing.

Maybe he was too worried to carry on his little fling-ding. Maybe he felt bad. But I don't think so. Or if he did feel something like remorse, it wasn't strong enough to make him stop. I pat Claire's shoulder and utter soothing words, but it's an old story. The oldest. It's hard to reconcile the independent, strong-minded person I know Claire to be with someone who would put up with this treatment. The human heart is truly unfathomable. I try to picture Daniel Chandler as some kind of Don Juan, but I can't. He's no George Clooney. But he is — was — a pleasant enough guy. Maybe that's enough, more than enough, for desperate, lonely women.

Again, I lead Claire gently back through her memories of the parking lot, the building, and finally the office. The desk, the chair, the body.

He'd been beaten to death, his head pulped by a blunt instrument. A hammer, a bat, a two by four. Someone who felt an extreme version of fear or rage. Knowing what I do now, I think: jealous husband, jealous lover. He'd diddled the wrong woman, and someone got revenge.

There's already been one murder. Are they related? Do I have two killers to find, or only one?

Maybe Claire finally got fed up.

No. I don't believe it. Too brutal. Women don't often beat people to death. They shoot, stab, suffocate, or poison. Sometimes, occasionally, they drown.

Out of the mouths of babes.

No. Victoria's killer is a man. I know it.

Do you?

21

I glance back as I leave the Chandler house. It looks dark and lonely, with only a single lamp glowing through the window. It's just after seven, and the eastern sky is pale as I click my car door open with the key fob. It's been raining, big surprise, and the pavement looks black and shiny, reflecting the street light in a dim yellowish circle. My car is beaded with moisture. The seat upholstery feels cool to the touch. As I drive away, the reaction sets in — the personal one. I'm shaken by what has happened to Daniel. I just saw the guy, healthy if not wealthy and wise. Or maybe he was wealthy; he had a fairly expensive car. Nice furniture, decent house. But he didn't get it working for churches. It's been my experience that, unless you're a rock star preacher with a celebrity income to match, church workers are notoriously underpaid.

So. Why kill Daniel?

Philandering comes to mind.

But to have his murder coincident with Victoria's death? What are the odds?

I'm no statistician, but my guess: pretty damn unlikely.

The two must be related.

So. Why Daniel? I mean, he's a bookkeeper, for crying out loud. At a non-profit. Robbery seems to be a non-starter. There shouldn't have been much cash on the premises, since there hasn't been a service.

But. There's entirely too much money in his life. My guess: fraud. Or blackmail.

People don't usually kill over fraud. They sue each other instead. But blackmail? That includes a recipe for violence.

What might Daniel have known?

Maybe he knew who killed Victoria Harkness.

Jumping over the moon to your latest conclusion, Lake?

Okay. It is a big leap. Set that aside for a moment. What else might he have known?

...

I can't think of anything. Some sexy secret discovered during an illicit tryst? Feels like a reach. But. It must be something that would generate anger or fear.

Blackmail presupposes evidence. I wonder if anything is missing from his office. I was just there, so I might be able to detect an anomaly that the police would miss. And I've already left my DNA on previous visits, so adding more trace evidence won't make any difference.

As easy as that, I've talked myself into going back to the scene of the crime.

I know, crazy. Not to mention unprofessional. But. I have to look at the place before it gets too messed up by the cops, and before my own memory fades.

When I pull into the parking lot of the Church of the Spirit, the clouds open and rain bullets onto the asphalt. Wonderful. Gloves, shoe covers: check. I run to the front door, splashing my pant legs. Rivulets of water drip off the hem of my jacket, creating a ribbon of wetness around my thighs.

The door of the church is crossed over by yellow crime scene tape that rattles in the downpour. I thought I might have to dodge some CSIs but no one is here. Sloppy. Could be because it's early, But still. I try the door and to my surprise it opens. Hooray, no need for the pick gun which I've forgotten in the car anyway. Before my nerve deserts me, I duck under the tape and go inside. Look out the window as I pull on gloves and booties. The big supermarket windows offer a wide, depressing view of Marine Drive. Once again, I feel like a target on a shooting range, but tell myself there's no one out there to see me. Besides, the light isn't on. I'm hidden in shadow.

The roar of rain falling on the metal roof covers the sound of my footsteps as I make my way back to Chandler's office. There's no sign of the numbered cones and tags or other detritus of forensic data collection. Doesn't look like the scene has been processed yet. They probably don't have a local CSI team. Lucky for me.

I hope they've at least taken the body.

Steeling myself to peek around the jamb, I'm relieved to see there's no corpse in the chair, no near-sighted bookkeeper with an eye for the ladies. The office doesn't have windows, so it feels safe to flick on the light and shift into observation mode.

The harsh illumination reveals bloodstains, sprinkles of reddish drops on the desk and walls and a big smudge on the chair back. A line of backspatter across the ceiling tiles. Even without the body, evidence of a severe beating is clear. I glance around, trying to remember what the place looked like earlier. Piles of papers, computer, sagging bookcase, uncomfortable guest chair. Check, check, check, and check. The office still looks untidy, but not searched. Or if it has been, it's been by a consummate professional. And I doubt that anyone of that caliber has any interest in Daniel Chandler.

I nudge the mouse a tiny bit to awaken the computer. I'd love to see an appointment schedule appear on the monitor, complete with names and addresses, but it's only the login screen. I never seem to get the same breaks the TV detectives do.

Look again at the papers. Is one of the piles shorter? It's hard to tell. And Daniel might have continued on working after I left. The truth is, I wasn't paying that much attention to his desk. I take a barrage of pictures to study later, and notice the small red spots that crisscross the papers. The arcs look uninterrupted. The papers haven't been moved since the attack; ditto flash drives and pens and post-it notes.

Whoever killed Chandler didn't care about what the bookkeeper was doing in here. They weren't after money, or incriminating documents, or blackmail material. Or if they were, they got what they wanted before the attack. There doesn't even appear to have been a fight. Just one guy walking up to another and beating his head in.

I glance up at the backspatter, mime a swing over my head and adjust my position until I'm under it. The killer seems to have been standing at the side of the desk. But. There's a lot of variables. Where Daniel was seated. The angle of the wound. The length of the weapon. All I know is the killer got close. My intuition goes clickety-clack. Chandler knew his killer. Knew him, and didn't expect the violence. Didn't see or recognize the weapon as a potential threat.

So, not an enraged husband. Or, a husband who kept himself so cool that Daniel didn't clock the threat. Was that even possible? Even if the guy was cool, wouldn't the bookkeeper have been a teensy bit nervous? Chandler wasn't stupid. Would he have stayed sitting down? Seems like anyone would instinctively address a potential threat by standing up.

He wouldn't have been afraid of Claire.

Shut up. It isn't her. Women hardly ever beat people to death, remember?

Hardly ever isn't never, though, is it?

I ignore Zoe, try to put myself in Chandler's point of view. Close my eyes. Imagine that I'm sitting down, working, it's late at night. I'm here alone...

A vision starts to form behind my eyelids. The ergonomic chair cradles my aching back, the computer keyboard is smooth under my fingers, clicking as I type. There's a sharp pain behind my right shoulder, and I massage the muscle. My eyes are burning with fatigue. But I'm almost finished. The spreadsheet numbers blur and I rub my eyes. The sound of the rain is a background hum, white noise. The door creaks open. I look up in surprise, expecting to see my wife.

A steel hand clamps on my shoulder, jolting me back to the present. I scream a little, jabbing an elbow into whoever is behind me. I feel a body twist away from the impact, a grunt of aggravation more than pain.

"Ms. Lake," says a masculine voice, "You are out of your jurisdiction."

Detective Olafson gives me the option to go without handcuffs, but makes it clear that I'm coming with him to the station. I'm numb, still in shock from my experience. I don't understand what just happened. I'd tried to imagine a sequence of events, and got something else, something more autonomous. Another vision? But how? What causes these? And why did Olafson have to interrupt before I saw the intruder?

Irritation replaces fear.

After a silent ride to the APD, we move past the curious gaze of the guy at the front desk and go right in to the same interview room we used when I came looking for a consultation.

"So, Ms. Lake, want to tell me why you've broken in to a crime scene which was clearly marked? I doubt you've forgotten what that means, despite the number of months you've been off the job." The detective sounds genial, but the flash of his canines behind his upper lip and the hard glint in his eye reveal that he's pissed.

I think about lying, but why? I think about not answering, but again, why? Just to annoy Detective Olafson? Doesn't seem like a smart choice at this point. So, the truth it is, then.

But first: "I think 'broken in' is too strong a term, Detective. I didn't break anything that wasn't already. No one was on guard. And the door was unlocked."

He rubs his forehead. "Don't play games with me, Lake. You may think you've got the edge here, but you don't. You may think you have a right to ignore the rules and regulations of police investigation, but you don't. You may think your status as some sort of 'criminal consultant'" — he raises his fingers and makes air quotes — "gives you some kind of immunity. Well, you can think again." He leans back in the folding chair until the screws at the joints creak. "Now. Stop wasting time and tell me what you were doing at the Church of the Spirit."

"I was investigating."

"I don't recall inviting you onto the team."

"Listen, Detective." I rest my forearms on the table and prepare to stretch the truth. "My client, Claire Chandler, asked me to look into it. It's her husband, for chrissake. I wanted to see the place for myself, before your 'team' starts to move things around. I know how to keep it clean." I indicate my gloves and the shoe covers that are still on my feet, now torn and muddy from being herded across the church parking lot by Olafson.

"Why?" he barks, leaning forward now, until we're almost nose to nose. "Why did you feel the need to 'see it for yourself?'" Annoying air quotes again.

I resist the urge to pull away. "Because I was just there. I talked to him yesterday. I wanted to see if anything had been disturbed, if anything was missing, that I could remember."

Olafson remains in his bent forward position, like a crouching wolverine. A vein is pulsing in his temple. I can smell whatever it is he uses for shampoo. Something faintly medicinal.

"Give me one good reason why I shouldn't arrest you."

"I haven't committed a crime." That you know about, anyway. "Okay, I trespassed on a crime scene. You got me on that. But since I was just in Daniel's office, you're going to find my traces anyway. I didn't touch anything." Almost. "And I had the victim's wife's permission to be there."

"What you should have done is come straight to me."

"I was going to, after I had a look at the scene." I run a hand through my hair in exasperated bewilderment. "Look, Detective, you and I haven't exactly clicked like Legos. I honestly didn't think you'd listen to me. If you knew I was one of the last people to see him, you'd still be grilling me and I'd have missed my chance at the scene."

I hear voices, unintelligible, beyond the door. Laughter.

At last he speaks. "How did you find out about the murder?"

"I told you. Daniel's wife. Claire Chandler."

He taps his pen on the table, first the nib, then the clicker. Tap. Tap. Tap.

"When?"

"She called me this morning."

"So. Why. Didn't. You. Call us. And tell us about your involvement?"

"There's no involvement. I just talked to the guy yesterday evening."

"Don't pretend ignorance, Lake. You know the procedure, better than anybody."

He's right. I shrug. My position is delicate. But he's not going to throw me in jail for this. There's nothing to gain, and a whole lot of paperwork to file. Since the scene was left unattended, he's got some culpability, too.

Yeah, keep telling yourself that, Lake.

Tap. Tap. Tap. "Describe your visit with the deceased."

I really don't want to end up in a cell, and figure a bit of cooperation is in order. So I tell him. About selling the art, the church finances, the things Daniel had said about Victoria. He asks questions, I answer. He repeats the questions, I answer again, adding new details. I ask for a soda and get a tepid can of cola. At last he runs down and we look at each other for a few silent minutes.

"Anything else?" Tap. Tap. Tap.

I hesitate. I'm reluctant to break Claire's confidence.

He picks up on my hesitation and leans forward again. "Anything else?" he repeats, with more emphasis.

I relent. "Only copper's suspicion." I tell Olafson about my sense that Daniel had been expecting someone else. I don't mention my own quivering antenna when I asked him about his past work experience. Or what Claire in her emotional distress had told me about her husband's affairs. Client confidentiality. Plus, dignity. However, I do mention that the possibility of infidelity was raised during the course of my investigation. And that Victoria's mother has threatened to sue the church.

"Her kind always does." He grimaces, and we share a moment of camaraderie. Then he says, casually, "Did you kill him, Ms. Lake?"

Eye roll. Splutter. "Of course not. He's my client, not my enemy.

Now I'll probably never get paid."

The silence stretches out between us. If I had been a real suspect, I'd be squirming to fill it with denials and justifications. But I'm an experienced interrogator. So I sit quietly, waiting for the next question.

The overhead fixtures emit a barely detectable hum. I feel a trickle of sweat run between my shoulders.

Finally, he says, "What did you think of the scene on your second visit?"

Relief relaxes the tightness in my chest. He's going to let it go. "It didn't look like anyone had tossed the place. It was a little haphazard before, papers and things lying around. I couldn't swear to the contents of every stack, but it didn't look any different from the previous day. It didn't have a vibe. That's what I was doing. Standing and trying to see if anything clicked as out of place. And then you scared the life out of me. Kudos on your ninja skills." A little butter never hurts. But actually, I feel grateful for that intrusive hand. In trying to bring forth the memory of the office, I'd somehow precipitated something else. Another vision. And I want — need — to think about the implications.

Olafson smirks. "You were pretty zoned out."

Subject change. "Have you released Takahashi?"

"Huh?" He blinks, and stops playing with his pen.

"I heard you arrested him."

Eyes narrow. "Don't believe everything you hear. We asked him some questions, no more."

"Learn anything?"

"Nothing you need to know." He taps his pen. "Where were you on the Wednesday a week before the vigil?"

Emphasis on the 'you.' He's checking my movements. Wednesday before last — the day before the service where Victoria turned up missing.

That must be when she died.

Tap, tap, tap. "I'm waiting."

"I'm thinking. Let's see — Wednesday, that was the day I first came in to the station to talk to you guys."

The pen stills. His face is expressionless, but the flicker of his eyes... he's thinking back himself, remembering.

"Yeah," I say, "I came in to chat with you guys. Voluntarily. And then —" And then I was so upset I went to a bar.

"And then?"

I shrug and stretch. "I went home, and later to the Portway Tavern for a burger. That's where I met Claire Chandler for the first time. She told me about the Church of the Spirit. Suggested I come to a service. You can check with her. She'll remember."

"Good. Because we will."

We engage in a staring match. I can feel the hard edge of the chair under my thighs, hear the distant patter of rain on the roof. The HVAC begins its cycle and blows a fresh gust of dusty air into the room.

"What else were you doing yesterday?"

Where to start? "I talked to Victoria Harkness's mother." I raise my hand before he can start a tirade. "She called me. I interviewed Seth Takahashi, before you guys dragged him in. That must be why Detective Candide showed up at my door and brought me back here." I look around. Had it only been yesterday? "When she let me go, that's when I walked down to the church and talked to Daniel Chandler." I give him times of day, as near as I can guess. I have the recording of my conversation, but I want to keep that up my sleeve.

"You were apparently the last person to see Chandler alive."

"Except for the killer," I remind him.

Tap, tap, tap.

Finally, Olafson rubs his eyes with thick, callused fingers. "Get out of here, Audrey. Don't enter any crime scenes. Don't interfere with us. And come forward if you find anything regarding either of these cases. Don't play a lone hand." He glares. "Understand?"

"Yes, Detective. I understand." It's all bluster, and I've heard the subtext. They've got nothing, and he doesn't want to lose a thread, however thin. He needs my help, whether he wants to acknowledge it or not.

"Stop at the front desk and have Larsen set you up to get fingerprinted. For elimination purposes."

It's a reasonable request, but all the same I feel the walls closing in a little.

Still, leaving the station, I walk a little easier, with head held high. I'm not going to be arrested. At least, not today.

22

My good mood is tempered by the fact that I have a two-mile walk in the rain to get back to my car, which is still parked at the church. This is getting to be a habit.

The visit to the cop shop has reminded me about my previous profession. The methodical plodding. The tedious ticking of boxes. The reports, the forms, the paperwork, the procedure, all intended to boost the prosecutor's case when it came to a trial. I haven't been doing any of that. I'm not used to working alone without the scaffolding and structure of the police force. Other eyes to examine findings and other minds to bounce ideas off of. But. No excuses. I'm a team of one; even more important to regroup and rethink.

At home, I shower, change, and head down to the incident room in the basement. I've posted pictures of the suspects and victim; now I add Daniel Chandler's to the collage. I use string to illustrate connections between victims and suspects, multiple strands to indicate stronger ties. I tie one between Morganstern and North, between Morganstern and Takahashi. I make the last one a double.

Finally, I sit with my back to the wall, laptop on my thighs, and begin to type. Collate my notes on each of my interviews. Make lists of bullet points: known facts, things I have to confirm, questions to follow up on.

SETH TAKAHASHI (minister at Riverside Christian)
- Motive for VH: didn't want Victoria to lead people astray.
- Opportunity: unknown, but talked to her before Thursday when she invited him to come to the

service and a discussion after.
- Motive for DC: blackmail?
- Opportunity: the police picked him up on the same day Daniel was killed. Was he in custody at the time of death? If not, would he have committed murder the same day? Seems unlikely.
- Connections: VH - both part of the faith community; DC - unknown
- Remarks: The police let him go. Meaning, there's no evidence to charge him.

JASON MORGANSTERN (welder and aspiring artist)
- Motive for VH: thwarted affection? No evidence, just a guess.
- Opportunity: unknown. He might have met up with her, Claire says V. worked with him to find a job and pursue art. V. probably trusted him.
- Motive for DC: blackmail?
- Opportunity: unknown. but the church was open.
- Connections: VH - congregant at her church; DC - unknown.
- Remarks: did he steal a welding torch? Why? Is it relevant? Eric North was teaching him about being an artist. Could this have inspired him to use Eric's picture as place to kill the pastor?

ERIC NORTH (professional artist/painter)
- Motive for VH: unknown, did she reject his advances?
- Opportunity: unknown, but she probably trusted him
- Motive for DC: he sold Eric's artwork? No evidence, but the picture is missing. Blackmail?
- Opportunity: unknown, but the church was open
- Connections: VH: knew her as a child; DC: unknown
- Remarks: his painting showed VH at the kill site.

DANIEL CHANDLER (bookkeeper for Church of the Spirit)
- Motive for VH: unknown. Related to money? Does

he get control of the insurance proceeds? Whatever, if he's a cheater and she's beautiful and vulnerable, that seems a recipe for trouble.
- Opportunity: they often worked together, it would be natural for him to set up a meeting with her. Was the last person to see her alive at 10:45 meeting on Wed.

I shake my head. In theory, any of these men could have killed Victoria Harkness. Or none of them. I don't know exactly when her death occurred, but based on Olafson's questions, I'm pretty sure it's the Wednesday before the aborted service. I haven't talked to anyone who saw her after her meeting with Daniel, but she arrived home after, so he didn't kill her at the meeting.

But what if he killed her later, and someone saw him do it? And that person later attacked him in revenge?

What is this, a mafia movie?

Okay, okay. It's unlikely. And I'm also going to bet that it wasn't Seth Takahashi. He might have drowned Victoria to protect others, but I just don't see him beating Daniel to death. Splattering blood all over his nice white shirt after a grueling session in a police interview room. I remember him from the first time I went to the church. He'd said it was his first time there as well.

Click.

His first time. That means he hadn't ever seen the painting of Victoria. It couldn't have given him the idea for the kill site. It wasn't him. I'm sure of it. It had to be one of the others.

Don't forget Claire.

I'm not. But the guys are much more likely.

You should make some notes for her too.

Okay, okay.

CLAIRE CHANDLER
- Motive for VH: jealousy
- Opportunity: wide open, she was associated with the church, trusted by VH
- Motive for DC: jealousy / revenge for philandering
- Opportunity: unlimited
- Connections: VH - friend and associate; DC: wife
- Remarks: the obvious suspect

* * *

Happy now?

I have to take a different approach. Look at Victoria herself, find out why it was necessary for her to die. I sit for a bit, drumming my fingers on the floor. Rain splashes against the windows and wind tosses the trees. I can't see the river beyond a boundary of mist.

Forget about who for a minute. Why would someone murder her? I think back over the cases of my career in Denver. Murder can be, and often is, incredibly banal. It's not usually the convoluted rigmarole portrayed in mystery novels. On the contrary, there's almost always a direct link between perp and victim. So, why kill?

Fear. She knew something someone was afraid she'd reveal. She was going to do something that was going to hurt someone else.

Anger. Revenge for a past wrong.

Greed. Her death would benefit someone monetarily. This is the mother of all motives. Her trust fund went to her cousins, all of whom are out of the picture. But if Harkness was insured, and the church was the beneficiary, who had access to the money? Daniel? And now that he was dead, who was next to hold the reins? Claire might know.

Or maybe she's the one with access.

Next. Jealousy. A slighted lover. No one could tell me about her love life — she seemed remarkably chaste, or discreet, or both. But. What about Daniel? Were they having an affair? Did a spurned boyfriend, or someone who wanted to have a relationship with her — maybe Jason, maybe Eric — kill Victoria, and then Daniel when he found out about their affair? Or, put it another way. Someone interested in Daniel discovered the affair, killed Victoria out of jealousy and then Daniel out of revenge? In that scenario, only Claire herself fits the bill.

The light dawns.

I don't want to believe that Claire is capable of murder. But. I know from bitter experience that given the right provocation, anyone is.

Part of a homicide investigation means determining what it is about the deceased that led to their death, what they did or didn't do. Sounds like victim-blaming, I know. But there's some reason Victoria was killed and not someone else, something unique to her. In each of my visions, the man said something about not allowing her to spread her lies. Does that fit with anyone?

Takahashi. He thinks her teachings are wrong and dangerous. But I've already ruled him out.

Morganstern? Nothing comes to mind. Ditto North. But North has the ego, and Morganstern had issues with women, according to Takahashi. Except, now that I think of it, I only have the preacher's word for that. As well as the information regarding Jason's criminal past.

Argh. I want to pull my hair out in frustration. People are dying. I'm afraid that, if I don't find the murderer, more people will die. I don't trust the police to get this one right. They've already consigned Victoria to the accidental death category. I pace around the small room, eyes glued to the collage of pictures and notes. When in doubt, just keep digging. Just keep shaking the trees.

I know Harkness lived in Astoria until she was thirteen years old. She must have gone to school somewhere. I access the district website, discover that there is one high school, one middle school, and two elementary schools. Click through to the middle school website, access the staff. Choose the oldest looking teacher, and discover in her profile that she's recently been recognized for teaching 20 years in the district. I do a search on the award, and find a list of five teachers who have been at the district for twenty years or more. Cross-reference with the current staff at the middle school, and discover that the principal herself is a long-time employee. Her LinkedIn profile indicates she was a former English teacher before becoming vice-principal and then full-fledged principal, a position she has held for three years.

Hooray. Someone in authority. As good a start as any. I don't expect her to answer her phone on Saturday, but I can at least leave a message. But after three rings, a brisk voice says, "Astoria Middle School, Principal Collins speaking."

"Oh," I'm thrown off-stride a little, but arrange to meet her at the school in half an hour.

The middle school building has a red brick veneer and one of those faux-mansard roofs, which looks weird on a one-story structure. The principal is waiting to let me in, and wishes me 'top o' the morning.'

Rhonda Collins is a spherical redhead with an open smile, a cheerful laugh, and green eyes that miss nothing. Her brow is furrowed with lines, the corners of her eyes with crow's feet. Her office is sparsely furnished and liberally inhabited by houseplants. The Easter cactus is getting ready to bloom and a philodendron drapes its leafy tresses along the edge of a bookcase filled with yearbooks, textbooks, and assorted three-ring binders. She gestures me to a squarish visitor's chair and leans back in her own upholstered throne, folding her hands on her belly.

"So, you are a private investigator."

"More like a consultant. I'm not technically a P. I."

"What are you investigating? I hope there's been no trouble with any of our students." She makes the statement an interrogative and cocks her head.

"Not a current student, no. I'm looking for information on a past student, one I'm hoping you knew personally."

This interests her, as I thought it would. But she says, "I hope you realize I can't share any information about students without parents' permission. Or a court order." She smiles brightly.

"And I'm hoping in this case you'll bend the rules." I recross my legs and straighten my jacket. I left my weapon in the car because bringing a gun into the school might send the wrong message, but I miss its comforting weight on my shoulder.

She laughs a rolling Irish laugh. "Oh dear, Ms. Lake. What on earth makes you think I would do that?"

"Because this student — former student — is dead."

She stops laughing. "Oh." She runs her tongue along the front of her teeth, puckering her forehead. She's thinking. I let her.

"Who is it?" she asks.

"Victoria Harkness," I say.

"Oh," she says again, and shakes her head. "Oh. Poor little Vicky. I remember her." There's a pause while she looks back into the past.

"Her body was recently pulled from the river."

She snaps to attention. "I heard something about that. That was Vicky? Oh, dear. How tragic." Her face pales, and she looks her age, which is probably late fifties.

"Were you her teacher?"

"English. Back in the day. Way before all this." She waves a hand, indicating her surroundings. "I was still hoping to discover an incipient Virginia Woolf. Or Graham Greene." She rolls her eyes at her own naïveté. "No such luck. But there were occasional sparks in the darkness."

I ask her about teaching, the rewards, funny stories, anything to get her comfortable with reminiscing. Plus, it's interesting. I admire her long-ago dedication to the art and craft of reading and writing, her ingenious plots to interest her students who really just cared about TV and sports and their own budding hormones. Finally, I wonder in a conversational tone, "Why did you call her 'poor little Vicky'?"

I learn that young Victoria was one of those sparks in the dark. That even back then she had a shine. When the class had to write and give speeches, she was the only one who enjoyed the assignment and treated it seriously.

"I still remember her speech," says Rhonda. "It was on the meaning of life."

"Pretty esoteric for a thirteen-year-old," I say.

"Yes, well. She wasn't ordinary." The principal's smile is melancholic. "It's so sad to hear this."

"And then she moved away."

"Not quite then. It was afterwards." Smile goes away.

"Afterwards?" I hate it when people parrot other people, so I say, "After what?"

Rhonda pauses, a small frown on her face. The clouds outside part and a ray of sunshine illuminates the Easter cactus and its tiny pink buds. I wonder if she's going to answer, or if she's going to go all private with 'I've already said too much.' Instead, she says, "If I'd had more experience I would've noticed the signs. Recognized the problem. Helped her."

"What do you mean?"

"She just shut down. Became incommunicative. Stopped doing her homework. I thought she was just being a rebellious brat, like thirteen-year-olds will." She shakes her head. "I wish I'd been more on top of it. But we know so much more now than we did then. And I was still seeing my students as children with all their little quirks, not as potential victims."

Her meaning is still fluttering just out of reach. "When you say victim, you mean..."

She sighs and steeples her fingers against her mouth. "I'm sorry, I can't say with any certainty, so you'll have to draw your own conclusions. Let's say, with twenty years of hindsight, that I think there was some trauma in her life."

I take a moment to digest her words. "So what happened? Do you know?"

"No. I don't. All I know is that for the last couple of months of seventh grade she turned into an automaton, and then the family moved away. Or at least, Vicky and her mother did. Telling, in retrospect." She looks out the window. "I should have seen it. Should have realized." Another pause. "It haunts me."

A silence grows between us. I don't know what else to ask her. So I stand up.

"Thank you for your time, Ms. Collins."

She walks me to the door without further conversation. I've only gotten a crumb, but maybe if I go deeper into the woods I'll find another.

23

Someone else knows about Victoria's past: her mother. I call her up. Ask if I can meet her back at Victoria's apartment. She agrees with great reluctance. I'm not thrilled with it myself, but once again I climb the stairs and enter the dead woman's home. Elizabeth Harkness is going through papers, as evidenced by the stacks on the dining table. Like my first visit, the blinds are closed, and the room is dim.

This time, she doesn't offer me a beverage.

"All this," she gestures at the papers. "It's all that's left of my daughter."

I don't know what to say to that. So instead, I repeat my request to talk about Victoria.

"Please, Detective. Have some respect for my privacy. You can't imagine what I'm going through."

"Maybe I can't, but there's someone else who can. Claire Chandler. Her husband — the bookkeeper at your daughter's church — has just been murdered. Last night."

"How tragic." But her voice is flat, and I'm not getting any sympathy vibes. It makes me angry, her assumption of self-pity that eclipses any one else's pain.

I say roughly, "Yes. It is. And this is why I need to talk about Victoria, before anyone else is killed. Before it becomes a three-act tragedy."

Maybe it's the cultural reference, but she thaws a little. She says she's told me everything, reiterates she doesn't know anything about her daughter's recent life.

"That's okay. I actually want to talk about her childhood."

"Oh?"

Is it my imagination, or is that syllable freighted with a lifetime's worth of denial and regret? I say, "Tell me about your family and living situation when you lived here in Astoria."

Ms. Harkness gives me a brief sketch, some of which I've heard before. Her husband was a city planner. The schools were of poor quality. The society lacked culture. Their neighbors were no doubt decent people, but working class. Her husband had an engineering degree but the rest of the family hadn't done much to rise above their background. The Harknesses were a local family that lived outside of town, in the rural backwoods of Clatsop County. Her husband's brother would often invite himself to stay with them for a day or two, sponging on their hospitality while doing errands or business in town.

Oh, my God. Somebody slap this woman.

I kind of agree with Zoe. But. The thing I want to talk about is difficult. There's no gentle way to broach the topic of abuse, so I don't even try. I tell her what I heard from Principal Collins, about Victoria's change in behavior and the suggestion of trauma. Ask her mother if she can tell me what happened.

Her tone changes. There's anger, the murderous kind. She says, "it was happening under my nose, and I didn't realize. When I did, I was horrified. And so, so angry. I confronted my husband, told him he had to face up to his brother and make it stop. That we would prosecute. But that — that *coward* did nothing. He said his brother would never do anything like that. That I was imagining things. But I knew I wasn't. Victoria went from being a lovely, angelic girl to almost catatonic overnight. She wouldn't talk, wouldn't leave the house. I knew something was wrong."

"What did you do?"

"I took my daughter and I left. I went back to Portland where my people were. I did everything in my power to counteract the — the poison that evil man had inflicted on my daughter. I enrolled Victoria in a private Christian school where I knew she would be protected physically and morally."

Sounds like she served her daughter right to the wolves. Why not just put an apple in her mouth?

Ms. Harkness pulls a handkerchief from her purse and presses it to her face. Then she fumbles for a compact and, looking in the tiny mirror, blots the smudged makeup. Repairing her image.

I try to pull the narrative together. One thing seems clear, but I have to confirm. "Ms. Harkness, I know this is painful, but I have to be sure.

Are you saying that your brother-in-law abused your daughter?"

She nods without meeting my eyes, placing the compact down on the table.

Daniel Chandler said Victoria was looking for a way to process emotional trauma through art in order to help her congregants. It sounds as though she was also looking for a way to help herself.

"Where is your brother-in-law now?"

"I don't know, and I don't care. I severed all ties with that family. I only kept my husband's name for Victoria's sake."

"But he could still be here?"

She closes her eyes and nods. "That's why I didn't want her to come back. Why I don't want to be here. It makes my skin crawl." Her voice is brittle with anguish and outrage. "What if he tried to contact her again?"

What if? "Did you mention this to the police?"

She bites her lip. "No. It's too disgusting. And long ago. What bearing could it have?"

I'm trying to get her to cooperate, so I refrain from giving her a lecture about withholding information. She doesn't strike me as someone who shares herself lightly. I need to get everything I can in case she clams up later. So I ask if she's heard anything more from the police.

She says they've told her there's no phone activity beyond the Wednesday before last, no financial movement since the Saturday previous to that. Ms. Harkness gets up from the table and goes to a window. She yanks on the blind cords, pulling it up with a metallic rattle. Sunlight streams into the room, and I glimpse a snapshot of the river and industrial buildings.

"The police tell me my daughter's death was a tragic accident."

"Oh?" I'm surprised. "Are they dropping the investigation?"

"Yes. Apparently they found the fingerprints of a maintenance worker on her purse and wallet. He claimed he was only checking the apartment, that the door was unlocked, and he never saw Victoria. The police seem to believe him. But his kind always lie. The man should be sent back where he came from. The detectives here are incompetent."

With an effort, I keep a cool countenance. "Did they have any other suspects?"

"They had one other 'person of interest,' as they called him. But they interviewed him and he had an alibi. They say there's no indication of foul play. She drowned after falling into the river, and there's an end to it."

The desolation in her voice is achingly real. And I feel for her, I do. Despite my annoyance at her self-imposed bubble of social superiority. I guess nothing can shield us from love and the associated pain. It's too bad I have to cause more of it, but in the end I get her to divulge the uncle's name: Abe Harkness.

After the interview with Elizabeth Harkness, I go for a drive. I spiral up the on-ramp to the Megler Bridge, past the backside of the houses on Alameda, until I'm on the road deck, two hundred feet above the water. Freighters and cruise ships and battleships can all pass safely beneath, even at high tide. I press my lips together as a gust of wind broadsides my car and makes me swerve away from the centerline.

Once I pass over the main shipping channel, the bridge drops to a more prosaic height. Cormorants and seagulls soar over the guardrails. To my left are swatches of brown; extensive sand bars sprawl just beneath the surface. During low tide, they become visible as monochrome islands outlined with foam.

When a detective interviews someone, she has to keep her feelings in check. It's important not to react, to record the facts and not add her own emotional baggage to the atmosphere. But after hearing about something like this, it's hard not to feel angry.

Victoria had been an abused child. First by her uncle, then by her well-meaning mother. Enrolling her in a private school fell far short of what was needed. Victoria should have had therapy. I mean, hello, doesn't Elizabeth read the news? A religious school and church are, sadly, no protection against further abuse, and it feels criminally ignorant that her mother just assumed they would be. The girl had been groomed and molested by an older man at an especially vulnerable age. She wouldn't have been able to protect herself, might even have unintentionally responded to attention in a provocative manner. And the overt morality of a religious school may have made her feel even more isolated and unworthy. I truly hope nothing further happened to Victoria, I hope the new surroundings were safe. But. It's perhaps not surprising that she rejected all forms of traditional worship.

It's incredible that Victoria was trying to turn her own tragedy into a positive. I admire her for it. But. What if her abuser heard about her church, and went to a service? Or she might have looked him up herself. Trying for closure, or maybe an apology. Knowing what I know about her, it sounds like something she might do.

Whoever reached out first, what if their meeting didn't result in hope or healing, but in harm?

The man in my vision had said he wanted to stop Victoria from spreading lies. Could that be a reference to her talking about the abuse? He might not want to admit he was a pedophile, to himself or anyone else. It might be buried so deep in his psyche that he truly believed it was a lie.

No one ever wants to see themselves as they truly are.

As the highway unfurls through mossy forest and over gleaming waterways, with their attendant herons and raptors, I turn the pieces of the investigation, trying to arrange an image. My latest idea has a resonance to it; I can't help but feel the past has a bearing on Victoria's death. If the police stopped their digging when Seth Takahashi had an alibi, if there's no forensic evidence to support an investigation, then the only one pursuing this is me.

I get it. Drownings are tough. It's hard to prove a homicide, especially when it's in a big body of moving water. Forensic evidence gets washed away. Plus, it's the third most common method of suicide among women. The Astoria Police Department doesn't have my dubious advantage of psychotic visions to help them.

Or maybe they just need to focus on the latest crime: the killing of Daniel Chandler.

I haven't allowed myself to think about this crime. Because it's the mother of all monkey wrenches. I don't understand what it means. Plus, Daniel was my client. Oh, Claire approached me, but Daniel signed the contract. Legally, I'm not sure where I stand. Do I continue with the Harkness investigation, ignoring Chandler's death? Do I broaden the scope to include Chandler? Or do I back off completely? I didn't really like him, but murder is murder.

My questions to myself are largely rhetorical — of course I'm going to continue. Of course I'm going to try to find out what happened to Chandler too. Because I just don't think two murders in the same small group of people are a coincidence. There's a unified theory that explains them both.

Corpses always show up when you're around. You seem to inspire people to murder. A regular Typhoid Mary.

I'm getting pretty sick of Zoe. Ignoring her doesn't seem to be working. She isn't going away, and I don't know how to get rid of her. She understands me better than anyone. She was present when I had my meltdown. And for that reason, it frightens me to hear her now.

On my way home, I pass the Three Bean Coffee Shop and screech across two lanes of traffic to wedge my car in between a Suburban and Silverado before sauntering inside to snag a tiny table by the window.

Could Uncle Abe Harkness be responsible for Chandler's death too?

The only way to find out is to discover where Victoria's uncle has been for the past few years.

Soon, I've got a toasted ham sandwich — a panino, in cafe parlance — and a cup of black coffee with a pinch of salt keeping me company as I rev up the search engine on my laptop, search for Abe+Harkness+Astoria+Oregon. I add the state after getting a bunch of false positives for people in New York. All kinds of results cascade down the screen: social media profiles, white pages, newspaper mentions. And something I don't expect: an obituary. After reading it, and associated *Astorian* articles published around the same time, I discover that Abe Harkness died in a car accident five years ago in which he was found to have a blood alcohol level of .23. Long before Victoria returned to the town she'd grown up in.

I'm disappointed. In some corner of my brain, I'd been hoping that somehow the abusive uncle would be implicated in the homicide. But if Victoria was writing a book about recovery, where she actually talked about her trauma, and if she named names, or even if someone only thought she had, that could be a strong motive for murder. He might even have approached her about it, and she would have gone to him in the hope of redemption. Now that idea had been quashed.

Another dead end.

But. Old sins cast long shadows, as they say. Maybe there are other members of the family who don't want the secret to come out.

So I call Elizabeth Harkness from the parking lot, pulling my hood up against the rain. I know she won't be too eager to talk about the past again, so I soften her up by asking about Victoria's book. She doesn't know anything about it. I ask about Victoria's laptop. She hadn't been able to break the password. I ask about other Harknesses in the area and there's a predictable silence. Then:

"If any of those people are still around they'd better keep out of my way."

"Listen, Ms. Harkness, is there any chance that one of them might bear some sort of grudge against Victoria?"

Another pregnant pause. When she answers, her words are laced with bitterness and gall. "What do any of them have to be angry about? We're the ones whose lives they ruined. If anyone has the right to a grudge, it's me."

And of course from her point of view, she's right.

But. I still get her to tell me some names.

For all the good they do me. At the end of the day, I've still got nothing.

Maybe the thought of being a woman, unprotected and alone, has dug into my subconscious. Because that night I dream I'm Zoe. I'm back in the squat, lying on the floor next to Blue and Kirstin. He's a runner for the Black Dogs. She's a girl from the cathouse on third. They're both passed out. I hear voices. I get up and go into the hallway. The world seems to tilt, and I hold on to the wall. The voices come closer. They don't see me. Men in suits. Men in DPD uniforms, walking and talking with Sonny and his lieutenants. I see money change hands. They walk right through me as though I don't exist. The men go back to where Blue and Kirstin are sleeping, and then I hear the screams.

I come awake, turtled in the center of the cot, shivering and sweating both. The window shades clack against the sash. Rain splats on the glass. Where am I? This isn't the Baxter Building. The air smells fresh and moist. The night is quiet, no traffic or sirens or shots.

Breathe.

My name is…

I can't remember my name. Panic closes my throat. I gulp air, clutching the blanket around me.

My name is Zoe Crenshaw.

No. That isn't right. Breathe. Eyes wide open. Get up. Find a light switch. Look around at the empty room, camp cot, suitcase.

The darkness recedes. I know this place. This empty house belongs to me. Me, Audrey.

My name is Audrey Lake. I live in Astoria, Oregon. I used to live in Denver, Colorado. I used to be a detective with the Denver Police Department. My father's name is Barney. My mother's name is Anita. My brother's name is — was — Dean.

My name is Audrey Lake. I am a police officer like my father. My mother is an architect. My brother is dead.

My name is Audrey Lake.

I repeat it to myself, over and over, until I fall asleep with the light still on.

24

When I wake up the next morning, I feel like a scarecrow left up through the winter. Last night's episode has unnerved me. I thought the disassociation of identity would get better over time, not worse. The sun is leaking around the window shades and I raise them to reveal a glittering morning, clouds pile up over the bar but the river is blue and lovely, gleaming like a sapphire set in diamonds.

I know it's Sunday, but I need help. Before I can change my mind, I dress in sweats and a fleece and walk next door. When I knock, Phoebe answers. I can see her surprise, but also her appraisal, eyes flicking over my uncombed hair and rumpled clothes.

"Audrey. Is everything all right?"

I take a deep breath. "Phoebe. I need to consult you. Professionally. Now, if possible."

She nods. Points to the outside stairs which skirt the house and lead to another door, the door of her office. I go down, and meet her there. The furniture is the same: desk, chairs, lounger. Unexpectedly, Delilah has joined us, and she gives my hand a friendly lick before settling down in the corner.

I sit in the armchair. Phoebe sits behind the desk. We fill out forms. Name, address, medical history.

"Are you taking any prescriptions?" she asks.

I hesitate, and tell her about the Zyprexa. "I threw it away."

Her eyebrows go up. "I presume you are aware it is an anti-psychotic medication."

"I don't like drugs. I don't like what they do to people."

She nods, pursing her lips. Finishes the form, and shuts down the computer. "All right, Audrey. What brings you here, now, to my office?"

I tell her almost all of it. About my stint of undercover work, where I'd posed for months as Zoe Crenshaw, a drug addict living in a squat in East Denver, a condemned eight story structure called the Baxter Building. I'd been warned about the difficulty in integrating a deep undercover identity. In my case, I'd assumed it too well. When the operation was over, when the police had stormed the building and arrested the small fry but allowed the big dogs to slip through their fingers, I'd been taken to the hospital. Practically catatonic, suffering from stab wounds, I'd woken up screaming about the police being in league with the criminals, how no one could be trusted. I tried to pull out my tubes. They put me in restraints and eventually the psych ward, until I'd recovered enough of my identity to be discharged.

Phoebe frowns. "None of that explains why you're taking an anti-psychotic."

So I tell her about the hallucinations, beginning with the one at the Baxter Building. Seeing the cops and suppliers together, mixed up in some nightmare terrain, killing people. Backtrack to a few years before, when my brother died. I'd seen his car going off the bridge, again and again. Not just in my head, but in front of my eyes. I couldn't go over the bridge without seeing it, like it was happening for real. I'd almost had an accident myself.

"Have you had any hallucinations since going off your meds?"

I hesitate.

None of your fucking business, lady.

Zoe's words decide me. I tell Phoebe about my vision on the Riverwalk. About Victoria's murder. About the almost-vision in Daniel Chandler's office. About the voice of my alter ego that I can't seem to silence. That, in fact, is getting stronger every day.

"I need help, Phoebe. All this is interfering with my work, my life. I can't function when I don't know if I'm about to go over the edge, if I don't know what's real. But I don't want drugs. They make me feel like I'm a ghost in my own life."

"Do you ever feel like harming yourself?"

"What? No."

Phoebe leans forward, elbows on her desk and hands in a pyramid. She's frowning. Not as though she is angry, but as though she is perplexed. She slowly resettles herself.

"Do you hear voices?"

"No. I never hear anything. Except in conjunction with a vision."

"Do you feel like someone is telling you to do something? Sending you a message?"

"No."

"What about Zoe?"

"Oh. Well, I guess I kind of hear her, but she's not associated with the visions. She's more like a running commentary in my head. But she doesn't give me orders. Just snide remarks. And she's not...outside, if you know what I mean. I don't *hear* her - hear her. Not like for real."

"Do you ever talk back to her? Or initiate conversation?"

I squirm in the chair. "Sometimes I talk back to her. Is that — is that crazy?" I laugh nervously.

"It's probably best that you don't respond. The more energy you feed to this delusion, the stronger it will grow."

Well, shit. I swallow hard.

Phoebe says, "Do you ever feel anything, or smell anything, in conjunction with the visions?"

"Yes. I feel physical pain, and falling. I feel the water as it closes in. The cold. And Phoebe, this is what terrifies me. I think — no, I know — that I experienced Victoria's death. For real. Before I knew anything about her, or it."

Phoebe doesn't say anything for a few moments, which triples my anxiety. Is she going to say I'm at a level of crazy that only survives in a nuthouse? That she's going to forcibly commit me right now?

Finally, she says, "Audrey, there are some aspects to your symptoms that don't make sense to me. You are definitely seeing things that aren't there, but most psychotic hallucinations aren't a replay of events like you are describing."

I sink back in my seat and close my eyes. I'm so done with all this. "I'm telling you the truth."

"I believe you, Audrey." She constructs a short chain of paperclips while she thinks. Delilah gets up from her corner and sits beside me, pressing her body against my leg. It feels strangely good; warm and supportive.

Phoebe pushes her paperclips away and says, "All right Audrey. I'm going to go out on a limb here. I think you may have been misdiagnosed. In that case, your prescribed medication may have done more harm than good. But with your permission, I'd like to consult with someone else. I'm not sure your problem is entirely psychiatric in nature."

I open my eyes. "Wait, what? Are you saying I have some other problem? Something *else* wrong?" This is a nightmare. One I can't seem to wake up from.

She holds up a hand. "I'll need to get more information before I commit myself."

"Or me?" I say weakly.

"Or you." She smiles. "But Audrey, take heart. Whatever it is, we'll get to the bottom of it."

Phoebe shows me some exercises, ways to curb my anxiety and generate a feeling of safety, and insists I do them twice. She knows I'm alone, so she gives me permission to get in touch if I need to. Her overprotectiveness raises my hackles, and I think the exercises are hooey, but I do appreciate her concern. Sometime soon, when I'm not too busy, I'll give them a try.

I feel better after talking to Phoebe, but also worse in some ways. I've exposed my craziness for someone else's judgement. The fact that it's to someone who is trained to diagnose and understand craziness adds another layer of fear and trembling. What if she insists that I go back on drugs, like ones that cut me off from reality and made me feel as though I were wrapped in a layer of lead? I won't be able to do my job if I can barely think. And who was this other person she wanted to talk to, about my other problem? Now my own symptoms, my own mental health, are out of my control. I imagine all sorts of dire things from cancerous tumors to brain-eating worms.

I hate having to rely on other people.

We should just blow this joint. Never trust a shrink, if you ask me.

Except I didn't ask you, did I? You're just another part of me, some submerged shard of my undercover identity, my legend. You don't even exist, not really.

Belatedly, I recall I'm not supposed to give her any energy.

The Legend of Zoe. Sweet. There oughta be a video game.

Maybe it isn't surprising that I decide to walk down to the Portway Tavern.

"How are you doing, Claire? Are you coping with all this?"

The light from the muted TV flickers over the polished surface of the bar. I had been surprised to find her here, actually. But many of us seek solace from stress and sorrow in work. It beats sitting at home alone in an empty house.

The Portway was actually closed. It was mid-afternoon on a Sunday, but I'd seen Claire through the window and she'd let me in. As she moved around, stocking shelves and wiping tables, polishing fixtures and squaring up the menus, I stayed. She didn't tell me to go home, and now we're sitting side by side at the bar nursing bottled beers.

She says, "The police have been talking to me. Asking me about Dan and my marriage, our finances, whether there was trouble between us." She shakes her head. "I want to believe they are looking into every possibility, but it feels like I'm their number one suspect."

Uh, yeah.

I snag a peanut from the bowl on the bar and crack the shell in halves. "Unfortunately, in a lot of cases, it's the surviving spouse who's guilty. So, until they're convinced otherwise, you're in the limelight." I've been the investigating officer in several cases where the wife was found guilty, but I don't mention that. "It probably feels awful, but it's not personal. Just statistics."

"Yeah, well, I'd rather not become one."

For a few minutes, the only noise is the sound of splintering peanut shells. Then Claire says, "You know, I keep thinking that this one is going to be the last. That I won't have to find another."

"'This one'?"

"This life. I really thought I could make it work this time."

"I'm sorry for your pain. All the death — it must be — I can't even imagine. It must be awful." There's some solace in knowing that there is suffering greater than your own. Not much, but some. "How long were you and Daniel together?"

"I met Dan about ten years ago. Just come up from L.A. Where I'd been for way too long, depending on the wrong guy again." She lays the sweating bottle against her cheek. "You ever done that, Audrey?"

The wrong guy. I touch the scar on my chest.

Such a thing as the right guy?

I swig a mouthful of my Hef. "I trusted a gangster once. He tried to kill me."

"You? Thought you were a cop."

"It's been a long and strange career."

"Huh." Claire takes a drink from her own bottle, puts it with the other dead soldiers and pops the top off another. "I always choose the wrong one. Before Dan it was Maurice, before him it was Harvey. Others. Bu' that's it. I'm on my own now." Her voice is slightly slurred; not a surprise, given the empties on the bar.

"Tell me about Harvey."

Like you care.

But I do care. Or at least, I'm interested. Can't be a good cop without being endlessly interested in the human story. Always got to roll that stone away, look at what's underneath. Plus, friendship. Maybe. I'm out of practice.

"He was the first person besides my mother to tell me that I was beautiful. That guy had a way with words and a taste for adventure, and he made me feel like I could do anything I wanted. That I could have an adventure, too. That's why I got on the back of his motorcycle to leave Iowa and never looked back. Because he made me feel pretty and powerful. I should've known it couldn't last. That he was just lying to get what he wanted." Claire shakes her head. "God, that motorcycle, like being on my own personal rocket ship. I wish I could feel that freedom again. That power. Someday, I'm gonna buy one of my own."

She slides off her stool and beckons me over to the wall. Among the haphazard decor — life preservers, bits of fishing net, floats — there's a small black and white photo in a metal frame. It shows a Black woman dressed in a white jumpsuit and knee-high boots, standing in front of an old-style Harley-Davidson motorcycle.

"Who's that?" I ask.

"Bessie Stringfield. She was a bad-ass rider back in the day, nineteen-thirties and -forties, won races, went cross-country on her Harley, the works. Didn't let anything slow her down. Had six husbands. Guess they couldn't keep up. She's in the Motorcycle Hall of Fame." She touches the frame. "I put this here to look at when the job feels too much like a death sentence."

More than anything else she's said, I get that. "So what happened with Harvey?"

Claire snorts. "We never got further than Des Moines. Harvey got drunk, beat another guy up, got thrown in jail. I ended up working at a bar, washing glasses, wiping tables. The start of my brilliant career." She waves a hand to encompass the Portway. "Always a need for bartenders. Even on the last day before the world ends, people will be calling for shots."

"Especially then." Nod. Head feels heavy for some reason. "How'd you get out of Des Moines?"

"That was Maurice. Slick talking man, said he'd take me to L.A. and make me a star. Again with the promises. But I had high hopes. Turned out I'd gotten hooked up with the wrong guy, again. I was trying to be an actress, but I had no qualifications. That's hard to realize when you're young and ambitious. I'd never taken a class, never done anything except Dorothy in a school production of The Wiz way back. I could sing, but I was no Tina Turner. It was so demoralizing going to auditions and to be dismissed before I'd said ten words. And Maurice turned out to be a scumbag. But when I walked away, I walked by myself, and got on the bus to Portland."

How much longer we got to sit here and listen to her sob story?

She's getting worse. Zoe, I mean. I don't want to be her. Ever again. Because I like Claire, and her story. And she needs to talk, a sympathetic ear. I ask her to pour me a shot of Jack Daniels, make it a double please, and I fire back those shots and follow with a beer chaser. I hear about her arrival in Portland, working in bars and restaurants, a series of short-term boyfriends. Then she heard a broadcast of Pastor Harkness on the radio, went to a service out of curiosity, returning over and over, until she'd become a member of the congregation. Saw Daniel around, liked his smile, his air of respectability, the fact that he actually had a professional job.

"And here I thought I was moving up in the world, when he asked me to marry him." Claire shakes her head. Her words have become blurred and rounded. She pauses, and the silence licks about us like the river.

I say, "I'm sorry."

"Sorry for what? That he cheated on me? That he got killed? Please." She prints wet circles on the bar with her bottle. "He always was too slick. There were other women in Portland, too. I always wondered — did he and Pastor Harkness? — but he wasn't her type, not really. She liked them a bit lost. A bit rugged."

"Did she — Victoria — have a permanent partner? Or...?"

Claire scoffs. "With all those willing boys to choose from, all of them wanting to worship at her feet?" She drops her gaze. "Shouldn't be mean. Shouldn't judge. Did them some good. Made them feel better. Women too."

I try to sort this out. "You mean she had relationships with women as well?" I feel my suspect pool expand exponentially, and my eyes glaze.

"Nah. I mean she made everyone feel special. Like they had something to offer. Like they could touch the Spirit like her, if only they tried."

Claire's plenty in touch with spirits herself.

I'm not far behind. The JD coats my senses like an ermine robe. I feel warm and snuggly, my problems a distant shadow on the shore.

"Did Victoria have relationships with many men?"

"Wouldn't say relationships. She liked to be of comfort, liked to show love."

"Physically, you mean? Sex?"

"Sometimes. It wasn't exclusive, with her. Never stuck with any one guy. Maybe she and Dan were birds of a feather." A taste of wormwood in her tone. "I wish — I wish —" Claire's voice breaks.

Here it comes. Please, can we just leave?

Shut up, bitch. I'm listening here.

"What do you wish?" I strive to focus my eyes, but it's so much easier to let them relax, let the bar dissolve into gentle blurs.

"Just that things could be different, that's all."

"Did you know she was writing a book?"

"Yeah."

"Did you ever read it? Or did she tell you about the contents?"

"She was abused as a child. She was pretty open about it. Said healing could only happen when the wound was exposed to the air. That the abuser was a victim too." Claire snorts. "Some victim. My opinion, someone hurts you, you don't go around hurting other people in revenge. Coward's way out."

"And the book?"

"Pastor's way out. Turning ugliness into something like love, something useful for others. Not revenge. Healing. Forgiveness." Claire empties her bottle. Again. "Don't think I could forgive something like that, myself."

I think of the evil that I've seen. "Yeah, me neither."

"Audrey?"

"Yes?"

"Do you know who killed Victoria?"

"No. I don't."

"Do you know who killed Daniel?"

"No."

We stop talking. The neon signs buzz. A truck rumbles by on the street outside. A drop of water falls from the bar sink faucet and hits the stainless steel basin with a plink like a musical note.

"Claire?"

"Yeah?"

"I'm sorry."

"Me, too."

"I'll keep trying. I won't give up."

"Okay." Claire peels the label off her bottle, using her thumbnail. It comes off in a single piece, slightly tattered at the edges. She smooths it carefully on the bar top. "Neither will I."

25

Who sang that song "Monday Morning Coming Down?" Or is it Sunday morning? Whatever, my Monday starts out like I stuck my head in a church bell right before Quasimodo started to ring it. I can hear my brain thumping in time with my pulse. And the spikes of sunlight that penetrate the shades are lasers aimed directly at my eyes. The ceiling spins slowly above. Seems like a good day to stay in bed.

When Phoebe calls later, I almost don't answer. Almost let it go to voicemail. But. I'd gone this far, told her unthinkable things. So I pick up, my voice a husky rasp. Phoebe says the other consultant she wanted to talk to is in her office now. He's a friend, and I can trust him absolutely. She assures me she hasn't told him anything about what she and I discussed, but he might be able to throw some light on my hallucinations. Could I please come over?

I whimper like a distressed animal. Do I have to? But. I need answers. Plus, Phoebe is sure to have coffee. So, out of the cot, down the suicide stairs, into the shower. Water beating like warm rain. Clothes. Hair. I carefully don't look at my face.

Trepidation knots my belly as I walk up the stairs to the street, up the sidewalk to the Rutherford house and down the stairs to Phoebe's office. No escaping the hills of Astoria. The cold hardness under my feet makes me realize I need some grounding. Need to know where and how I stand: on the brink of madness, completely over the edge, or somewhere else entirely.

I knock and the door opens.

Phoebe greets me with a smile. "Hello, Audrey. I'm glad you could make it on such short notice."

Over the threshold. Bluebeard, or the good fairy? Only one way to find out.

She gestures to a man beside her, saying, "This is the colleague and friend I told you about. Bernard Flowers."

He says, "Call me Bernie." We shake hands. His is warm and dry. Mine is cold and a bit damp. He's white, older, dressed in a chunky cabled sweater and wide-waled corduroys.

Phoebe says, "Bernard is a psychotherapist with an expertise in psychic phenomena."

Wait, what? I'm confused. "I don't —"

Phoebe lifts a warning hand. "I know you're skeptical. As am I, frankly. But please, just listen to what he has to say. Then you can decide for yourself."

Skeptical? Try flummoxed. At sea in a dinghy without oars and no land in sight.

Flowers glances from one to the other of us, shrugs, and leans back in the arm chair, putting his hands behind his head. Phoebe goes to her desk, and I lean against the edge. I feel the corner poke into the flesh of my left buttock, but don't change position. It's a counterpart to the pain in my head. My arms cross my chest, and I feel the hard lump of my weapon.

Phoebe hands me a glass of water. "Do you want a chair, Audrey?"

"I'm good." Standing, I can get a running start if I need to leave the room. "So. What is this?"

The man's voice is pleasantly rumbly. "It's difficult to know where to start. I'll just blather, and you can jump in with questions, okay? I don't claim to have any psychic powers myself, but I have worked with various members of the sensitive community who are struggling to integrate their abilities, so I know something about it." He pauses for thought.

Shut up. A psychotherapist named Flowers? The 'sensitive community?' What the fuck?

What Zoe said. My confidence in Phoebe takes a deep dive.

Bernie clears his throat. "Most people have a mistaken idea of what psychics do and are. The ones I know are very low key. No one is sitting behind a crystal ball with big earrings and a pointy hat." He rubs his jaw, glances at Phoebe, and adjusts the neck of his sweater. "So. There's different kinds of ESP — extrasensory perception. It's literally perception of things beyond our normal five senses, although what psychics 'feel' is translated through those sensory templates that we are familiar with. Clairvoyance, for instance, is visual in nature, images seen with the 'inner eye'. Clairaudience is auditory, sounds perceived with the 'inner ear.' Am I making sense so far?"

Ye gods. "Well — I guess — I don't really know." My head is killing me, and I squirm against the edge of the desk. "Truthfully, I don't believe in this stuff. No offense." Except, what did I think the vision was, a complimentary movie from the gods? Like that was any more credible. The truth is, I simply hadn't wanted to think about it.

The queen of denial.

I look over to Phoebe, raising my eyebrows in appeal. She shrugs and inclines her head toward Flowers.

He laughs and says, "You're not offending me. It's not an easy thing to assimilate. Like explaining color to someone who was born blind. Really, ESP is just a different way of perceiving the environment. For instance, I know a woman who can pick up information about another person by touching an object they have owned."

Struggling to be polite. "I frankly don't see how that's possible."

"Phoebe says you used to be a detective. Think of how a forensic scientist can utilize DNA from clothing or jewelry, and the information that can be gleaned from those traces. How is that so different from what you might call psychic residue?"

"Because it's physical — tiny bits and pieces. It's really there, even if you can't see it with the naked eye."

"Okay, think about sound then. Purely an energetic phenomena that we pick up with our ears. Vibrational disturbances that our brains translate as music, noise, or speech. Why shouldn't there be other kinds of energetic information patterns? Echoes of personality, of events?"

"If that's true, why can't we all see or hear these things?"

"Why can't we hear radio broadcasts without a radio? Or see colors beyond the rainbow spectrum? It doesn't mean those things don't exist, just that we need specialized equipment to 'tune in,' so to speak. Many creatures have more acute senses than we — just because a dog can hear a noise that we can't, we don't discount the existence of the noise. We accept that a dog can hear better than a human. Well, some humans have more acute perception than others."

"But." I struggle to justify my unbelief. "A dog is hearing a noise that is happening right now. How can a person, no matter how acute their senses, be seeing something that has already happened? Days or weeks or years ago?"

Bernie glances at Phoebe and steeples his fingers. "I don't know the actual mechanics, but think of an echo. If I shout in a canyon, the echo bounces back and back, and can be heard even after I have stopped shouting. The sound goes on and on. An animal may hear reverberations of an echo for a much longer time than a human might. In some way, perhaps an event gets imprinted on an object, or the environment. Maybe because of intensity. Maybe the greater the emotional energy, the stronger the imprint — the psychic 'echo,' if you will."

"Are you saying the environment — the world — remembers the things that happen on it?" I can't keep the incredulity out of my voice. And yet, a part of me wants to believe, to latch on to this explanation of what is happening to me, as an alternative to mental illness.

"Not in the sense that you and I remember, but maybe in the sense a computer remembers. It's just information, stored in a matrix that can be accessed by a particular type of antenna. Metaphorically speaking, of course." He crosses his legs. "Haven't you ever been in a place with an atmosphere? A place that seems eerie, or forbidding, or even evil?"

I think of the Baxter Building, the miasma of human pain and misery that seemed layered into the walls along with the paint. I think of jail cells; interrogation rooms; the back alleys of Denver where unspeakable crimes were committed.

Yeah. Atmosphere. Vibe.

Bernie speaks again. "You have, haven't you? I have too. I don't know if Phoebe told you, but I'm also an antiquarian. I own From Time to Time, an antique store downtown. Sometimes I get a piece that has its own story, its own resonance. My friend who can feel the past can identify a doll that has been loved, a rocking horse that has been part of imaginary adventures, or a shackle used to imprison a slave that contains horrors."

He falls silent, and I struggle to process what he's said. Why Phoebe had called him. She must think my visions are some kind of ESP.

I can barely bring myself to think it. It sounds so much like late night television. B movies.

If they are ESP — I don't think so, but if they are — does that mean I'm witnessing an actual event?

A memory of murder.

The thought makes my head throb even more. I have been banking on that idea all through the investigation, but haven't made the effort to rationalize my own behavior, or follow the logic to its end. I've been treating the visions as I would a hunch. But if Flowers is right, it would mean I'm not crazy. That I've been basing my investigation on something authentic. But it also means that the terrible vision I'd had at the Baxter Building, the cops — my colleagues — being directly linked to what happened there. It means that one might also true.

Fireworks explode in my brain. Was that the real reason behind my meltdown? The recognition of evil combined with the confusion of identity engendered by my undercover operation?

I realize that the other two are watching me; Phoebe with clinical calm, Bernie with head cocked and an inquisitive expression.

I lick dry lips. "Do you know anyone who sees things that have happened? How reliable is this — ability?"

He spreads his hands. "I would say, just as reliable — or unreliable — as any other kind of witnessing. As with any sensory perception, it's all down to the observer."

Phoebe chimes in. "We all filter the information of the world through our particular viewpoints and emotional states. What touches me may not touch you, or not in the same way. We won't invest the same meaning into any one experience."

"And," Bernie smiles disarmingly, "some people just like to make stuff up."

No worse than any other eyewitness, then. And no better. I've been dealing with that my whole professional life.

Grain of salt. Trust, but verify.

Okay. I think I can handle that.

I have to leave them. Go walking to wrap my head around it all. Thoughts and beliefs ricochet around in my skull. I used to despise people like Bernie Flowers, irrational nonconformists, who want to skirt concrete facts and solid substance. In the course of my job as a homicide detective, I've known too many self-seeking, self-aggrandizing psychics who prey on the tragedies of crime and murder, seeking emotional fulfillment at the expense of people whom death had made vulnerable. There is no way I would join the ranks of those praying mantises.

And yet...

And yet, Bernie isn't profiting. He's an interested, if bombastic, professional. And my visions. The images. Things I thought were imagined. The horrid visual of my brother's car plunging off the bridge, each time I passed the stage of his suicide. The lurid montage I had seen in the Baxter Building, the one that had pushed me into catatonia and enabled Zoe to cut permanent footholds in the ice cliff of my psyche. And now the killing of Victoria Harkness. I used to think the choice was between crazy and not crazy. But now the choice is between crazy and psychic. Even the word makes me cringe. The magnetic field has realigned and left me with two negative poles.

I walk through jumbled neighborhoods of Victorian, Queen Anne, and Craftsman houses. I frighten deer from the street-side buffet of ivy, rhododendron, and buttercup. My calves ache from uphill asphalt, my knees from downhill sidewalks. I pass free furniture left on the curb, vacant lots buried in blackberry brambles with the remnant of concrete foundations and steps that go nowhere. The eyes and caws of crows follow me like a smoldering telegraph of black wings.

I find my way up to the towering Astoria column decorated with a spiraling history of the region, a DNA of events leading to the present day. On one side of the park it's possible to see the broad Columbia with its anchored ships and hustling pilot boats; on the other I look out over Youngs Bay with its feeder rivers, serene and green as a landscape painting. The Megler Bridge arches like a salmon's leap over the deep channel of the river; the New Youngs Bay Bridge curves across the junction of bay and river, low and practical, without embellishment. Choices and solutions. Each bridge is what it is; a solution to a set of particular circumstances.

I have discovered my own beliefs are not based on immovable concrete abutments, but rooted in false bedrock that is now eroding. I've always associated so-called psychics with lies and con games, with people profiting from someone else's pain. The worst kind of selfishness. It shakes me to the core to think I might have been wrong, that I'm now one of them.

Does this new ability make me evil, like those others? But if that's true, then it means that choice and free will are meaningless. And if *that's* true, then what the hell are we all doing here?

No. It's up to me how to assimilate the new material, whether to struggle against the turbulence or harness its energy. Build a bridge to another shore. Victoria Harkness took something terrible and tried to transform it into something good. If her legacy means anything, it means I must try to do the same.

By the time I'm almost home I'm exhausted, my legs and feet pulsing with a deep-seated ache. But now I know I have to move forward with the investigation of both myself and Victoria. The two are so intertwined as to be one and the same.

26

I'm exhausted from my long walk and from coming to terms with the latest revelations from Bernard Flowers. I just want to get home and put my feet up, knit all the thoughts and implications together. But as I turn up Rhododendron Street, my phone throbs in my pocket. The caller ID announces Claire Chandler.

I sigh, but pick up. "Audrey here."

"Oh my God, I need your help! I've discovered something and I don't know what to do."

I press the phone against my right ear and cover my left, turning away from the street. "Where are you?"

"The church. I was looking at some of the computer files."

"Wait, Claire, that's a crime scene. You shouldn't be there. You could get in trouble."

Irony. That's what this is.

"I know, but I couldn't wait, I had to know. And Audrey, the books aren't right! At least, I don't understand them. Please, I don't know what to do." Her voice cranks up a notch and I pull the phone away a titch. Take a breath for calm.

"Okay, first, you should get out of there before someone discovers you." My own capture gleams sharp in my memory, and Olafson probably wouldn't be so generous with another intruder. Then reality clicks. "Wait, the computer is still there?"

"The detectives told me they had to get a forensic team from the State police, and they haven't come yet. So I thought it would be okay."

"Claire, you're contaminating the scene. Get out, and go home, and then call me back." I end the call.

Well, aren't we concerned about law and order now that you're not the one

171

breaking the rules.

I know, I know. But I knew what I was getting into. Claire doesn't.

Like you knew what would happen when you agreed to go undercover? What are you, psychic?

I'm a cop! I knew there might be consequences! I knew things might go to shit. But if that's the price to prevent what went on at that place, then it was worth it. Worth it to see Sonny and his gang apprehended. Worth it to get those kids out of his clutches.

Please. Those 'kids' were all more streetwise than you'll ever be. Do you think any of them were surprised that the cops were involved up to their eyebrows? 'Justice' isn't a word in their vocabulary.

Not all cops are crooked. I wasn't.

Does it matter? Tar, brush. Even if you weren't feeding at Sonny's trough, you chose to shut your eyes to what was going on.

No. I was there to get information. Not to arrest people.

Too bad you didn't get the relevant stuff. You know, like the other dirty cops. Maybe that's why you had a 'psychic vision,' since you weren't very adept at putting two and two together. How convenient, that you couldn't participate in the trial.

No. The breakdown. I wasn't fit —

That's exactly right. You're not fit to be a cop, or a detective, or anything else. Go hide in your hole, little mousie. Let other people deal with the dead.

"Shut up! Leave me alone!"

Sweat, streaming down my face. The sound of my own voice jolts me with a fearsome realization. I'm standing alone on the sidewalk. Talking to myself. Waving my arms like a lunatic. Knees buckling. With an effort, I look around. Don't see anyone, but it doesn't mean I'm not observed. Go back up the street, toward my house. Three-sixty-degree glance at the top of the steps before I dash to the door. This time my perimeter walk is outside first. Look for footprints, try the windows, any sign of intrusion. Don't go inside until I'm happy with the outside, and once through the door I do the whole thing again. House is empty, entry points secure. Gun is nestled at my shoulder.

Still shaking, I go into the bathroom. Force my gaze into the mirror. The face is my own, white and padded with extra flesh. Scar, thin line ridging the skin below my collarbone. Hair, disheveled. But the eyes are Zoe's. Frightened, feral, and mean.

My fist cracks out, into the glass. Full impact. It shudders up my arm, into my shoulder. A spiderweb shivers across the reflective surface, turning my face into a fractured mosaic. This image is closer to the truth. So close it burns my eyes with tears. I shut them, quick. Run cold water over my hand. Leave the room, shuck my coat. Realize I haven't eaten anything so I pour out some cereal. Put my gun on the table beside me. The flakes are cold and crunchy, and the spoon rattles against the bowl.

I will not have a breakdown. I owe it to my client — my friend — to finish out this investigation. And I owe it to the dead.

The phone rings. Claire. Don't want to answer but I do anyway.

"Okay, Audrey. I'm home." She's breathing hard.

Tighten the screws. Cop mode, not crazy mode. "Okay. What did you discover?"

"I was looking at the books. It should be straightforward, but I don't understand it. There's all these entries for artwork being sold, eBay accounts and shipping addresses. But I don't see any matching revenue for the church."

"How did you know what to access?"

"I just started looking at the flash drives on the desk. I didn't know what was important."

Something is off here. "Claire, why did you want to look at the church books in the first place?"

"I was trying to find a copy of Pastor Harkness's manuscript. But then I find all this stuff about art. It must be the spirit offerings. Some of them have been sold for hundreds of dollars. And when I tried to check the church books to confirm, I didn't see any revenue. Audrey, I think — I think Daniel might have been stealing." She hiccups past a sob.

"Just hang on a second." I pace, thinking. "Okay, just to clarify, do the spirit offerings belong the church, officially? Like donations? Or are they on loan from the congregants?"

Claire sniffles. "Well, I don't think anyone ever asks for them back. But I'm sure Pastor Harkness would have returned them if anyone did. The value isn't monetary, it's spiritual. A celebration of, of sacredness. Touching the Spirit."

"Your husband told me he was having a hard time paying the bills for the church. Maybe he was selling them to help with that."

"Maybe. But then wouldn't they be in with the other church revenues? Along with cash donations?"

"You'd think so, wouldn't you? But if the artwork had never been listed as an asset in the first place, it's off the books anyway. Maybe he's just being cagey to maximize the return for the church." That's a pretty generous interpretation, but plausible. "He might have just deposited it to the checking account without running it through the books."

Claire doesn't speak, but her breathing comes through loud and clear. "Is that legit?"

"I'm not an accountant or an auditor, but if the art belongs to the church, I don't see any problem. It's sloppy bookkeeping, but not illegal. Unless..." I pause. Do I want to go further? The woman has been battered about a lot recently. But. She's my client. And maybe, sort of, my friend.

"Unless?"

"Unless he was taking the proceeds for himself." I wait for the angry denial, even hold the phone away from my ear, but nothing comes, just the sound of sniffles.

"Claire? Do you know where the money went?"

"No." Her voice is firm.

"Are you sure you don't know where it might be? Any big expenditures?" I think about his car compared to hers.

A minuscule pause. "No."

"Then leave it to the police. They'll go through the accounts, looking for motive for his killer. Believe me, you want to stay away from that. If there is some skulduggery, they'll dig and dig until they find something. If they ask — *when* they ask, be honest. Come clean, if there's anything to be clean about."

Her tone is bedrock, hard and unyielding despite the tears. "I've never stolen anything. Ever."

"Good. Then you're safe."

Claire sucks in a breath and lets it out slowly. "What are you going to do now? Honestly, a little action would be welcome."

Ouch. Her tone makes me wince. But. Her husband is dead, her life a shambles. It's amazing she's as self-controlled as she is. "Shake the trees some more. Something will give. It always does."

"If you say so, Audrey. But I can't hang on forever."

"You won't have to. I promise."

Talking to Claire gave me a rope to hold onto, snapping me back into professional mode. But after I hang up, I realize the knuckles on my right hand are dusted with tiny scuffs and cuts. My slip in the street comes back to haunt. Not like a creak or a crack you can put on the wind, but a full-on phantom with a scythe and a flaming skull.

I am losing my mind. Talking to myself. Smashing things. No other interpretation possible. Only the job, the facade of being a cop, gave me a strong enough mask to hold the pieces together. But it's not working anymore. I won't be able to keep my promise to Claire.

I walk out the door, up the steps, up the sidewalk, down the steps, to knock on Phoebe's door. It's only been a few hours since I was there. She'll think I'm desperate, possibly unhinged. But there's nowhere else to go.

It opens. Phoebe, not the judge. Thank all the goodness of the universe.

One look. "Let's go downstairs, Audrey. You'll be more comfortable in my office."

When we arrive, I choose the hard chair. It has more structure.

"Audrey, talk to me. Are you all right? What's wrong?"

Our discussion of the morning seems like year ago. Or a lifetime. Now, I'm afraid if I open my mouth the pieces that are my face will fall off. I can't let that happen. I can only breathe, in and out. Then, "I can't see the face of the man in the vision. Why can't I see his face?"

Phoebe blinks, visibly recalibrating. "Are you sure you want to?"

"He's a killer, Phoebe."

"Is he?"

"I know it."

"How do you know it?"

"I felt him do it. I felt him grab her. Push her under the water. He called her by name. He's evil."

"How do you know he's evil?"

"He's a murderer."

"So?"

My voice rises in anger. "So, murderers are evil." Why doesn't she see that?

"Are they?"

It's been a mistake to come here. If this stupid woman can't understand that murder is evil, there's nothing more I can say. I stand up.

"Sit down." A doctor voice. Authority. She hasn't moved from her chair.

I sit down.

She looks at me for what seems an eternity. Then she makes an unfamiliar gesture, and Delilah, who I hadn't noticed was in the room, comes over and leans against my legs like she did before. Puts her big square head on my knee. Steady and warm and calm.

"Audrey, I'm worried we're moving too fast."

"Phoebe, please. Help me." I stroke Delilah's smooth head.

Phoebe purses her lips, nods once. "Are you facing the man in your vision?"

"I'm running from him. She is." I'm confused. "We are."

"Do you ever look directly at him?"

I squirm against the hard wood. "Yes. I — she — we look back. At him."

"What do you see?"

"A shape. A shadow."

"Does she know who it is?"

"Yes." I'm positive of this. She knows and fears him.

"Then why don't you?"

Blankness. "I don't know."

A wire of silence stretches between us. Humming, jangling.

Phoebe speaks again. "Do you know what an occluded memory is?"

"What?" Shrink jargon. Out of my depth. Hate that. I want to stand, but can't seem to get my feet under me.

"It's when you associate a particular memory with something that you don't want to deal with, so you block it out."

Absorption moment. "So?" Belligerent. She's so irritating.

"There's something you don't want to see."

"What's that?"

"The face of the man in your vision."

Silence. I'm struggling. She's wrong. "You're wrong. I do want to see."

"Why?"

Patiently. "So I can catch him. Put him in jail." Ye gods. This woman has advanced degrees. Why isn't she smarter? My hands clench the arms of the hard chair.

"Why?"

Slowly, so she gets it. "Because he's evil."

"And evil people need to be punished?"

Finally. "Yes."

"And he's evil because...?"

I lose it. "Because she killed an innocent person!" My voice is loud and shrill, and seems to echo in the small room. It gets louder, reverberating. I expect the window to shatter. The vase on the desk. I expect the sheetrock to crack, the carpet to curl and scorch, because my face has fallen off and my cheeks are scalding with tears.

"Who did she kill, Audrey?" Phoebe's voice is gentle and implacable, like the small rain that permeates the seams of my jacket whenever I go outside. I can feel the wetness spreading, my chin, my neck, the top of my chest. There's a strange sound coming from somewhere; an odd, hitching gasp.

Who was the corpse in the closet? Who did you kill, Zoe?

Who did you kill, Audrey?

My heart thumps weakly in its lonely cave.

I don't know.

27

I'm home, sitting cross-legged on the floor in an empty room as the rain beats on the roof and windows. Phoebe wants to do some EMDR sessions with me. Eye Movement Desensitization and Reprocessing. Whatever that means. I can tell she's very worried about my past trauma. She's left two unanswered voicemails on my phone. I know she wants to follow up but I've got to think.

Phoebe made me realize that I'm the one obstructing my own investigation. I'll never see the whole vision because I'm afraid to. Afraid to see the face of the murderer.

But now I know that somehow, I'm a murderer, too. I'm one of the evil ones that need to be captured and punished. I'm trying to pull that all together, make a coherent picture, but it keeps slipping out of my grasp.

Yeah, you take the blame. I'm cool with that. I'm just a figment, remember?

Zoe. My undercover identity, nemesis, and evil twin all in one. User, transient, petty criminal. As Zoe, I met lots of street kids, pimps, prostitutes and drug dealers. The pressure to uncover more and more information was tremendous. The raid kept getting put off and put off, my stint getting longer and longer. I got confused about where my loyalties lay. When the raid finally came, with bullets flying and hand to hand fighting taking place in the hallways, I hid in a storeroom with a mattress and a corpse, overcome by visions of police officers making back room deals with the same criminals I was trying to get evidence to convict.

That whole night was a jumble of circumstance and emotion. Terror. Horror. Nowhere to run. Afraid the police wouldn't recognize Zoe as one of their own and she'd be gunned down by an overeager rookie.

Afraid the squatters would realize she's a cop and slit her throat before she had a chance to be rescued by the thin blue line advancing through the premises, floor by floor and room by room. Afraid the drugs in her system, the ones she couldn't avoid taking, were twisting her consciousness into a morass of real and imagined images. Zoe had no better option than to hide like a rat in the darkness and hope the terror passed her by.

For a long time after my assignment ended, I didn't look at those memory. I didn't repress them, exactly — I knew I'd been hiding in a room with a dead body — but I didn't look directly at them. Couldn't. Because Zoe killed someone.

No. Not Zoe. Me.

Denver Police Department detective Audrey Lake.

Who swore to serve and protect. And who has an obligation to Claire Chandler, and Victoria Harkness, not just because of a piece of paper I signed, but because this is my life's work. But somehow this other thing, this trauma, is getting tangled up in my perceptions. And because I won't allow my own weakness to make me a victim, I intend to face my fear, look at the monster full on.

Eventually.

But before I think about that, I have to think about Victoria Harkness. There's a case to be solved, and right now, I'm the only one who can do it. I don't have time to engage in therapy.

I steel myself to go down to the beach again.

Third time's the charm, baby.

I'll deal with Zoe later, maybe with Phoebe's help. Right now, I have a crime to witness.

Clarity, I need clarity.

I hope it's like seeing a movie for the second time. The first time you're too caught up in the plot to be conscious of all the background information and cinematography that work together to create an overall emotional effect. But later, if you watch it again, you can appreciate all the little details that go into telling the story.

In the case of Victoria's murder, I know what's going to happen. I hope I can be more detached this time, not get steamrolled by the emotional turmoil, and take note of the telling details.

I wait until night, thinking that it might help to have all the elements in reality as similar as possible to the vision. I drive down to the parking lot of the Holiday Inn, and walk down to where I can see the beach. The bridge looms overhead, reaching into the darkness. A truck vibrates the concrete deck. A pair of mallards bob amongst the broken piers snaggling up above the surface of the river. I'm alone. Good. And the rain has stopped, for now.

With a deep breath and a half-formed prayer, I step onto the featureless sand, wiped clean by wind and rain and tide. Walk slowly down to the water's edge. Try not to think, just feel the moist cool darkness of the night. I wait, breathing easily, feeling the pulse in my veins and the gentle roar of blood in my ears. I close my eyes.

Footsteps. The slow cadence of walking, then nothing. The soft scuff of shoes on sand, picking up speed, not running but coming with purpose. A voice whispering my name: Victoria.

I don't want to look. I don't want to see the face.

No, that's not right. Because Victoria looks. I can't prevent her.

I turn, see the dark shape of the killer, his tousled hair, his dark eyes illuminated by the dull glow of a street lamp. Even as the familiar fear washes over me, I do not close my eyes. I can deal with this. I can. Because now I know the face is not my own.

He says, "It was just a game. Nothing more."

The words are soft, civilized even, but rage blazes from his eyes.

I recognize the man whose hands are around my neck, who shuts off my breath, who pushes me down and forces me into the water until I am permeated by darkness.

It is Eric North. And he growls, "I won't let you wreck my life. You made me do this. With your lies."

28

I spend the night tossing and turning, trying to get my head around Eric North as Victoria's murderer. Why, why, why? His final words are inexplicable. What game? What lies? And how can I possibly find out if my vision is a depiction of true events? There's just no evidence. No forensics that I know of, nothing that points to him.

I wonder if Olafson & Co. ever acted on my tip about possible witnesses at the Best Western Hotel. That might be my best bet. In between my worried conjectures, I dream about knocking on endless doors looking for long-absent guests. As quality sleep goes, I've had more restful stakeouts.

The morning finds me groggy and grumpy. I remain on my cot, snug beneath my sleeping bag while a noisy bird twitters outside and some critter scampers over the roof.

But. Thinking isn't helping. What's needed is evidence. Finally, I figure that the only thing I can do is to see if I can induce a vision about Daniel's murder. Like I did with Victoria's.

I don't like this idea, and it takes me some time to figure out why. My vision about Victoria came unannounced and unprepared for. Even when I evoked it again for clarity, I felt like I was following up on a clue given to me by the universe. But looking at Daniel's last moments feels vaguely pornographic. A breach of ethics that I can't even really define. Plus, it's not easy to choose to watch terrible violence while being unable to do anything about it. There's a certain level of — distaste. I can't intellectually justify my repugnance, but, in the end, I don't have to. As a former homicide detective, I've seen and done a lot of distasteful things. Sacrificing personal disquietude in the name of justice.

Yay, you. A big gold medal for Audrey.
Shut up, Zoe.

My phone rings, and I see Phoebe's name on the caller I.D. I let it go to voicemail. Because I'm sure she wouldn't approve of what I'm about to do.

Olafson and Candide have learned their lesson. There's a combination lock like the kind Realtors use bolted over the hardware of the Church of the Spirit. I feel like a kid standing outside a candy store with my nose pressed to the glass, dreaming of the sweets therein. Since I can't get inside, I do the next best thing. I call the cops. Specifically, Detective Jane Candide. For some reason I think I'll have a better chance with her than with her boss. I can always work my way up the hierarchy if that assumption turns out to be wrong.

She picks up on the third ring. "Candide."

"Hello, Detective. Audrey Lake here."

Long pause. I count to ten before she says, "You've got a lot of nerve, I'll say that for you."

"Listen, Jane — I know we got off on the wrong foot, but I've been in your shoes a thousand times. I'd like to help you. And for you to help me."

My count reaches twenty when she says, "I'm listening."

"Okay, well — I heard that Daniel Chandler was killed with blunt force trauma. The thing is, I'd like to get access to the crime scene, see if I can remember anything that could be used as a weapon that's now missing."

I can hear her breathing on the line.

"Unless you've got the weapon already, in which case..." I let that trail off.

Another long pause. "We don't have the weapon."

"Any idea what it might be?"

She sighs, long and gustily. "Something narrow, cylindrical. But there's also some wounds with anomalous shapes."

"All right, let me see if I can help you."

"Steve pulled you out of the scene once already. Unauthorized entrance. Why do you want to get back there? What's the real reason?"

"I was trying to do the same thing, see if something was different from how I remembered it before."

"You said you didn't see anything wrong."

"Olafson yanked me out before I could get a proper look. And I didn't have something to look for specifically. Now I know something about the weapon."

Yet another long pause. I wait her out, walking in circles. I hear background office noises. A man laughs, a phone rings, someone answers it.

Finally, she says, "You'll contaminate the scene."

"I won't. I've already been there — once more won't make any difference. Your techs have been there, haven't they? What have you got to lose?"

"My job, for one."

"But if I can give you something to help, it might go a long way to solving the crime. You could look for the weapon."

Silence. I count to thirty-seven.

The detective sighs. "All right. I'll meet you there. And don't make me regret this. Or you will too, I swear it."

Candide arrives shortly, parking her SUV carefully in one of the many spaces on the sea of empty asphalt. Silently, she leads me around the back of the building, to what was once the loading dock. We're on the scraggy edge of Youngs Bay. Cormorants float in the spaces between the broken pilings. The black birds perch on the tops, wings spread to dry after an afternoon of diving for fish. An occasional tuft of grass sprouts from the rocks along the shore, and the thorny curl of blackberry brambles twines from the undergrowth. I'm struck by the sheer verdancy of even the waste spaces. Every cranny is filled with moss or lichen or dandelions, sometimes all three.

Candide gives me some gloves and opens the door, keys jingling. "Don't touch anything. Don't run off. Don't pick anything up."

"I know how to manage a crime scene. Plus, I already touched things when I was here on Saturday. You've got my prints on file."

We make our way through the maze of halls to Daniel's office. The room is much as I had last seen it. Fingerprinting dust is everywhere, and to my surprise, the papers and computer and books are still all present.

"Aren't you guys going to analyze the computer?" I can't believe they haven't taken the electronics into evidence. Not only does it likely contain pertinent information, it has intrinsic value. Someone might steal it.

"We don't have all the resources you had in Denver. Gotta wait for a forensic team from the State Police to help us out, and they've been tied up with a shooting at one of the parks."

"Aren't you originally from Portland?"

"Yeah, so?"

"So, don't you have some pull? Can't you get some CSI guys from your old home county? Favor for an old friend, that kind of thing?"

"I don't have those kinds of relationships."

She must have left some bad blood behind her. But I'm one to talk. "Candide, it's been over three days since the crime."

She glares. "Leave it, Audrey. It's not my call. Or yours."

"Okay, okay." It's not okay, but whatever. She's right. It's not my call.

"Well? Any weapon ideas?"

"Let me just look, all right? I need a few minutes to stand here and remember, and then see what's different." I walk over behind the desk. Close my eyes. I want to sit down but I know Jane won't like that. I understand — preserve the scene, especially if the forensic guys haven't been here yet.

Plus, there's blood in the chair.

I don't know what I'm doing, and having Jane hovering in the background is distracting. The memory of the office, and what I'd seen while talking to Daniel previously, are vague and unformed. I'd been concentrating on him, and not on the surroundings. The images that come to mind are hazy, and I don't know if they're more my imagination than not.

I count backwards slowly, trying to simply let it happen. Slowly, the pressure of the chair forms behind me. The feeling of plastic under my fingers, the click of keys. Papers, slightly haphazard, on the desk. I glance at the clock: just after midnight.

It's not the same as my experience on the beach. This vision is less immersive. I'm aware of Jane's presence, of the blood. I screw my eyes shut. Clock at five past twelve. Fluorescent light. Hot and stuffy room. The doorknob turns, creaks open. Is it who I've been expecting? A tall figure. A man. It looks like Eric North — but is that because I *want* to see him? And he's carrying something in his right hand. But I don't feel the same sense of menace that I felt with Victoria, the invasive unwelcome awareness of danger.

I'm afraid I'm making it all up in my head. Flowers said sometimes people do just that.

I think you're pulling it out of your backside.

Ignoring Zoe's interjection, I open my eyes and look around, back to my detective brain and Jane's toe-tapping impatience. The desire to find something amiss, something that will justify getting her to break procedure, is strong, but there's nothing.

I close my eyes again, letting the image of Eric coalesce, focus on what he's carrying. This time it seems like a narrow cylinder of some kind, hanging down from his hand. But he isn't holding it like a pipe. I try to get a clearer image, but the object changes to a paintbrush, and then to a beer bottle. His face flickers to that of Jason Morganstern before reverting back to the artist.

Okay, I have to stop. There's too much chance of my imagining things. I should have known it wouldn't be that easy. Just exercising my super-power to solve crimes like Wonder Woman. I rub my eyes and blink the room back into focus.

"Sorry, detective, I'm not remembering anything. I don't recall seeing anything like what you've described. It was all papers and files and stuff. My guess is that the perp brought whatever it was with him. I wish I could hand it to you on a platter, especially after you've taken the trouble to bring me here. But I can't, and I don't want to give you a false lead."

My honesty could elicit a couple of different reactions, but it succeeds in disarming the detective. She sighs and runs a gloved hand through her hair, then grimaces because she's just possibly shed a few fibers into the forensic traces in the room. "I didn't think it would work, anyway. Too much to hope for." She gestures for me to precede her out the door.

To offer a carrot, I say, "You might want to check into the church finances. Chandler told me he had sold some of the artwork to pay bills."

"We'll do that anyway. Money is usually right up there in the top tier of motives for murder."

"Yeah, it is."

"We've got our eyes on some possible perps."

"How, when you haven't even processed the crime scene?"

"Don't start. Forensics aren't everything. Means, motive, opportunity — those things are telling, too."

"Any tie to Harkness's death?"

"That's been ruled accidental."

"And do you believe that?"

The detective doesn't reply. There doesn't seem to be anything else to say. Candide closes the office door and ostentatiously makes a big X over the portal with yellow crime scene tape.

"Listen," I say. "Thanks for this. If I come up with anything I'll let you know, okay?"

She nods, but also frowns. "You should do that anyway, as part of your civic duty. Anything else is concealment. You know that."

"Yeah," I say. "I know." Then something insinuates itself into my awareness. "Hey, Detective. Do you smell smoke?"

Jane and I look at each other. The acrid scent of smoke has already filled the narrow hallways of the admin suite. A thin haze hangs near the ceiling, making the overhead lighting yellow and wan.

I cough. "What's burning?"

I have my answer when we burst into the fellowship hall. Someone has thrown flaming bundles of rags, soaked with accelerant, in through a broken window. The foam-filled chairs and sofas have gone up like the devil himself is sitting on them. Palls of black and stinking smoke swirl around the hanging lights.

"Come on!" I yell. "Out the back way."

"The computer! We need to analyze it! If we lose it, we lose everything."

"Don't be stupid!"

But Detective Candide has already run back into the warren where Chandler's office is.

"Goddamn it!" I cough again, deep hacks that wrench my chest. Already the heat is stifling.

Let her go. She made her choice.

Reflexively, I push Zoe out of my mind. "Detective! Come back!" Cursing, I make my way back towards the office, expecting to meet her in the hallway. But it isn't until I stumble through the ragged ends of yellow tape and into Daniel's office that I find her, yanking plugs and cords from the box of the CPU.

Both of us are coughing like last-stage emphysema patients.

"Get the flash drives!" yells Candide, as she bundles the computer into her arms.

"There's no time!"

"Get them! It's evidence!"

Rather than argue, I scoop the memory sticks into my pockets from where they lay on the desk. "Now, come on!"

We stumble into the hallway. The heat from the fellowship hall has increased, and smoke billows above our heads. I bend double, following Jane with her awkward load.

The fellowship hall has filled with smoke and an acrid chemical smell. Plastic chairs and tables warp and twist. The carpet smolders, and flowers of flame bloom from the nap. Pictures form squares of heat and light on the walls. My eyes water and burn.

Jane yells, "We need to get out!"

No shit, Sherlock. What was your first clue?

I push Jane ahead of me, toward the back exit. Where the hell is the fire department?

Then she trips, and falls face down. The computer flies from her arms and crashes on the floor, the box breaking open.

"Leave it!" I shout. "We have to get out!" The carpet is in flames, with streamers of fire licking towards us. I can scarcely breathe.

"No!" She fumbles for the hard drive amid the broken components.

The heat makes a twisting, searing tentacle that wraps around us both. I grab Jane's collar, and pull her away from the computer and towards the exit. I hit the crash bar and feel her weight against my back as she careens into me. Then we're both outside, filling our lungs with sweet damp air that feels like a gift from the gods.

Candide stumbles past me to her car. She grabs the mic and chokes out an emergency call. I can hear the calm voice of the dispatcher as the detective requests fire trucks. Someone else has already called, because the sirens split the air while she is still talking. I bend over, hands on my knees, coughing and sucking oxygen deep into my lungs, coughing again. Behind me, the Church of the Spirit continues to burn.

The back alley is too hot to bear, and we run around to the front. I am shocked at the extent of billowing flame. Sheltering my eyes, blinking back tears, I can barely make out individual piles of material set at discrete intervals along the base of the building. I try to take pictures with my phone, zooming in through clouds of smoke and quivering heat waves. The heat is like a breath from hell, and I retreat back to the edge of the parking lot. Candide joins me. Her face is red and ash sprinkles her hair.

"Audrey, are you all right?"

"Yes. You?"

She nods.

"It's arson, Detective. Look." I point out the flaming piles, now almost gone.

After the pumper trucks arrive, Jane and I just watch the building consume itself. Those big interior open spaces fan the flame like a wind tunnel, and the water jets take care of what's left.

No pictures. No papers. No files. Nothing.

So. Now what?

I think I know who killed Victoria Harkness. I don't know who killed Daniel Chandler. I don't know if the image of Eric North was cosmic residue or overactive imagination. If I were still a cop, I would get some backup and go over to see North and try to rattle his composure. See what shakes loose. But I'm not a cop anymore. And what's worse, I'm not used to not being a cop. I'm not used to playing a completely lone hand. And being almost burned alive has given me pause. As it is no doubt meant to.

29

When I go downstairs the next morning, the first thing I smell is smoke. My jacket is hanging in the basement to air out — even after a whole night, I can smell it. Now that I'm safe, the thought of that fire gives me the shakes. I'd like to think whoever did it thought the building was empty, but that doesn't pass muster. Our cars were in the parking lot. Either we were the targets or acceptable collateral damage. Either way, the killer has escalated his behavior. I've got to tie up all the loose ends, get proof positive. Before someone else pays the price.

Might be you next time, Lake.

Thanks for the reminder.

Because it's always the innocent who get hurt, isn't it?

Yes. The innocent. Like the body on the mattress. I still can't look directly at it. Instead, I see it darkly, through a distorted funhouse mirror; fuzzily, through a layer of distorting gauze; distantly, through the wrong end of a telescope.

I feel the ringing begin, the high pitched tone, and I shake myself. I can push the image away, but I can't focus on anything else. It lurks behind my every thought like a half-seen stalker in the woods.

Maybe that's why, despite the pressure of the investigation, I stay in my house all morning and into the afternoon. It's not fear. Or anxiety. It's not. I'm giving my subconscious the time to process and collate, and come up with a solution for what to do next. I don't want to be distracted, which is why I ignore Phoebe's phone calls.

The scanner app on my phone is playing non-stop, a curtain of white noise, and between bouts of static I hear about loose dogs, an argument on a downtown street corner that becomes a fistfight, complaints about noisy neighbors. And then I hear an arrest go down.

It isn't that explicit, but I know the codes and can read the intent contained in terse bursts of dialogue. Backup units called to aid in apprehending a dangerous suspect. My anxiety spikes. I get a hollow feeling in my belly. The address is one I recognize. Because I was just there.

Claire Chandler has been taken into custody. And my brain snaps back into focus.

Within hours the Church of the Spirit social media page is crawling with speculation. All comments are couched in appropriate rhetoric, offering prayers and thoughts, but everyone has an opinion. The majority agree her motivation is supposed to be revenge for his philandering.

I guess Daniel's secret life isn't so secret after all. Astoria is a small town, and there's no one like your neighbors for rooting out the dirt.

Honestly, I'm reeling. Claire, guilty? I just didn't get a resentful, good-riddance vibe from her, when she told me about her husband's death. She didn't say anything about his 'getting what he deserved' or 'well, at least I have the life insurance.' Although she was angry and hurt because of his cheating, she'd known about it for years. So why kill him now? And what about Harkness's murder? I had half-assumed both killings would have the same perpetrator. But the M.O.'s *are* different: forced drowning versus bludgeoning with a blunt object.

I pace around my house for what seems like ages. The lack of furniture enables me to cover a lot of distance without tripping over anything. Bonus.

The police couldn't have arrested Claire without evidence for the warrant, so there must be something. Strong circumstantial evidence, plus the statistical likelihood that the surviving spouse is the guilty party. Depends on how stringent the judge is.

I don't believe that Claire is guilty. But. Is it just because I know her, and don't want to think of her that way? Anyone can be a killer, given the right provocation. But a murderer? No. Murder demands a certain detachment, a certain coldness, a certain level of ego. Or desperation.

But. My beliefs don't mean anything. What's needed is evidence. And I don't have any. Not yet.

I go down to my incident room. Stare at the collage of photos, strings, and notes. Who among my suspects had connections to Daniel? Jason Morganstern: I remember how Daniel treated him at the vigil, Morganstern's flash of belligerence and anger. My own evaluation of 'no love lost.' Next, Eric North: he gave a picture to the church, but his relationship with the bookkeeper was minimal. There is a connection between Jason and Eric, though. A successful artist mentoring a beginner.

Could they both be involved? That might explain the difference between the two killings.

Or am I completely wrong, and Claire has been guilty all along?

First, I go to Jason Morganstern's place of work. The sound of welding and metal banging on metal echoes throughout the warehouse. Shouts. Ribald jokes. Smell of diesel and heat.

"Morganstern's not here," says the foreman.

"Where is he?" I ask.

"Let go."

"When?"

"Yesterday."

"What for?"

The foreman looks around, shifts a toothpick in his mouth from one corner to the other. "Stealing. I heard." He shrugs.

"Stealing what?" I remember the missing tools Jason talked about when I interviewed him last time.

"Don't know. He was caught breaking into the tool shed."

"This is separate from the other incident, right?"

The manager nods, shrugs again, looks bored. He glances over the busy floor of the warehouse. Boats up on blocks.

I persevere. "Can you tell me where he lives?"

"No."

"Have you seen him recently?"

"No."

"Do *you* think he was stealing?"

"Doesn't matter much what I think."

"But really. You're the guy who's out here, who really knows what's going on." Just a bit of butter. "What do you think?"

Finally he takes the toothpick out of his mouth and spits on the ground. "I think Jason's a dumb fuck who can't control his impulses. I don't think he's dishonest, but I wouldn't put it past him to just 'borrow' some tools. Company has lots of money. They can always buy more, right?"

"Right."

Nothing more of value from the foreman. I go back to my car, find an unsecured wifi channel. It takes me a while on various search engines, but eventually I find Jason's digs, an old apartment building on Bond Street a few blocks from the shelter. There's no buzzer system, but the front door of the building is propped open and a wall of mailboxes is visible with names and numbers. I shake my head. Bad security. Anyone could just walk in. Jason's name is on box 224, so I head upstairs and knock on his door. He actually answers, looking somewhat the worse for wear. A patchy beard stubbles his jaws, and his hair looks like he slept on it wet. The place is a sty, with dirty dishes and beer cans and soiled laundry everywhere. It smells like hamburger grease and unwashed dude.

"What do you want?" he asks.

"I heard you got canned," I say.

He mumbles something and looks away, wandering into the kitchen. I follow him. "Want to tell me about it?"

"Nah, not really. Assholes. I was putting something back, not taking something away."

"Oh. So, anti-stealing, you mean."

He looks at me blearily, unwilling or unable to follow my verbal repartee. He just shakes his head. "I didn't take nothing."

"What were you putting back?"

"Welding torch." His voice has taken on a sullen note.

"Wasn't that missing when I talked to you last?"

He cracks his neck from side to side, not answering.

"Did you maybe borrow it, for a project or something, and then need to return it when you were done?"

He looks suspicious, but his brow clears. "Yeah. That's it."

"What did you need a welding torch for?"

"Art project."

"Can you show me?"

"Wasn't mine."

"Whose then?"

"Friend."

"So, you borrowed a welding torch for a friend to use in an art project. She gave it back to you, and you snuck it back in to the toolshed. Is that how it went down?"

"He."

"What?"

"My friend is a he."

Ye gods. "Okay, then, he. Is that how it went?"

Not the brightest tool in the shed, is he? Maybe that's why he needs a torch.

To light the way.

Jason nods, digging his fingers into the hair at the back of his neck, and scratching as though beset by fleas.

"That was nice of you. But did your friend know you could get in trouble for doing what you did?"

Jason shrugs.

"Why can't your friend buy his own welding torch?"

Jason shrugs again.

I sigh. "Listen. Jason. You've already gotten fired for this little stunt. It sounds to me like your friend hasn't been much of a friend at all. Suppose you tell me who put you up to this?"

Morganstern's face settles into the stubborn mask that I know all too well from past perps who didn't want to cooperate, whatever was in their best interests. I'd gone after him like 'the Man' and that's how he was reacting.

Smarten up, Lake. Let me take over, why dontcha?

In your dreams, Zoe.

C'mon. At the end of the day we're one and the same. Get used to it.

I turn away from Jason for a moment, stomach roiling. But she — I — she is right. Zoe is part of me, an aspect of my psyche that I'd called into being when I'd accepted the undercover assignment. I can't just dismiss her as a figment of my imagination. Her traits are my own, seamy side up.

When I turn back to face Jason, Zoe looks out of my eyes.

"Listen, fuckhead," she begins.

He glares and pops his knuckles. "It's Jason."

"Whatever. Listen up. I'm not a cop, get it? I'm not bound by their rules. So don't mess with me." She flips the edge of my blazer back to reveal the but of my gun. "I'm looking for who killed Victoria. You care about that, don't you?" Zoe steamrolls over his stammered reply. "Forget about what you think you owe your fake friend. He's hanging you out to dry, unless you roll on him first. So, give. Who wanted the welding torch?"

He hems and haws, but in the end he gives Zoe what she wants.

A name: Eric North.

30

Clickety-clack. I finally put it together.

Welding torch. Arson. Disgruntled artist. Eric North.

My memory of murder.

I know he killed Victoria, but what about Daniel?

Do people really burn buildings down, or kill someone, because that someone had sold their painting without asking? That seems like over the top narcissism, or just plain craziness. All these are the acts of someone in the throes of a deep and corrosive rage. A person who has to resort to destruction because they feel so threatened, or so disrespected, or so angry they have to lash out like an avenging angel. Is that North?

The only way I know to figure that out is to confront him directly. Confront him, and goad him, and see if that destructive tendency reveals itself. Not a great idea — certainly not a safe idea, but I don't know what else to do. The police think Victoria's death was an accident; they aren't going to pursue any leads I give them. So I go by his studio, hoping to find him there. Upon arrival, I start recording with my phone nestled in the breast pocket of my blazer.

When I open the door, the first thing I see is his back. But he isn't alone. A young woman stands in the nude, cradling a large pinkish conch shell, looking out into the middle distance. The artist stands behind an easel, a canvas slashed with color. Although the background is abstract, the image of the woman is emerging.

He turns at the sound of the door, emitting an audible sigh. "Audrey. What do you want now? I'm busy."

"Just a few more questions, Mr. North."

I think he's going to refuse, but he looks back to his model and says,

"Take five." She stretches like a cat, puts down the conch and pulls on a flowered silk robe.

"I'm going out for a ciggie, Eric. Back in a few."

When she's gone, the artist frowns. "I really can't take the time to talk with you, so make it quick."

"Okay. Why did you kill Victoria Harkness?"

The tension in the room rises, like the silent twanging of a string, reverberating throughout the sunlit space. He blinks, slowly, his hand tightening on the brush.

He says, after too much delay, "Why do you think I did?"

Even if I hadn't had the vision, even if I hadn't made the links through Jason, I would have known then. I expected denial, outrage, disbelief, all the reactions of someone falsely accused, or someone seeking to emulate them.

"Because she made you angry."

He actually laughs. He throws back his head, opens his arms as though to embrace the world, widens his stance, and laughs long and loud. Again, a thoroughly fake performance. But not evidence.

"Audrey, if I went around killing everyone who pissed me off, there would be a lot fewer people in the world."

"Why did you burn down the church?"

"What church?"

"Don't play games."

"Are you talking about the Church of the Spirit? I heard about the fire on the radio. Terrible. Someone might have been killed." And he looks directly at me.

I feel a frisson of cold horror.

He says, "I don't know why you think I was involved. It meant nothing to me. I wasn't even a member." He turns away and puts his brush in a jar of mineral spirits, then goes to the window and adjusts the shades to increase the brightness. "I can't help you with your investigation if all you're doing is throwing baseless accusations around, hoping something will stick. I thought you were more professional than that. I thought you were some big-city hotshot, but now I see you're just a failed has-been, trying to bolster your ego by pinning the blame on someone — anyone — who you don't think will fight back. Well, let me tell you, *Detective*, I don't take this kind of thing lightly."

His words strike home, and for a moment I'm at a loss for words. I say nothing as he picks up his phone from where it lays on a wooden stool. He punches a number and lifts the phone to his ear, looking at me all the while.

"Hello, police? There's a woman here in my place of business, and she's harassing me." He pauses, listening to the voice on the other end.

"She's accusing me of things. Slanderous things. I think she might be crazy."

A high-pitched tone begins to sound. Maybe it's inside my head. I don't move.

"Her name is Audrey Lake." He puts down the phone. Looks at me with cold, unfriendly eyes. "I suggest you leave. The cops are sending someone."

My gut tenses. My face burns. My palms feel cold and I clench them reflexively. I want nothing more than to puncture his bubble of arrogance and self-satisfaction.

When he moves, it's too quickly for me to respond. I thought he'd shot his wad, that he'd wait, smiling, for the cops to arrive. But he lunges and bunches the fabric of my jacket in his fists. I feel the heat of his breath, and see the individual stipples of stubble on his jaw. His voice rasps with purpose and barely throttled anger.

"If you ever come around making accusations like this again, I will do more than call the cops. I. Will. Kill you." He gives me a single shake, and pushes me away.

And Zoe, the woman who can't stand to be pushed around by anyone, bursts through her barriers. She straightens my rumpled jacket, and pulls my pistol from the holster. Aims for the center of his body mass, and her grip is rock steady.

"Go ahead, asshole. Try it now." Her anger seethes under my skin like the lava under Yellowstone.

The sound of an approaching siren wails in through the open window. I back toward the door. "You better watch yourself, Mr. North. Or you'll be assisting inquiries from inside a prison cell." With that empty threat uttered, I slam the door behind me hard enough to rattle the glass.

31

I holster my weapon and walk down the outside stairs just as a black SUV with the word POLICE emblazoned on the side draws up in the parking lot. The model smirks as she blows out a stream of smoke through ruby lips.

"Leaving so soon?"

"You should leave too — he's not a safe man to know." I feel like I've got a gallon of adrenaline coursing in my veins, like I might have a heart attack any second.

She smiles like a ferret. "Who wants to be safe?" Then she crushes her cigarette butt under her heel, smiles at the cop car, and walks with a sway and a purpose back up the stairs.

Get the hell out of Dodge, Lake.

I've done nothing wrong, Zoe.

Tell it to the marines.

The door to the SUV opens, and Jane Candide steps out.

"Do detectives usually answer random citizen calls?" I ask.

"I came to make sure you leave the premises."

See? Told you.

"Oh, shut up." Too late I realize I've verbalized my comeback to Zoe.

Candide glowers, putting her hands on her hips. "What did you say?"

Great. "Not you, Detective. I was talking to myself."

That'll go over well.

"Ms. Lake, I really am in no mood for your antics. I don't care if you've been hired by someone. You are harassing citizens and hampering our investigation at every turn." She sounds exhausted, and it's no wonder. After last night's fire, she was probably up until the wee hours filling out paperwork.

I take a deep breath. "Listen, I'm following up on a lead. I have to ask questions that sometimes make people uncomfortable. You know that."

"What does this artist have to do with anything?"

I can't tell her about the vision. She'll think I'm loony. "He has connections with Victoria Harkness. He knew her when they were younger. He painted a suggestive picture which he donated to the church."

"And you didn't see fit to show me this picture when we were there?"

"It isn't there anymore."

"Where's the picture now?"

"I think Daniel Chandler sold it."

She nods, pursing her lips.

"It showed her with wings in a beam of light, floating over the water."

"Sounds like an alien abduction to me."

"Given that she ended up in the river, I think there's a connection. It showed a specific place, piling fields with the bridge in the background. That painting was hanging in the fellowship hall where everyone could see it."

"You're grasping at straws."

"Jane, listen —"

"No, you listen, Audrey. Steve wants you out of the picture. He's tired of running into you, and this call from a citizen complaining about you is just the icing on the cake. I've seen your file. I know you had a meltdown back in Colorado."

Speaking through gritted teeth. "I'm not having a meltdown."

"Audrey, look. I know what it's like to have to start all over again. I know what it's like to make mistakes, okay? I pretty much wrecked my career in Portland. I was just lucky that Steve and the APD were willing to give me a second chance. I'm telling you, acting like a rogue agent is not the way to rebuild your credibility."

"That's not what I'm trying to do."

Oh, really?

"Well, good. Because it isn't working. What are you trying to do, then?"

"I'm trying to solve the murder of Victoria Harkness, since no one else seems to be doing that."

Jane's face darkens, and I think maybe I've gone too far. But my frustration level is just below critical. It doesn't help that it's mostly my own fault.

"Jane, I'm sorry. But maybe it's time to pool our resources. What have you got?"

She doesn't answer, tapping her fingers against the hood of the car. Then she motions sharply. "Get in."

I get in.

I think she's going to take me to the station, but we pull out of the parking lot and head south instead of north. She circles the roundabout and follows the highway along the north shore of Youngs Bay.

"Where are we going?"

"You want to know how the investigation is going. Well, I can tell you, it's not."

"Oh?"

Detective Candide gives me a fierce glance. "If you ever say anything to Steve, if you mention to anyone that I told you about an ongoing investigation, I will break you in this town."

"Got it." So tired of threats.

She heaves a sigh. "When North's call came in, Steve told me to follow it up. He wanted me to deliver a message. He wants you to stop your investigation. If you don't, he'll make sure that everyone knows about your breakdown. Your mental state. He'll do it, too. You know what gossip is like in a small town."

I've had a taste of it already. "So, you're delivering his message."

Jane nods. "Yes. But frankly, I'm concerned that we didn't get further in the investigation. I talked to church members, all Harkness's known associates, and got nothing. Her mother is breathing down our necks, and she's a real piece of work. But there's no evidence, no motive. I've heard more about petty jealousies and squabbles in the congregation than you would believe. I've heard about Daniel's philandering. But I can't identify any motive, any reason to kill the pastor."

"What about forensics?"

"Nothing conclusive. We don't know where she went into the water. Someone left a tip about the Holiday Inn, but that didn't pan out. There was nothing on her body — the water destroyed anything there might have been. Her apartment was clean, nothing missing or that shouldn't have been there."

Except the money.

I'm not bringing that up.

"Harkness's death has been ruled an accident. I can't continue investigating a non-case. And neither should you."

We ride in silence for a little while. The road unspools before us, houses and commercial properties on the left, the ruffled waters of Youngs Bay on the right.

Finally, I say, "You don't think it was an accident." That's been the subtext to everything she's said.

"Audrey, Steve would kill me if he knew I was asking you for help. But I am. We've got nothing — and honestly, we're not very experienced when it comes to investigating homicides. If it's not the result of a bar brawl or domestic violence, some close associate that can't keep their mouth shut, we don't have the expertise or the manpower to get much further. So if you know something, if there's something we've overlooked, please tell me. Help us get to the bottom of this crime."

She talks a good game, don't you think?

Zoe's right. I'm moved by Detective Candide's plea. It can't have been easy for her to ask for help, to go behind her boss's back and admit that they were stumped, but I respect her more for it. She's been more open with me than I have been with her. I feel the imbalance of obligation between us. But there's no way she'll believe I had a psychic vision of the murder, or if she did, there's no way she'll treat it seriously.

"Okay, Jane...I know this isn't going to sound very convincing, but I *know* that Eric North is involved in Victoria's death. I can't tell you how I know," I raise a hand as Jane starts to question me, "but I do. That's why I was at his studio. Trying to shake something loose. It didn't work, but I can tell you he didn't react like an innocent bystander. He didn't admit anything, but his responses were off."

"What do you mean?"

I run a hand through my hair. "I've been a homicide detective for a long time. Questioned a lot of people. You just get a feeling for when someone is concealing something, or holding something back."

She nods slowly, eyes glued to the road ahead.

"Plus, he threatened me. He grabbed my coat, said he'd kill me if I kept harassing him."

"Well, from his point of view, you were."

"This was more than just testosterone posturing. He was angry.

Enraged. If you hadn't arrived just then, I don't know what he would have done. He let me go when we heard your siren, and I still drew my weapon. He was that intimidating."

"What? You pulled a gun on someone? Audrey —" She takes a turn too wide, and has to swerve away from an oncoming truck. Its horn blares a warning.

I'm squeezing the armrest as my seatbelt presses against my chest. "Jane, listen. I was afraid for my life. You would have been too, if you'd seen the rage in his eyes. It's him. I know it." I take out my phone and play back the recording.

When it's finished, she says, "Jesus Christ."

"I know, right?"

"You think he's the arsonist?"

"I know he had access to a welding torch." I tell her about my interview with Jason. "Plus, he uses paint thinners and other possible accelerants. Those piles we saw? Maybe rags from his studio. We both saw some in the fellowship hall."

She doesn't say anything.

I press my case. "He's already shown disregard for human life, Detective. He knew we were there."

"What I heard on your recording was him expressing dismay at the thought of someone being killed."

"It was the way he looked at me when he said it. And his tone." But my heart sinks.

Jane drives me back home. Judge Rutherford is in his front yard and waves as we flip a u-turn in front of the house. Great, my law-abiding neighbors see me arriving in police custody.

But. Other things to think about.

"Detective, there's one other thing." She rolls her eyes, but I continue. "You've arrested Claire Chandler for her husband's death."

"Yeah, so?"

I take a deep breath, committing myself. "So, I think she's innocent. I think Eric North is responsible for both murders."

Jane rests her head briefly on the steering wheel. "Audrey, just stop. We have evidence. Her fingerprints were all over the crime scene. She has ready access to the church and has no alibi for the time of death. Opportunity. Chandler was having an affair. Had a history of cheating. Motive. There's a life insurance policy for him that lists her as the beneficiary. More motive. You know yourself the surviving spouse is usually the perp in cases like these."

"You guys didn't get a crime scene team in there for days. She called me from his office the day after they'd taken the body away. She was actually on the computer. I told her to get out of there, but that explains the fingerprints. Plus, they were married. It's not unlikely her prints would be on anything of his."

"She called you? What for?"

"Because she'd found evidence of financial fraud on Daniel's computer. She thought he was selling the church assets — the artwork — and doing something else with the money. Jane, just look at the accounting records. It's additional motive."

"Yeah, for *her*. It sounds like Daniel was going to wreck their lives."

Shit. "You've got it wrong, Detective. She didn't know until after he'd been killed. She was nosing around, trying to figure it out. Her call to me proves it."

"So she says. It could all be staged to make her look better."

"And the Earth could be flat." I unbuckle my seat belt. "I'm trying to help you. The evidence is only circumstantial at best. If your case isn't completely watertight, you're going to be accused of implicit bias."

Candide scoffs. "Because she's Black, I suppose?"

"Yes. Because she's Black, and a woman, and because she's innocent. Don't do this to yourself. Don't do this to her."

"Audrey, just get out, all right? Out of my car, out of this investigation, out of the whole damn business."

"I'm going, but Jane — don't trash your career a second time."

She peels away as soon as I've shut the door and I watch her drive away. Despite my appeal, it's all too likely that Claire will be convicted. There's no other suspect. I'd be suspicious of her too, if I didn't know about Eric North.

32

The next day I decide to visit Claire Chandler. My coat still reeks of smoke, so I pull on a sweater and fleece vest before setting out.

I'm surprised to learn the jail — the 'corrections center' — is right downtown behind the first Baptist Church. It's a brutalist concrete affair, and it's difficult to find the entry. The maple tree in a concrete planter is just beginning to bud, and some joker has put a 'no vacancy' sign in one of the windows.

So, jail.

I wish I could say I didn't know what to expect, but that's not true. There's no glossing over what is an essentially grim experience. Still, I discover that the visiting process is casual as far as these things go. But of course, Claire hasn't been convicted yet. She's being held pending her bail hearing; apparently, she's a flight risk. Because, you know, murder. Capital crime. Oregon has a death penalty, although it's been in abeyance for a while; it's still on the books.

Be calm. That's the best way I can help her.

Soon I'm in a big conference room sitting at a white plastic table, and a female guard who looks like she missed her calling as a linebacker for the Broncos escorts Claire inside. She's wearing a polo-style shirt and baggy pants in broad black and white stripes. Her expression is stern and angry. The lines around her eyes have taken on a new depth, and look as though they are etched down to her skull.

As she sits at the table, she says, "Audrey. Get me the hell out of here."

I feel at fault somehow, as though I am to blame for her current condition. If I had caught Victoria's killer. If I had caught Daniel's killer. If.

But. This is not about me.

They don't allow us to touch, so I put my hands together. "I'm trying. I'm positive I know who killed Victoria. I just need evidence."

"I don't really care about that now. What about Daniel?" Her eyes sheen with unshed tears. "Find out who killed him. That's the only thing that will help me."

"I think it's the same person."

"Who?"

Do I tell her? Without evidence, it's outright slander. She doesn't need that. I explain why I'm withholding my suspicions for now.

She grits her teeth. "I don't give a shit for all your legal niceties. Get me out. Find out who did this. Have they processed the scene? Who else was there?"

"Claire, I've got some bad news. The scene has been demolished. Someone tried to burn down the church Tuesday night."

Her mouth drops open. "What?"

"I was there at the time. With Detective Candide."

"Oh my God. Who would do such a thing?" She shakes her head, and her expression becomes bleak. "So many haters. Did you see who it was?"

"No. We were inside Daniel's office at the time. But logic says it's the killer."

I wait while she moans a little to herself, then mutters, then slaps the table. A guard at the wall jolts to attention, then settles back down when I raise a palm.

Claire puts her face in her hands. "I've lost everything. My husband. My freedom. My church. What's happening to me? What's going on? Why is my life being ruined?" She looks up, to the industrial light fixtures and perhaps beyond. "Why?"

She closes her eyes.

"Claire, I'm sorry. I'm so sorry. I can't imagine what you're going through, how it must feel." I lean forward. "Did they say why they think you did it?"

Her laugh is hollow, without mirth. "Revenge for his cheating and life insurance. I didn't even know there was a policy! They don't have the weapon but they say they don't need it, that I must have thrown it into the river. They keep trying to get me to confess."

Trying to be encouraging. "It sounds pretty circumstantial."

"You're the one who told me the police don't arrest innocent people. But I should have known better." She laughs again, with a sound so bitter it makes me recoil.

I wish I could tell her that's not true. But I can't.

"So who do you think killed Daniel?" I ask again.

"Aside from a jealous husband? I don't know."

"A specific jealous husband? Do you know for sure who he was having an affair with?"

"I can't talk about this, I really can't."

"Claire, please. I'm trying to help you."

She sighs, rubs her eyes. "Victoria. Maybe. But really, there could be others." Her smile is twisted. "There were always others."

I recall my own earlier suspicions. "The pastor? Why didn't you tell me?"

She shrugs, looks away. "I actually don't know for sure. It's not the sort of thing you want to broadcast. It's too hurtful. Plus, it just gives me more motive."

My head is spinning. What if Daniel *had* killed Victoria? Or if someone thought he had? I remembered a sullen voice, Jason Morganstern, saying: "I'd kill anyone who'd hurt her." What if he thought Daniel had? Or — if he'd known Daniel and Victoria had a sexual relationship, would his devotion to her turn into jealousy? Enough to kill his perceived rival?

Enough to kill the woman he adores?

But no, *Eric* killed Victoria. I'm sure of that.

Evidence. I need evidence.

"Knock knock, Audrey. What's going on in there?" Claire taps the side of her own head.

"Just trying to figure things out."

"Taking you a long time to do it." Claire's hands are restless, clenching, unclenching, and finally ending up in her lap. "I need help. Please. I can't pay you from in here, but —"

"It's not the money. That's the least of it. This case is just — slippery. I can't seem to get a foothold. But," I say, standing up, "For what it's worth, I don't believe you killed anyone."

"Why don't you tell Detective Olafson that? Or the D.A.?"

"I will. I've already told Detective Candide."

"Why were you two at the church?"

I'm thrown for a second by her change of subject. "We were looking for evidence. We tried to get the computer, but the fire had already started and we didn't get it out. At least, not whole. I think the detective got the hard drive. But only after she dropped the whole thing on the floor."

"There's backups at the house."

"Whose house? Yours?"

"Daniel always brought the backups home with him. Said it was good practice to keep them in a different place than the main computer."

I feel a surge of hope. "Would you grant access to the cops?"

"Would it help my case?"

"It might. Create goodwill. Show you have nothing to hide. You should tell your attorney. You do have one, right?"

"Tips at the Portway don't begin to cover the cost of a lawyer. They've assigned me a public defender. In theory. I haven't actually seen him."

"Use the computer backup as a bargaining chip. Tell your lawyer you'll grant access in exchange for bail."

"I see you know all about twisting the system."

"Court cases are all about negotiation."

"So much for justice, then." Her voice is sad and bitter.

I suck in a breath. "Look, Claire, I know I haven't been spectacularly productive so far. But I will do my best to nail the killer, and I won't give up until I do. I'm close, I know it."

She shrugs and raises a skeptical eyebrow, but I mean every word.

I drive back home, get out, and lean against the car. It's all out of control. I'm shaking with repressed emotion.

I've never seen a friend get jailed before. Never been so sure of a miscarriage of justice.

Hey, that's just how it is. Hook 'em. Book 'em. Let the lawyers sort it out.

"No, that's not how it is!" I kick the side of the garage in frustration. I want to howl at the heavens. "Help me save my friend, for God's sake."

"Something wrong?" The voice is Lincoln Rutherford's gravelly baritone. "Shall I get Phoebe?" He's dressed in overalls and gardening gloves with deep grass and earth stains, a trowel in one hand.

"Everything's just peachy," I growl, extremely irritated that he thinks I need a therapist. Even if I do. "Where's the public defender's office?"

He blinks, but reels it off from memory. Afterwards, he says, "Don't tell me anything more. I really, really don't want to know why you were with the police yesterday, or why you want the P.D. It's a small town, and too easy for me to hear something that I shouldn't."

"I thought you were retired."

"Am. But active judges still have vacation, sick leave, or have to recuse themselves. I'm back on the bench every six weeks or so."

My phone rings. It's Seth Takahashi. With an apologetic wave to Link, I go a few yards down the sidewalk. The preacher says he's at the homeless shelter, and that one of the residents has something important to tell me. He wants me to come and talk to this man, right now.

So, of course I go. Because at this point, I'm looking for a miracle.

33

I find Takahashi and his companion in a small room at the shelter, in a space set aside for counseling or meditation. There's a table and four chairs. I take one, try to keep my eagerness and anxiety and hope in check, but I can feel sweat between my shoulder blades.

The Reverend as usual is dressed in black jeans and a white shirt, buttoned up to the neck. His companion is the opposite: a white man with stringy brown hair to his shoulders and a patchy beard. He's dressed in stained blue jeans and a red sweatshirt. His shoes are torn and full of holes. He clutches a tattered spiral notebook and looks down at the table. With a start, I realize that I recognize him.

Takahashi says, "Audrey, I'd like you to meet Mr. Travis McGuthrie. Travis, this is the woman I told you about, Ms. Audrey Lake."

"Hi," I say. "I saw you at the shelter last week." I extend my hand to McGuthrie, and he barely touches it with his fingers before dropping his hand back to his notebook. He doesn't look at me.

"Travis, I'd like you to share your poem with Audrey. Is that okay? You can read it aloud, or give it to her to read herself."

Oh lordy, a poetry reading. There was a detective from Denver...

Shut up, Zoe. Seth wouldn't have asked us — me — here without a good reason.

Who stuck her hand in a blender...

I remembered Phoebe's advice not to talk back to the voice, not to give it any more attention and energy. The recollection of her firm, no-nonsense tone is a lifeline.

It's getting crowded in here, gonna have to build an addition.

I should never have given her free rein.

Ignore Zoe, concentrate instead on the tableau before me. Seth sitting quietly, hands in his lap, looking at Travis encouragingly. Travis opens up his notebook and pages through it. It bears many brief notes, some sketches, and some dense handwritten passages which I think might be a sort of journal. He stops at a page with a rough series of single written lines marred by smudged fingermarks and begins to read.

"The night is cold. The ground is hard. But river seen through screen of grass is beautiful.

I hear footsteps. I see a woman. She comes along the path.

Her hair is long. Her shoulders hunched. She looks back more than once.

She leaves the path. Goes to the beach, her footprints on the sand."

I catch my breath. Seth flashes me a warning glance. Travis doesn't look up, continuing his recital.

"I hear the tread of someone else. Faster. Harder. Louder.

A man comes through. He follows her. His feet sink in the sand.

I see him reach. She dances back. I hear him yell. I see him strike.

I hear her cry. I see her fall. Her hand is on her cheek.

I see him kneel and shake her hard. Her words to him are sharp.

He strikes again. She speaks again. He reaches for her.

Knocks her down. Then puts her into the water.

For a moment they are one, then two.

The man walks away alone."

Travis puts his notebook down. Takahashi looks at me and raises his eyebrows.

Holy shit. He was there.

Yeah. He was.

I've got to proceed carefully here. This is a vulnerable witness. I don't want to lead him, or scare him, or make him retract his story.

"Wow," I say. "That's a pretty striking poem. Was that something you actually saw?" I deliberately don't use the word 'witnessed.' I don't want to be all policey and intimidating. Who knows what his interaction with law enforcement has been before now? Not good, I'll reckon.

Travis nods.

"Where did this happen?"

He shuffles his feet. Looks around the room. At Seth. But not at me.

Seth says, "Is it close by? Can you take us there, Travis? Can you show us where you were camping?"

Shuffle. Shift. Sniffle. Finally, a nod.

"Okay then," I say. "Let's go. You lead the way."

Travis walks out of the shelter onto the narrow sidewalk. Takahashi follows him, and I come last, trying not to crowd. Travis leads us toward Marine Drive, where we wait at a crosswalk in silence. When the light changes, we cross five lanes of steaming bug-splattered grills and a parking lot to get to the Riverwalk. The Holiday Inn looms. I feel a shiver across my shoulders, my skin pimpling as though caressed by an arctic breeze.

Our guide stops at the end of the boardwalk where it joins the paved trail that runs between the hotel and the river. "I got a place down underneath here," Travis mumbles. He points at the boardwalk. "Above the tide line, some shelter when it rains. I like to be by the river. It wasn't raining that night. So I laid up over there." He points to a clump of yellow-flowered Scotch broom. "Thick. No one can see me in there."

I don't doubt it. The broom is woody, gnarly, the tight-packed stems discouraging casual visitors. But someone who wasn't worried about scratches or stains could wriggle into the copse, snug as a bug in a rug. And invisible to a casual glance. Especially at dusk. I circle the thicket, tramping through tall, dew-covered grass. Assuming Travis had been seated, peering through the stems, the beach where I'd first had my vision is clearly visible.

I ask, "Do you remember when you saw this happen, Travis? What day it was?"

He looks at Seth, and shakes his head. "Naw."

Seth says, "The calendar is pretty meaningless when you don't have places to go or people to see. No reason to keep track."

I nod, disappointed. Maybe there's something else in the journal that would help to narrow down the date. Although the fact that it wasn't raining should help. Because it always seems to be raining in Astoria.

We return to the shelter. Travis goes back to his room and Takahashi and I stand on the front porch. A few sparrows are twittering on the sidewalk, pecking at some crumbs. They scatter at the approach of a brindle cat who pretends he isn't on the stalk.

Takahashi breaks the silence. "It's important, isn't it? Travis's story."

"Yeah, it's important. He witnessed a murder. Victoria's murder."

There's a sharp, intake of breath before his next words. "We need to be careful with him. He's fragile."

"I know. I can tell. Will he stay here?"

"A few days, maybe. These guys are called transients for a reason. He'll start to feel confined and get on the move again, maybe across the bridge, maybe down south to Seaside."

I reach out, put a hand on his arm. "Reverend Takahashi — Seth — please, if you can, keep him here. Convince him to stay. Or if you can't, find out where he's going."

"I'm not his keeper, Audrey. He has the right to go where he likes, when he likes."

"I know, but please. An innocent woman may go down for this."

He covers my hand with his own. "No promises, but I'll do my best."

We stand for a few seconds. Then I say, "Why didn't you contact the police?"

He takes a step away. "Because Travis wouldn't talk to the police. But you're not a cop, and he remembered you."

34

I go back home, too agitated even to walk the perimeter. I can't explain how I feel. Vindicated. Terrified. Relieved. Incredulous. A gigantic mix of emotions that swamp my inner tidelands with a tsunami of feeling.

But all that feeling is detrimental to criminal investigation. So I push it away, wipe it off my shoes and wring out my socks and try to look at the situation objectively.

Okay. I have a real witness. Someone who has actually seen and heard what to date I have only experienced inside my own head. Although I've been assuming my vision is authentic, to know that the events had an objective reality outside my mind that someone else could and has perceived takes a tremendous load off my shoulders. I feel light as a feather. A pink balloon, bouncing.

So. Now what? Still far away from catching the guy. Evidence is lacking. Eyewitness, sure. Sorta. Think of the questions from the defense. 'Was he sober? Of sound mind?' Would he even testify? I have doubts. He'll be classed as an unreliable witness at best.

No shortage of those around here.

Come up with a useful idea for once, will you?

Get North to confess.

He doesn't seem like the confessing kind. And it's not like I have access to an interview room, with other cops to help with the interrogation. Plus proof. As in, none.

So? You've got the details. Convince him you know everything. Get him to admit something no one else could know. Jog his memory. Take him back to the scene of the crime.

I think about that. I mean, what if? But I need more than just my own or Travis's testimony. I needed someone else to hear and understand what they are hearing. I need some help. Preferably someone official. Another cop.

Detective Jane Candide.

Yeah. Good luck with that.

I have to tie up all the loose ends before I approach her. She isn't going to be interested in half-baked theories. I look through my scrawl of notes taken over the last few weeks. One anomalous item catches my attention. 'Welding torch.'

I'd forgotten to ask Eric why he wanted it. Or needed it. And also why he'd had Jason get it for him. What could you do with a welding torch besides, well, weld?

Burn down a building.

I scroll through the internet but am no wiser. Except, now I know what one looks like. It's a nozzle with a pipe-like fitting that attaches to a fuel tank.

A pipe-like fitting. A narrow, cylindrical fuel tank.

The murder weapon for Daniel Chandler. I'd stake my life on it.

I try to imagine what might have happened. Maybe North approached Chandler about the unauthorized sale of the artwork. Or maybe Chandler had figured out North's involvement in the murder and confronted him. Whatever, North had shown up with the torch. Not an ideal murder weapon — why hadn't he brought something more appropriate, assuming this was pre-meditated?

No, it must have been spur of the moment, using the tool he had to hand. North had made the decision at the scene. He'd either been surprised by something Chandler had said, or hadn't expected to find him there. But it still seemed unlikely. Why bring the torch at all?

Maybe North had intended to burn the church *then*, and Chandler had surprised him. Then for whatever reason, panic, or something else, the artist had left without finishing the job. Only to return a few days later, when Candide and I were inside.

Right, and then he just returns the thing to Jason? Hello, DNA? The guy's not an idiot, Lake. Unlike some I could mention.

No, he wasn't. But how likely was it that the police would make the connection? It was pretty thin. And even if they somehow got a line on the weapon, it would only lead them to Jason Morganstern. Who'd been fired for stealing tools, and had a record for criminal mischief. Even if he said he'd taken it for North, North would only have to deny it. Morganstern's word would be nothing against a respected local artist.

And I still don't know why he killed her.

How in hell am I going to get this guy? Before Claire goes down for his crimes?

I head down to the basement to the incident room, feeling useless and guilty. Check the locks on the walkout door, circle to check the windows. Dislodge some spiders. Spot my coat hanging on the nail where I'd hung it after the fire. Still stinks a bit, but this is the only coat I have that repels water. Lifting it off the nail, something rattles in the pocket. Can't be keys, I've got those. I reach in, exploring, and encounter a handful of flash drives. Memory sticks. The ones I snatched off Daniel Chandler's desk when Candide was grabbing the computer.

I run upstairs, tripping on the treads in my haste. Open my laptop and jam the first one into the USB port. Spreadsheets, lists of Ebay auctions, bids and buyers. This is what Claire must have been talking about when she called. I eject the flash drive and shove in another. More spreadsheets, tax records. I'm not an accountant so I don't even bother to try to interpret them. Third one has a single text document entitled Creative Healing. I double-click on the icon and the first page blossoms on my screen. Treating Trauma Through Guided Creation by Victoria Harkness.

This is the book she was writing, the one Daniel Chandler was going to help her publish.

I stop. For some reason I feel like I'll be violating her privacy. But this is her voice, her master work, what she wanted to share with the world.

Plus, she's dead.

Yeah, there's that.

So I read. Or at least, I skim. Most of the book is dedicated to creative exercises, guided drawing with pencils or watercolors; journaling with prompts; collage and even cooking. Victoria has chosen a multitude of vehicles and tools that most people should have access to, nothing that requires a lot of expense. It's all designed to help people get in touch with their feelings to better recover from trauma. But it's the part where she talks about herself that I go over carefully, word by word.

She describes her childhood, her happy home with strict but loving parents. I barely recognize the literary portrait of her mother. And then I read about her interactions with the neighbor boy. Several years older than Victoria, he began drawing her, and teaching her how to draw as well. They played sketching games, completing each other's work, or making comic book stories with a cast of characters. She looked up to him, and as they both got older he became more serious about his art and began to pose her. And then he began to touch her. When he was seventeen and she was twelve, they had sex for the first time.

The Harkness household was religious. Victoria was confused and thought what was happening was wrong, but she didn't know how to make it stop. And she didn't want to get her friend in trouble. Her fear of her parents' disappointment kept her from opening up to them. And then her mother and father started fighting. They split up, and she believed it was her fault. When her mother took her away to Portland, leaving the rest of the family behind, Victoria believed she was to blame, that she was evil, and that nobody wanted to be around her. In one stroke, she'd lost most of her family and her best friend. It took her years of searching and following her inner muse to recover from the trauma. In a final chapter of self-healing, she returned to her childhood town to face the pain and look for healing. For both herself and her abuser.

I look up from the laptop. The inside of my cheek is sore where I've been biting it unknowingly. This explains everything. Why she came back to Astoria. How she could connect so well with the damaged members of her congregation. And it gives me the motive for murder. Not just hers, but Daniel's as well. Because Daniel read the book. Daniel must have known. Because throughout the narrative are marginal comments from the bookkeeper. One of the last reads "Do you want to name names?"

It confirms what I already know. Eric North is a murderer. And an abuser. And unless I can do something, he's going to get away with it.

35

The visiting room at the Clatsop County Corrections Center hasn't changed in the course of one day. It's still frigid, and I keep my coat on. The acrid odor of smoke wafts up from the material, reminding me uncomfortably of the fire. I wait for Claire, and when she finally arrives, escorted by a guard, I'm shocked at how haggard my friend looks.

My friend. Because Claire *is* my friend, not just my client. In any case, I mean to help her in any way I can.

"Morning, Claire."

"Yes. It is." Clair settles down in the chair opposite. "To what do I owe the pleasure?"

"I know who killed Victoria."

"Oh?"

Claire's guarded expression isn't what I had expected. "Yes. It was Eric North."

A multitude of expressions cross her face, flitting by too quickly for me to interpret. But she seems surprised.

"He did it, Claire."

She leans forward "Did he? For sure?"

"Yes."

Her next question is barely above a whisper. "It wasn't Daniel?"

"What? No."

She closes her eyes and puts her head in her hands. "Oh, thank God. I thought..."

Sympathy, empathy, compassion, they all well up from some fissure beneath my cynicism. Because I understand, finally. That Claire has been afraid her husband was guilty. That she loved someone capable of murder.

She says, "Do you know who killed my husband?"

"It was Eric."

"He murdered Daniel, too? But why?"

My reasoning for this is not something I can share, it's so tenuous. But. "Your husband was helping Victoria with her book, the one about trauma from abuse. She was sexually abused as a child here in Astoria." I lean forward. "I've read her book, Claire. She describes what happened. There's no doubt. Her abuser was Eric North. And he didn't want that fact to be published. His life would be wrecked if that happened."

"Can you prove it? Can you get me out?"

"I'm working on that. I think I can get people to listen. I mean, what are the chances that two different murderers are operating at the Church of the Spirit at the same time?"

"But no real proof? Great. That means I'll be accused of both crimes."

"I'm going to get him, Claire."

"You do that." All the emotion seems drained out of her. She sits back, listless.

"Listen, Claire. I'd like you to contact your lawyer. Let them know I'll be coming in to talk to them. Give him proof of reasonable doubt."

She laughs. "My lawyer? Only rich white folks have lawyers on call. My public defender hasn't even bothered to put in an appearance."

I'd suspected this might be an issue when I'd asked Link for the address yesterday. "You haven't had any contact with anyone?"

"Not yet. My bail hearing hasn't even been scheduled."

I say, "I'm going to find whoever has your case, and light a fire under them. Don't give up, okay?"

She looks disbelieving. "Don't give up? My friend and my husband have been killed. Oh, and they were having an affair. And I'm the one on trial for murder. And you tell me not to give up?" She shakes her head. "You're unbelievable. Maybe if I was some suburban soccer mom I'd get a break. But come on, a middle-aged bartender wronged by her man? Jesus, Audrey. Why should the cops look any further? I'm the perfect fit. They've got me tied up with a bow."

"No, Claire, they don't. I'm in your corner. *I know who did it.* I just need a little more proof."

"Proof." She scoffs. "They don't seem to need that for me." Her gaze slides into the middle distance. "One thing. I'm not going to live the rest of my life in prison."

Her assertion fills me with dread.

The public defender's office is on the second floor of an office building across from the court house. After leaving the jail, I walk the three blocks in the drizzling mist that blows in from the river.

The waiting area is full of square chairs that look like they were upholstered in the seventies and haven't been altered since. The magazines on the table are almost as old. At least the receptionist is a little younger. Her name plate reads 'Juanita.' I march up to the counter and ask to speak to whoever is handling Claire Chandler's case.

Juanita looks at me over the top of her glasses. "Who?"

"Claire Chandler. She's being held over at the jail."

"When's her trial?"

"Hasn't been scheduled. She needs someone to put things in motion." Although now that I think about it, the whole speedy trial thing might not be in her best interests right this second. "I'd like to speak to her counsel. I think — no, I know — she's innocent."

Juanita's eyes glaze over. Too late, I realize she's probably heard that line a million billion times.

I strive to mitigate the damage. "Listen, I know what I'm talking about. I'm working as a private investigator. I used to be a cop. I was actually working for her when she was arrested."

Just then, a youngish Indian man approaches the receptionist from an interior office. "Juanita, have you gotten a copy of the warrant for the Carlisle case?" Then he sees me. "Sorry for interrupting, but I'm preparing for a trial." Looks back at the receptionist. "Juanita? The warrant?" His accent is low and rolling and slightly British.

"It's in your inbox, Mr. Biswas." She pronounces it biz-WAHZ.

"Thank you." He looks back at me. "Are you receiving the help you need?"

Juanita says, "She wants to know who is representing a Charlotte Chandler."

"That's Claire Chandler," I correct. "I have some information about her case. I'm a private investigator." Rinse. Repeat.

"I'm sorry," Biswas says. "We don't have the resources to pay a private investigator. You could go to the police and maybe they'll turn it over to us, if it's exculpatory."

"I'm not asking for money. I want to help her."

He closes his eyes briefly. I get a sense of deep tiredness. "Juanita, who's on the docket for incoming cases?"

"I think you are, Mr. Biswas. Ramirez and Jones got the last two."

"Has Chandler's case been assigned to us yet?"

"I haven't seen anything come through."

"Well, call over to the courthouse and get it expedited." He looks at me, then glances at the wall clock that reads 11:50. "I have exactly ten minutes to speak to you before my lunch meeting. Do you know what the charge against Ms. Chandler is?"

I hesitate. "Probably something like first degree murder."

"Who did she kill?"

"No one. The police think she killed her husband."

"Premeditated? Or an accident?"

"Not an accident."

"Paid to do it? Torture, multiple victims, prior convictions?"

"None of the above."

"Probably murder in the second degree, then. What's your angle?"

At least he seems to know his law. "As I said, I'm a private investigator. I was working for her at the time, and the circumstances don't add up."

He raises a skeptical eyebrow. "What were you doing? Investigating the husband for infidelity before he died?" Glances at his watch.

I wince at his summation. "No — I was looking into the death of Victoria Harkness."

"Huh. She hired you to investigate another murder? Then killed someone herself, while you were still on the job? That sounds unlikely."

"I'm saying she didn't kill anyone. I know who the real killer is."

Both eyebrows go up. "You should tell the police."

"I tried. They weren't interested."

Biswas stands. "I've got to leave now, but it sounds like we should definitely talk. Make an appointment with Juanita before you go." He bustles out of the room, straightening his tie as he goes.

"Wait! Mr. Biswas!" I run after him. "Please, go talk to her. Soon. I'm afraid —"

"What, Ms. Lake? I really have to go."

I swallow hard. "I'm afraid she may try to take her own life."

He closes his eyes briefly and grabs his briefcase. "Juanita, set up a consultation with Claire Chandler at the jail. And an appointment for Ms. Lake." And he's gone, practically leaving a dust cloud behind him.

36

Things are moving. Claire's lawyer is engaged. Now I need to follow Zoe's advice and get Eric to confess. And for that I'll need assistance.

The ring tone sounds three times before someone answers.

"Candide."

"Jane. I need your help."

She sighs with gusto. "Hello, Audrey. Are you having a nice day? Me, not so much."

"Listen, Jane, I've got a witness."

"A witness to what?"

"To Victoria Harkness's murder."

A pause, where I can hear background noise of people talking and phones ringing.

"What? Who? Why hasn't that person come forward?"

"He's...got some issues."

"What does that mean? He's crazy? A criminal? An alien abductee?"

"Listen, Jane. He has details that no one could know. I believe he was there, that he saw what he says."

"Details that no one knows. Maybe he made them up."

"He didn't."

"How do you know?"

And what am I supposed to say? That Travis's story tallied with my vision of Victoria's murder? Jane's question is reasonable. I would have asked it myself, if I was in her shoes. And if someone said they had psychic powers, I would probably hang up on them. And then make a little whirlybird symbol at my temple.

"Audrey? How do you know?"

"Sources." Like a damn journalist. I rub my forehead.

More background noise. I can hear a regular clicking, which I realize must be Jane drumming her fingers on her desk.

"Sources. A mystery witness who has issues. Jesus, Audrey."

"Jane, I know. I wouldn't blame you if you hang up now. But please. I think we can prove this. I think we can put this to bed. But I need your help. I need backup."

"Backup. For what?"

"I want to bring the killer back to the scene of the crime. Get him to admit his guilt. Get him to crack."

"Jesus, Audrey. That's dangerous. And you're not even a cop. Not any more."

"I know it's dangerous. That's why I need you for backup. To corroborate. And — for protection."

There. I'd said it. And deliberately asked for backup, one cop to another, even though I was technically a civilian now. Admitting my vulnerability. Phoebe would be proud. Or she will be when I tell her.

"You know I can't condone this. Leave it to us. Tell your witness to come forward. Or you come forward yourself. Divulge your sources. You know better than this." Whack. She must have smacked her desktop.

"I can't explain. You wouldn't believe me. I wouldn't believe me. And there's no direct evidence. I have to do it this way. Are you in, or out?"

"I can't help you. You know that. I could lose my job."

"Jane, an innocent person is in jail. Is your job more important than justice? Wait, don't answer that. I don't want to know. When I have this all set up, I'll send you the details. Regardless of whether or not you choose to sit on the sidelines, I'm going in."

"Audrey —"

"Oh, and Jane? One more thing." I tell her about the flash drives, that they will be arriving soon by US Mail.

And I hang up the phone.

My hands are shaking. I'm panting like I've just run a marathon. And for once Zoe is silent. She hasn't intruded into my conversation with Jane at all. I don't know if I should be relieved or terrified.

I write a note to Eric and tape it to the door of his studio. It reads:

"Eric. I know you killed Victoria Harkness. I have a witness. And I've read the book. Meet me at the scene, tonight at midnight. You know where, if you want to make a deal."

Then I send a text to Jane: The beach behind the Holiday Inn at midnight tonight.

Then I talk to Seth, and tell him what I have planned, and what I want him and Travis to do. As expected, he tries to talk me out of it. As expected, he tries to shield Travis.

"Let it be his choice," I say. "It isn't up to either of us to coerce him either way."

"He isn't in a fit state to make meaningful choices."

"Sez who? You? I know you mean it for the best, but who are you to decide?"

In the end, he agrees to put my request to Travis.

Would he come? Would she come? Would they come? Would this turn out to be the biggest mistake of my life? But so be it. One way or another, I have to know. And it's all I can do to save my friend from a lifetime of prison.

Nighttime. Darkness. Dank tendrils of mist and the mournful hoot of foghorns. The path winds away to my right and left. Three or four windows in the hotel behind me glow with a welcome yellow light. Everyone's curtains are closed.

I'm alone, except for Zoe, and she's not great company.

Don't talk about me as though I'm not here.

Terrific.

I mean, I haven't heard back from anyone. Not Jane, or Seth, or Eric.

Then I hear footsteps. I make sure my sidearm is ready, tucked away in my shoulder holster. I move onto the sand. It's hard to see, but a dark silhouette walks slowly down the path. The figure also steps onto the beach, and after a pause, heads in my direction.

A feeling of deja-vu suffuses me. It's the vision all over again. Is what I'm seeing real? Or is it actually happening?

The figure is obscured by the thickening fog. I draw my weapon, keep it close to my side. The sound of traffic on Marine is muffled and far away.

The mist thins, and the figure is only twenty feet away.

I say, "That's close enough." I begin recording on my phone, tucked into my breast pocket.

He stops. "Audrey? Is that you?"

"It was a night like this, wasn't it, Eric? Dark and foggy."

"I don't know what you're talking about."

"You came down the path, just like tonight. She heard your

footsteps."

"Who?" He takes a couple of steps forward. I back up. The water sloshes against the pilings.

"You know who. Victoria Harkness."

"You're crazy, you know that? I'm going to complain to the cops. This is harassment."

The mist condenses on my cheeks and forehead. "And yet, when you got my note, you knew where to come. This is the crime scene. This is where she died."

He stiffens, then visibly relaxes. "*You* told me."

"No. I didn't."

"You did. When you came to my studio the first time." He steps closer. "You were ranting about it, how I'd killed her on the beach."

"You know that's not true."

"And who are they going to believe?"

I feel a chill, like cold water running down my spine. "Stop." I don't raise my gun, not yet. I don't want to escalate the situation. But he's demonstrated a master stroke. There's no way I can prove what I had or hadn't said to him. Even though I recorded our conversation, since I did it without his permission, it's not admissible in an Oregon court. What I thought would be my trump card, his knowledge of the place Victoria had been killed, is now null.

He growls, "You said you wanted to make a deal."

"Sounds like you think I say a lot of things." I step back. I feel a wetness at my heels. The river. "What else did I tell you?"

"You said I ran after her. That I chased her onto the beach. This beach. That I strangled her. And threw her into the river."

"I said all that?"

"Yeah, you did."

"So did you do all that?"

"No. I did nothing."

"You didn't chase her down?"

"No."

"You didn't put your hands around her neck?"

"No."

"You didn't say, 'you made me do it?'"

"I — what?"

"Did you say, 'you made me do it'?"

"No — I didn't say anything."

"Nothing?"

"Nothing."

"You didn't apologize for killing her?"

"No."

"You didn't say 'it was just a game'?"

"How did — no."

"You just pushed her in the river without saying anything?"

"It wasn't — I didn't kill her."

I take a step toward him, out of the water. "A witness says otherwise."

"There was no witness."

"Yes, there is."

"It was dark, and foggy. No one could have seen."

Gotcha, gotcha, gotcha. The fish is on the line.

"So, in other words, it was a night like this."

He doesn't say anything. Then he starts to tremble, his shoulders and arms and hands, shaking.

"Why did you do it, Eric? What threat was she to you?"

"I didn't — she wasn't — she wouldn't listen to me!"

"What did you try to tell her?" Was that a movement behind the drift log?

"We were just kids. It didn't mean anything. And if she didn't like it she could have said."

The words feel ugly, a monster under the surface. "What didn't mean anything?"

"She liked it. She liked me. We were just kids. It would have been okay."

"Was this before she moved away?"

"That bitch. She wouldn't leave it alone."

"What? Who?"

"Her mother."

"Whose mother?"

"Vee's." His voice is angry and impatient. "I didn't hurt her. She liked it."

"That's what you told yourself, wasn't it? But it did hurt her. I've read the book. When she revealed the childhood abuse. And when she talked about reparations, and resolution." And redemption.

"We were just kids."

"You were seventeen. She was twelve. She trusted you, she thought you were her friend, and you betrayed her in the worst way possible."

"We were just kids."

"Technically, yes, you were still a juvenile. And maybe that will play for you in court. But you were old enough to know better." Now my voice is shaking with anger. "When she published her book, the whole world would know what you did. And you had to stop her, didn't you?"

"She had it all wrong. You have it all wrong. It was just a game. We were kids! She wanted to reveal it all and ruin my life!"

"Like you ruined hers?"

His breathing comes in hoarse pants. His hands clench and unclench.

Look out!

He lunges at me. I take an involuntary step back. But Zoe's voice put me on alert. Water sloshes into my shoes. He keeps coming. I dodge, and splash along the shore. Backwards. Not daring to turn my back on him.

At least you're not wearing heels.

Zoe's sardonic tone steadies me. "You killed her, Eric. You ruined her life and then you killed her."

"She ruined her own life! She could have gotten over it, but no, she turned it all into a sympathy shit-show at that godawful excuse for a church."

"Maybe she wanted you to apologize."

"I gave her the painting. What more did she want?"

"A painting isn't an apology."

"A picture is worth a thousand words."

"Oh, please. That painting was for your own glorification."

"Not for me. For her."

Zoe's strident sarcasm emerges from my mouth. "She didn't want you, did she, you pathetic fuck? She told you to stop bothering her as a child. And as an adult, you tried to make her love you by giving her that painting. But she put it in the church — not what you had in mind, was it? And then Daniel Chandler sold it to cover church expenses. It wasn't a religious icon — it was just another painting. Not any more remarkable than dogs playing poker."

"You're wrong. It was a masterpiece."

"So not only was Victoria going to bring your 'youthful misdeeds' home to roost, neither she nor Daniel appreciated your genius. I guess that's why you had to kill them both."

North's face goes white. His mouth curls in a snarl. "They had no right."

"Poor baby. So misunderstood."

He lunges at me, once again faster than I would have believed. I fire my gun, but the shot goes wide. He's too close. His hands close around my neck. His momentum carries us both down, and I land on my back in the water. It covers my face, my nose. I thrash, kick, try to force his hands apart, losing my grip on the weapon.

He's too strong. Far stronger than I.

Wake up! Find a weak spot! Fingers, eyes!

A weak spot. I stop trying to pull his hands away, and grab for his pinky fingers. His skin is slick with moisture, and slips beneath my hands. My sinuses sting as water enters my nose. At last I have one small finger in my grasp. I yank it down and out, away from his clamping hand, and feel the thin bone snap.

He screams and stumbles back, clutching his hand. I sit up, coughing and retching. I hear the sound of pounding feet, and Jane's strident voice.

"Don't move! You're under arrest!"

A warm arm circles my shoulders and I blink the water out of my eyes. Seth Takahashi kneels beside me.

"Audrey, are you all right?"

I gasp for air, coughing. "Yeah, yes — I'm good, I'm okay." I let him help me to my feet, and then unwind his arm and go to where Jane is holding her gun on a kneeling Eric. His rage ripples off him like heat waves.

"Got cuffs?" I ask.

She nods. "On my belt. Want to do the honors?"

I unhook them, and walk to where the artist crouches on the sand. He doesn't struggle as I put the handcuffs on, only wincing as I brush his broken finger. Accidentally on purpose.

"My hand — I can't paint — what have you done to me? This is police brutality."

What a princess. It's always all about him.

You said it, Zoe. You said it.

Straightening, I say, "What took you guys so long?"

Jane beckons to another officer that has materialized on the beach. Through the fog, red and blue lights strobe. As the officer begins to read Eric his rights, she says, "He had to confess. I had to hear him. The further he went, the more damning the evidence." She shrugs. "You chose the risk. I figured you could handle yourself. Although I didn't expect him to attack you like that."

"The man's a sociopath. Of course he was going to attack me."

"We've got him now."

"Well." I'm still annoyed — but I *did* choose the risk. "Thanks for coming."

"You're welcome." She nods, and joins the other officers surrounding Eric North.

I am absurdly grateful that Jane had come, despite all the reasons not to, and brought the cavalry with her. At the very least, they can charge him with assault or even attempted murder for his attack on me, and second degree murder for Victoria.

My feelings about Takahashi are mixed. He'd helped me out of the water at the end, but where had he been before that? Watching? How much had he seen? If he saw the assault, why didn't he help me sooner?

Jane, I could understand. She'd been waiting till the last second to get evidence to charge him. Plus she almost thought I was a criminal myself. But Seth? The man is standing nearby, and I ask him why he decided to come, and whether Travis was with him.

"Travis wouldn't come. He didn't want to see the place again, or identify the man he saw. As for me, I thought you wanted a witness. That's what I thought you meant when we last talked. When I got here, I saw you struggling in the water, and Detective Candide pointing her gun."

I guess I can't expect him to be a hero. I don't even know what I want from him. So I walk over to Jane. She's talking to another officer but nods him away when she sees me.

"Thanks Jane," I say. "I think you saved my life."

She nodded. "I'd say so. That guy was serious."

"Did you hear what he was saying?"

"Some. But I need to get a statement from you."

"Okay." I repeat what Eric had said, and what I suspect. That he sexually abused Victoria when they were younger. That he killed her because she was talking about it in her book, and he thought she might incriminate him. Or maybe he just couldn't bear to hear about it. Either way, he was responsible for her death. And also for Daniel Chandler.

Jane nods. "You put everything together. How? Eric North wasn't even on our radar."

I look at her. The woman isn't my friend. But she did listen to me when her partner hadn't, and she had just saved my life. But.

Gotta trust someone sometime.

That's not your usual schtick.

So sue me.

Life advice from Zoe? That's a first. But we've reached an understanding, or at least an acceptance, and if I can reconcile with her, I should be able to do the same with Jane.

The detective is looking at me quizzically.

"Okay." I say. "Okay. But it's a little bit weird." And I tell her, as simply as I can, about the vision. And how I'd followed up the clues in order to catch a killer.

"So," she says, "you're telling me you're psychic."

"No." I pause. "Well, maybe." I pause again. "I don't really know what that means. I only know what I've experienced."

Jane nods, her expression thoughtful. "I guess it worked out this time."

I think of all the stumbles and mistakes I've made, rookie errors while I sought to reconcile the visions with reality. "I guess."

She looks away across the river, at the bridge or maybe the hills.

"Detective, can you come over here?" calls one of the officers.

We both look up, but it's Jane who answers, "In a minute." Then she says to me, "I'll be in touch." And she walks away.

I go back up to the trail where the Reverend Seth Takahashi is waiting. He puts a blanket around my shoulders, and we watch as the police take Eric North away.

37

The next day, after spending the morning making statements and filling out forms at the police station, I get a call from Elizabeth Harkness. She asks me to come to Victoria's apartment one last time. I have mixed feelings about this, but I do it.

The apartment is clean and barren. All the odds and ends of a life once lived are gone, the closets and cupboards are bare. Elizabeth is taping the top of a cardboard box as I enter. Her face bears its usual armor of impeccable makeup.

"Audrey."

"Elizabeth."

Her hands pause in their duty, and she stares down at the box. I wonder about the tectonic shifting going on inside her spirit, none of which is apparent on her features. I'm surmising that there's something, anyway. No one can lose a child and be unmoved.

She says, "You found the killer."

"Yes."

Her hands shift slightly, picking at the tape on the box. I stand at parade rest, waiting, wondering why she called me here.

"Audrey..."

"Yes?"

"Do you think I did the right thing? With Victoria? How I raised her?"

I blow through my bangs. "I think you did what you felt was right."

"But was it? Am I, somehow, at fault?"

I sigh. Impossible to unweave the tangled snarl of the universe and all its might-have-beens. But. "You didn't make North do what he did. Those choices were his own."

Nichelle Seely

She nods, distracted by some inner thought process. "Still. I should have been a better mother."

It's easy to criticize, to judge and engage in armchair quarterbacking. Easy to opine 'I wouldn't have done that but this.' And with no guarantee that anything would be better in the long run. There's only one universal, so that's what I say: "All of us should be better than we are."

Another long moment of silence, both of us thinking our separate thoughts. Elizabeth Harkness leaves the box and opens her pink Fendi handbag. "I have something for you." She takes out an envelope and hands it to me.

"What is this?"

"Payment for services rendered." She squares her shoulders. "To thank you."

"Ms. Harkness — Elizabeth — I don't need you to —"

"I know I did not hire you. That you may have already been paid. Call it a reward, if you like. It's all I have to offer."

Conflict. Chagrin. And a tiny bit of greed flickering in the corner.

I did observe that we should all be better.

"All right. Thank you." I put the envelope in my pocket, unopened. "I am sorry, Ms. Harkness. For your loss."

She nods, and there doesn't seem to be anything more for me to say, except, "Have a safe trip back to Portland."

The familiar sights and scents of the Portway Tavern feel bittersweet. The place is still warm and familiar, but one thing is changing. Claire Chandler, newly released from jail, is leaving.

"The place won't be the same without you," I say.

"Come on outside. I've got something to show you."

I follow her to the gravel parking lot in back of the building. Braced on its stand is a brand new Harley-Davidson motorcycle. Our faces reflect in the glossy teal paint of the tank and saddlebags. The chrome gleams with the promise of the open road. It's a beautiful machine.

"Wow," I say. "Sweet ride."

"Thanks." She takes a deep breath. "It's a Road Glide Special touring bike, with a Milwaukie-Eight 114 V-twin engine. I can go to the horizon and back on this baby."

I nod, pretending to know what she's talking about.

Claire caresses the handlebar. "I need to get away from here for a while. Going on a little trip." We stand quietly and she states, "Daniel's life insurance paid for it."

"Bessie Stringfield would be proud. I'm glad at least one good thing came out of all this."

"Me, too." She looks at me sidelong, then extends her hand. Her grip is firm. "Thanks, Audrey. For catching the killer. Lighting a fire under my lawyer. Saving me from the Big House."

"You're welcome. But you didn't need my help, not really. You were innocent." I think back to our original conversation in the coffee shop, regarding why people disappear: men because of finances, women because of danger. But the stats don't reflect the nuances, or the courage it takes to change direction, when that change is undertaken voluntarily.

I'll miss her, but I respect and admire Claire for her decision. She'll be back one of these days, and even if she isn't, just the thought of her crisscrossing the country on her Harley makes me smile.

Claire's eagerness to start her journey shames me into continuing my own. I set up an appointment to talk to Phoebe.

"This is a comfortable chair," I say.

"It's meant to be." My neighbor and therapist cocks her head and waits.

"We arrested a murderer Friday night."

Her eyebrows go up. "Indeed?"

I nod. "I knew it was him. But getting him to confess was another matter."

"Why do you think confession is so important?"

"I didn't have any evidence." But that doesn't really answer her question. And I know she will just keep asking. I struggle for a bit. "We needed to arrest him. And confession makes it easier. So we don't have to fight him so much later."

"Why is that?"

"Once he admits what he's done, some of the resistance goes away. He knows he has to face the truth."

"And did he stop fighting? Once he had confessed?"

"No." I remember the coldness of the river. "He tried to kill me."

Her eyes widen for a split second, but she quickly regains her aplomb. "It seems didn't succeed."

"No."

"Why do you think he tried to kill you? Even after he confessed?"

I snort. "Because he still didn't want to admit it. Not really. Anyone who knew he'd abused Victoria had to go." In the end, he couldn't face the truth about himself; even as he was driven to reveal it. An endless cycle of internal conflict.

Phoebe says, "Sometimes we can't control who we are. But we can accept it, and work to be better."

Zoe. The visions. Stepping stones to an unseeable future. A bridge going off into the fog. But I have to take those steps, because if I don't, I'll end up like Eric and so many other perps. Doomed to an endless mental cycle of denial and anguish and concealment.

I see a long road ahead. But somewhere in the fog, I hope, I'll get to the other side of the river.

Safe in my own house, with sunlight flooding the empty rooms and a view of a freighter navigating the deep river channel, I can face the question I've been avoiding for days.

Who did you kill, Zoe?

For once she is silent. I poke at my own hazy recollections.

When the raid went down at the Baxter Building, I had no advance warning. Whether that was an oversight on the part of my handler, or a policy decision by someone higher up, I truly don't know. The cocaine I'd ingested earlier with Sonny and Blue and Kirstin was singing in my head. The late morning sun wasn't cheerful; it only illuminated the squalor and smears and accumulated trash. The residents were all sacked out in their rooms sleeping off another night of business and self-poisoning. But even then I'd thought the place was unusually quiet.

I hiked up the stairs to my own room. I heard the footsteps a flight or two below, but didn't clock them as a follower. The space I'd laid claim to had once been a studio apartment. No place to hide but the closet and I made sure it was empty, per my usual habit. But I forgot to lock the door. And then I swallowed a downer to counteract the coke, so I could get some sleep.

The opposing drugs fought a civil war in my system. My tolerance was far less advanced than the typical user, and I could barely make sense of my surroundings. When Sonny barged in, it was so unexpected I thought he might not be real. He disabused me of that notion soon enough, yanking me up from my bed and slamming me up against the wall. I thought he was going to rape me. Instead, he pulled a wicked blade and held it up for me to see. It glittered in the dirty sunlight.

"I hate cops," he said.

"What?" I said, struggling to stay in character. To be Zoe, feisty but responsive to the psychological power of a dealer. I forced a giggle. "I'm no cop."

"Liar." The back of his hand smashed my cheek, and the back of my head bounced off the wall. Colored lights exploded in my vision. He pressed a forearm against my throat. I scratched his face, tried to knee him in the balls. Then felt the cold plunge of the blade into my upper right chest.

"I got you, pig." I'd drawn blood on his face, and it dribbled across his teeth as he smiled. Then he punched me again, kicking my back, my gut as I hit the floor. My blood felt warm and liquid as it left my body.

I don't know why he didn't kill me. Maybe he thought he had, that I'd bleed out. Or maybe he didn't want to be known as a cop-killer and suffer all the bad juju that would bring down on his head. Whatever it was, I doubt he had an attack of conscience at the last minute.

I didn't see him leave, but I knew I was alone. Blinked in and out of awareness. When the shots and shouts began to echo up from the street, I was overcome with terror. Didn't know what was happening. With the desperation of a wounded animal I crawled to the closet. There was a nasty mattress in there, for the nights when I wanted to hide. And in my drug-and-pain addled state, I knew I didn't want to be found.

Wadded up some bedding and pressed it to my wound.

Left the door open a crack so I could see.

Heard someone calling Zoe's name.

In. Out. Grayness. Blackness.

Someone is here, in the room.

Someone is here, on the bed. There's a knife on the floor next to my hand. Shouts. Shots. Screams. The vision comes, overlaying what I can see of the empty room. I see police. Colleagues. Detective Janke. Detective O'Malley. Narc squad. Talking with Sonny. Exchanging packets of cash. Jokes and feral smiles. I blink. It's not real. Is it? No. It can't be. Anger. Disbelief.

I'm alone, aren't I?

Who is with me? Who is this figure of cooling flesh? What happened?

Just taking care of a little business. Don't worry, I've got your back.

That was the first time I heard Zoe's voice as something separate from my own internal monologue. Of course, at the time I didn't realize a splinter of my identity had peeled away from the core. I seemed to drift away from my body, looking down on the humped form beside me. External vision interrupted by flashes of the internal one.

What was happening to me? Something more than coke. And I remembered with languid terror that the downer had come from Sonny, too. Made with God knew what.

If something new had been born from my psyche that day, something else had died. Because after it all went down — the stabbing, the raid, the hospital — I was a different person.

Who did you kill, Zoe?

I gulp, swallow, shudder. Come back to myself, back to the house in Astoria. Look out the windows to the river, blue and beautiful and ever-flowing.

Maybe I don't want to know the answer.

The house smells like fresh air and newly-mown grass. I've opened all the windows. The filmy sheers flutter in the wind. I sit cross-legged on the floor, contractors' business cards arranged like game of solitaire. The commitment, both monetary and metaphorical, makes my chest constrict.

Move forward, remember?

I choose one, take a deep breath, and punch in the number.

A gruff voice answers. "Joe Ferguson, construction."

"I have a foundation that needs repair."

He asks for details, I give them to him. The cracks, the subsidence, the broken slab. I hide nothing, and he takes everything in, arranging to come by in a day or so to see for himself. I hang up, satisfied.

Outside, a heron swoops over the roof of the neighboring house, heading for the river. I can imagine looking out at this view forever. At last, I can imagine making this place my home.

Author's Note

I hope you enjoyed your sojourn in Astoria with Detective Audrey Lake. I'd be eternally grateful if you'd take a few minutes to leave some stars and/or a review at Amazon, Goodreads, and/or Library Thing. Writers need readers, and reviews are a great way to show your support and spread the word to other folks who might enjoy this story. And please, tell your friends!

If you're interested in hearing about Audrey's next adventure, sign up for Case Notes, my free newsletter. For more information visit my website at www.nichelleseely.com. You'll get early notice of the next book plus other tidbits. Thanks for reading and sharing.

If you'd like to contact me directly about this book, I'd love to hear from you. Drop me a line at nichelle@nichelleseely.com, with this book's title in the subject line so I know you're not a robot. No offense to our mechanical friends.

I wrote this novel during the Covid-19 pandemic, so most of my research was conducted on the Internet by necessity. Apologies for any mistakes. Many of the places described in this novel are real. None of the people are. The officers and staff of the Astoria Police Department have always been courteous and professional when I've encountered them; not at all like the detectives in this story. In addition, the allegations made against officers in the Denver Police Department are entirely fictional, as is the Baxter Building and what happened there.

Read on!

Acknowledgements

I'd like to thank Kendra Griffin, Kathy Mendt, and Phyllis Neher, my Colorado writing group for their tireless support and marvelous critique. They helped make this book a thousand times better. Thanks also to my mother Norma Seely for showing me first-hand the persistence and dedication it takes to be a writer, and my sister Elia Seely for reading the work over and over again even as she was working on her own novel.

My husband Aaron deserves a trophy of his own for his unfaltering support, his cooking ability, and his willingness to read and comment. Believe me when I say an honest reader's perspective is just as valuable, maybe more so, as that of another writer.

Lastly, thank you, the reader, for taking a chance on a debut author. I hope you enjoyed meeting Audrey Lake and immersing yourself in the mossy streets of Astoria. To hear about Audrey's next case, sign up for the Case Notes newsletter from my website at www.nichelleseely.com.